PRAISE FOR BETH K. VOGT

"I adored this sweet, funny, clever story. Vogt handles a large cast of loveable characters splendidly, but Kylie and Joe absolutely *shine*! A touching, original, and utterly romantic tale. You won't want to miss it!"

DEBORAH RANEY, AUTHOR OF *BREATH OF HEAVEN* AND *BRIDGES*

"Charming. Another winner from Beth Vogt. This delightful romance will be with you long after you read the last line."

RACHEL HAUCK, *NEW YORK TIMES'* BESTSELLING AUTHOR

"*Dedicated to the One I Love* is a fun, sassy romance between two people who are determined not to fall in love. Reminiscent of *You've Got Mail* and *The Lost City*, Vogt pens a sweet romance with quippy characters, charming antics, and a tender look at grief. Readers will want to keep turning the pages as they cheer for Joe and Kylie's happily ever after."

LISA JORDAN, AWARD-WINNING AUTHOR WITH LOVE INSPIRED

"*Dedicated to the One I Love* is more than a lighthearted "will-they-or-won't-they?" romance. And that's just what you'd expect from Beth K. Vogt. She portrays the love between father and son, longtime friends and new competitors, brothers and sisters, and the writer and story, taking readers on a journey to the heart. There, we discover that the joy of what is found transcends the pain of what was lost. Funny and Spirit-filled, *Dedicated* grabs you right away, and you'll both chide and cheer for Joe and Kylie from the very first page."

ROBIN W. PEARSON, CHRISTY
AWARD-WINNING AUTHOR

"Beth K. Vogt's long-awaited return to the romance genre is chock full of all my favorite tropes: pen pals, professional rivalry, love after loss. Following in the footsteps of gems like *You've Got Mail* and *Beach Read*, *Dedicated to the One I Love* is sure to please Vogt's long-time fans and earn her scores of new ones. Don't miss this fun summer story!"

CARLA LAUREANO, TWO-TIME RITA
AWARD-WINNING AUTHOR

"*Dedicated to the One I Love* has it all. I truly don't remember the last time I enjoyed the experience of reading a book like I did with this latest offering from author Beth K. Vogt. First, it was literary and who doesn't love books about books and those who write them? But the best thing of all was how hard I fell for the characters. I never wanted the story to end, yet when it did, I was utterly satisfied! A fun romp, with all the feels! Definitely, a book that will become dog-eared as I read it again and again and again."

EDIE MELSON, DIRECTOR OF BLUE RIDGE MOUNTAIN
CHRISTIAN WRITERS CONFERENCE

"Charming, engaging, and relatable – *Dedicated to the One I Love* is an absolute pleasure to read! I love a good push and pull between a hero and heroine, and Kylie and Joe have that in spades. From their tangled writing careers to a surprise romance, they tugged on my heart and kept me turning pages. Beth Vogt's latest is a delight!"

MELISSA TAGG, *USA TODAY* BESTSELLING,
CHRISTY AWARD-WINNING AUTHOR

DEDICATED TO THE ONE I LOVE

Beth K. Vogt

Dedicated to the One I Love

Published in association with the Books & Such Literary Management. www.booksandsuch.com.

Scripture quotations marked "NASB" are taken from the New American Standard Bible®,

Paperback ISBN: 979-8391682882

Dedicated to Rob, the one I love

CHAPTER 1

Good morning, Joe. It's a beautiful May morning here in Monument. By "beautiful," I mean it's snowing. Springtime in the Rockies, right?

There's just a dusting on my back porch, so I won't attach the all-too-familiar photo of lawn furniture covered in snow. Here's a question for you: What's the largest snowflake ever recorded?

I still can't believe I got stumped by your last trivia question. I had no idea the speed of a computer mouse is measured in "Mickeys." The only Mickey I'm familiar with is Mickey Mouse. Hope all is well in your corner of Colorado. Kylie

Despite what some people thought—specifically her mother, her best friends, and her agent—Kylie was fine. Just because her cat Remington kept her on schedule didn't mean he ran her life—what was left of it.

Remington leaned his furry body up against her legs as Kylie sat at the kitchen counter, his purr a soft vibration of comfort.

"Come on, Rem." Kylie abandoned her tepid cup of Irish Breakfast tea, tucked her phone in the side pocket of her leggings, scooped the cat into her arms, and headed for her office.

She paused in the hallway before entering through the open door. Her favorite books were color-coordinated on the built-in white shelves—writing books and fiction of every genre. Copies of her novels, in order of publication. Awards and favorite photographs with her agent, editor, and other author friends hung on the walls that were painted a lush periwinkle—her favorite color—thanks to her husband.

Her laptop sat in the center of her desk. Nothing else. No open books, pages of notes, no bowl of salted popcorn with a glass of cold ginger ale, no ice—nothing that hinted at the creative mess caused when she was in pursuit of "The End" for a story.

Kylie released Remington, who strolled away without a backward glance, and sat behind her desk. Opened her laptop. Closed her eyes as it powered up. Offered a silent prayer for inspiration. Waited ... waited ...

No spark. Nothing.

Kylie buried her face in her hands with a groan. She was a writer. Writers produced words—spark, or no spark. Today wasn't a writing day. Yesterday hadn't been a writing day. She'd ignored her unfinished manuscript for one thousand ninety-five days. *Three years.* She resisted the urge to pick up her phone and open the Words with Friends app. Escape to something fun. Easy. Or she could always check her email.

Her phone buzzed, causing Kylie to jerk upright, her chair skidding away from the desk. Shannon, with her midweek check-in. She could let the call go to voicemail, but that would just worry her agent, and then she'd start her traditional "Are you okay?" texts until Kylie called her back.

Kylie put her phone on speaker. "Hey."

"Hello. And how are you today?"

Ah. Shannon's extra-cheerful voice.

"Fine."

"Did you see the article I sent you?"

A not-so-subtle way of asking if Kylie was at her computer. Writing.

"No."

"Because you're too busy writing?" Shannon maintained the same upbeat tone.

"No. But you'll be happy to know I'm at my desk"—she eased her chair closer—"and my computer's on."

Every word she spoke was true.

"*Ky-lie.*"

"Shannon." Kylie braced herself. Would Shannon transition to the compassionate approach or the assertive approach?

"You need to be thinking about your career. Readers have been waiting for another Veronica Hollins book for three years. Thirty-six months. One hundred fifty-six weeks."

"I know how long it's been, Shannon."

"As soon as you finish the manuscript, the publisher can rush it through the editing and printing process. They. Want. This. Book."

"Creativity can't be rushed."

Especially when creativity had gone AWOL.

"Read that article. You've got competition."

"This from the woman who always told me other authors aren't competition and that another writer's success didn't mean I was failing."

"That was when you were writing!" Shannon's words flew across the phone. "If you'd read that article, you'd know there's a romance author in the house who people are calling the 'new Veronica Hollins.'"

Okay, that information stung.

"Her debut sat on the *New York Times* bestseller list for weeks. She's gained one hundred thousand followers on social media. Each one of them should be following *you*. And she's doing a national tour for her next release, book two in her series, which comes out in six months. Talking to the readers, the television hosts, that you should be talking to."

"She's one of our authors?" Kylie opened her inbox and found Shannon's email. Clicked on the link. "Madison Thomas? Why did the publisher bring her on?"

"There's no denying her voice is reminiscent of yours. More importantly, she's cranking out books. You're not. Your followers are reading *her* books because the last book in your series is sitting in your computer, unfinished."

"That's their choice to read her novels."

"You're not giving them a choice if you don't have *Worth the Risk* out there—a novel you promised your oh-so-loyal readers. Where's your pride, girl?"

Dead and buried with Andrew.

Kylie bit back the melodramatic words, twisting her wedding rings around her finger. It wasn't Shannon's fault her unfinished book was forever connected to Andrew's death.

"It's rumored her next advance is six figures."

"I'm happy for her."

"You could be signing your own contract—"

"If I finished this book and had another series idea." Kylie finished Shannon's sentence in a monotone.

"Exactly."

"I'm sorry, Shannon."

"I don't want an apology." Shannon's growl reached across the phone and crawled up Kylie's spine one vertebrae at a time. "I want you to do whatever it takes to finish writing that book."

Her agent was most definitely going with assertive today. "I will."

"Do you mean it this time?"

"Yes. I'll do whatever it takes to finish." Kylie's words sounded mechanical. As if she was reciting Shannon's words back to her. Which she was.

The thought of writing used to get her out of bed every morning. That, and the aroma of coffee because Andrew set the timer each night for a pot of their favorite dark roast to start brewing at five forty-five each morning. Now Remington woke her up by sitting on Kylie's stomach and tapping her face with his paw. She should be glad he didn't use his claws.

She drank tea all day and talked to her cat. Empty teacups littered different rooms of the house—except her office. Every evening, she'd gather them up, load the dishwasher, and start again the next day with clean cups.

"Kylie, I'm your agent, but I'm your friend too."

"I know you are."

"Andrew wouldn't want you living like this."

Now Shannon wasn't playing fair.

"You know I'm right."

"I know you *like* being right." Their laughter blended across the phone.

"He was so proud of your books." Shannon's tone softened. "Remember how he introduced you to everyone as 'my wife, the famous author'?"

Kylie had to laugh again at Shannon's attempt to sound like Andrew. "He'd pull that routine with every single waiter or waitress at every restaurant. 'Have you read any of my wife's books? She's a famous author, you know.'"

"He'd come to your book signings and walk around the store, gathering people up to come and meet you."

"He'd tell them how happy I would be to meet them—and then he'd get them to buy a book."

"Or two. Andrew would want you to keep writing."

Kylie couldn't argue with her. But she also couldn't write.

She'd lost her happily ever after, and the ability to write them for imaginary characters too. In the early days after Andrew died, she thought if she didn't get to have a happily ever after, why should anyone in her books have one? Why should anyone in the world have one? But that would be selfish. Her tragedy didn't negate happiness for everyone else.

Three years later, she was almost thirty-five and living this new Andrew-less life. Mostly. But creativity required more of her than she had left.

"When was the last time you read the manuscript?"

"It's been ... a while. I'll start reading it again today."

"That's great!" Shannon sounded as happy as if Kylie had promised to turn in the completed manuscript tomorrow. "Just relax and get the feel of the story."

"Right."

"Before you know it, you'll fall in love with the characters again and then you'll have to finish the book."

Fall in love. Wrong choice of words. That was the whole problem.

"I'll start reading it."

"Now."

"Yes."

"Right now."

"We're still talking."

"I'm hanging up. You go read."

Shannon disconnected the call. Remington stared at Kylie from the doorway of her office. "I know. I know. She means well."

Remington meowed.

"Yes, I said I'd read the manuscript."

Kylie promised herself she could take a nap after she read the first ten ... *five* chapters. Who was she kidding? Opening the Word document would be considered a success. It wasn't that she didn't ever go in her office. Or open her laptop. She did, every single day. Looked at emails. Deleted emails.

And read the emails from Joe.

Just-her-friend Joe.

They'd connected five months ago through Words with Friends after discovering they were both Colorado natives, with a love for trivia and funny one-star book reviews. He'd asked, "What musical keys do most cars honk in?" and she'd replied, "F or F-sharp." Silly questions like that. Then one night he asked if he could email her, and she figured why not? Since then, they emailed back and forth daily, talking about harmless things like the weather, movies, and the Broncos. Kylie said her background was literature, which was true since she majored in journalism and minored in English. Joe probably thought she was a librarian. He'd said he'd been in the military. Their correspondence was casual. Fun. Platonic.

Kylie forced herself to stay seated behind her desk, pressing her palms against the clean glass top. When she was in deep writing mode, her desk was a mess, and she warned the cleaning team not to touch anything. Now they came and went twice a month, dealt with her teacups, cleaned her bathrooms, their vacuuming and dusting causing Remington to hide under her bed.

She tossed her phone in the top desk drawer. No time to play Words with Friends. Instead, she found her manuscript. Opened it.

Dianna wasn't looking for love. Not now. Maybe never. All she had to do was convince Jeremy of that fact—and forget how he'd kissed her senseless last night—and there wouldn't be any trouble.

Thirty-five words. Only seventy-thousand-plus words to read, rewrite, and then thirty-thousand words more while she figured out the rest of the book to satisfy her agent. Her editor. Her readers.

Writing had been reduced to a math problem. How many words did she have to produce? This wasn't about falling back in love with characters, like Shannon had said. Of course, she had to write a happily ever after to ensure her readers were satisfied. That was one unchangeable rule of the romance genre.

The words in front of her were just that—words. Black consonants and vowels on a white page. No color.

She wasn't looking for love either—in her life or in the pages of a story, even if she'd written it.

...

Joe tugged on his gray Broncos T-shirt. Grabbed the towel he'd dropped on his bed and dried his hair, so it stuck up all over his head. The alarm clock on the bedside table glowed 1:20 p.m. in bright red numerals, which meant he had ten minutes before Liza called. Just enough time to grab something to drink, maybe something to eat, before they discussed the manuscript he'd submitted to his publisher six weeks ago.

He'd turned in a good story. One of his best. He'd likely secured his "favorite client" status for another year.

He stuck one earbud in and then took the stairs to the main floor two at a time, sliding sideways into the kitchen. Opened the fridge and retrieved a cold bottle of water. Scanned the shelves that boasted a store-bought rotisserie chicken, eggs, packaged lettuce, low-fat milk, and a six-pack of Pepsi.

There. The remaining half of a cold cut sub he'd brought home yesterday. He could finish it before Liza called, unless she—

His phone vibrated in the side pocket of his sweatpants.

—called early.

He palmed the sandwich, the paper wrapper crinkling against his fingers, and dropped it on the kitchen counter. Pulled his phone from his pocket, answering so it went through his earbud. "You're early."

"Interrupting a brilliant writing streak, no doubt."

"I'm eating."

"Go right ahead." Liza sounded bored. "It won't be the first time you chewed in my ear."

"Very funny."

"You have the manners of a thirteen-year-old."

"I know you love me."

"Yeah, you're my favorite client. You tell me that all the time."

"Can't let you forget."

This was one of the reasons Joe liked having Liza as his literary agent. Talking to her was like talking to his sister—and that was one of the best compliments he could ever give Liza. His favorite person in his family was his younger sister, Abbie, not that he would ever admit that to his mom.

He bit into the sub, savoring the smoky, mildly spicy bite of ham, mortadella, capicola, and provolone cheese topped with shredded lettuce, tomatoes, and just the right amount of mayo and olive oil.

"Tell me the good news already." Joe took a swig of water as he carried his phone and the remainder of the sub to his favorite chair in the living room, stretching out to continue the conversation. For Liza's sake, when he turned on the flat-screen TV, he kept it on mute, only paying partial attention to whatever sports show was on ESPN. "They loved the manuscript, right?"

"Not exactly, Joe."

"Wha—?" He choked on the wad of bread, cold cuts, and cheese. Sat up. Coughed. Wheezed.

"You okay?"

Joe grabbed the water bottle and took small sips. "What do you mean 'not exactly'?"

"You know sales for your last three books have slipped."

"Every author I know has struggled with sales numbers this past year." Joe gulped more water. "Well, except for that romance writer who hasn't even had a book out in the last few years ... what's her name?"

"Veronica Hollins?"

"That's the one. But she can probably live off the royalties of her last two books alone for the rest of her life."

"It's interesting you mentioned Veronica Hollins."

"Because?"

"After reading your manuscript, the editors suggested you should add more romance to the story."

"There's romance in the story, Liza."

"Barely. No one holds hands. No kisses. It's elementary school romance. You could cut the sexual tension with dental floss."

"I write about espionage and double agents and—"

"I know what you write," Liza interrupted him. "Your editor wants you to up the romance angle to pull in more female readers."

"I have female readers."

"Joe, I need you to listen to me. Really listen." Liza's voice lost any sense of humor. "Romance is the top-selling fiction genre. Women read romance. Recognize these two facts and add a strong romantic thread to your book and you will automatically reach more readers."

"Wow." Joe closed his eyes as he pressed his fingers to the bridge of his nose.

This was not what he'd expected when Liza scheduled this phone call. He'd lost Liza's favorite-client ranking. He'd do anything to improve his manuscript.

Almost anything.

Joe pointed the remote at the TV screen and turned off the muted sports show. Tossed the remote aside. "This isn't a discussion, is it?"

"You and I are talking."

"Liza."

"This is me bringing you in on the discussion."

"I turned in a good manuscript."

"You did. The story is classic Tate Merrick. But this is about making your manuscript better. About reaching more readers."

"I've been doing everything I can to connect with readers."

"I know." Liza's voice was calm. Supportive. "We've endlessly brainstormed different ways to do that. You spent your own marketing dollars. But people are tired of war and political infighting. Readers want happier stories. They want romance."

Joe huffed out a breath, paced the length of the room, searching for something—anything—he could say to change Liza's mind.

"If you think about this for a minute, you'll realize the idea has great potential."

"There is a romantic interest in the book." Now he was repeating himself.

"Again—we need you to make it stronger."

"I've never read a romance in my life—not even something as basic as *Cinderella*."

"Maybe that's where you start."

"As if I'm going to walk into the children's section of the library—"

"Joe! If you keep being such a grouch, you'll fall out of favorite-client status."

He hadn't already?

His award-winning author status was slipping through his fingers. He was as unsettled as if he were waiting to see if his first manuscript would be accepted by a publisher. Any publisher. Right now, it sounded as if *Lethal Strike* wouldn't be published at all, not if he didn't do what they wanted, which meant changing how he wrote his stories.

A few moments later, Liza signed off with a quiet goodbye.

This wasn't the first time his life hadn't turned out the way he planned.

Joe retreated to his office and collapsed in the chair behind his grandfather's rolltop desk. He didn't mind the disorganized bookshelves with books stacked however they came out of the packing boxes when he'd moved into the house near the Denver metro area five years ago. Fiction. Nonfiction. Even some textbooks from his favorite college classes. A large glass jar sat in the corner beneath the window, filled with all the pennies, dimes, nickels, and quarters he emptied out of his pockets at the end of the day.

No photos of Cassidy—of course.

No family photos.

He just didn't do photos.

Awards, yes. Tangible reminders that he was a good writer. A successful writer. Not that he looked at them every day. Liza always let him know when he received some sort of accolade. He'd celebrate with a glass of good cabernet. Call Abbie so she could shout, "Bravo, brother!" Call his mom because he was a good son. Let her tell Dad because, well, he wasn't impressed.

Never had been.

Never would be.

He couldn't explain why he'd given up a "perfectly good career in the military" to write stories. To this day, despite the fact that he was thirty-four years old, his dad's words echoed in his mind, no matter how many awards he racked up.

"You're being irresponsible, but of course, I'm not surprised."

Joe shoved away from the desk, walked out of his office, shutting the door with a decisive click.

CHAPTER 2

Dear Kylie, Have I mentioned I'm a sore loser? I come by it
honestly. Everyone in my family—both my parents and my
only sister—are super competitive. (She's younger than me
by three years.) Growing up, game nights in my house were
cutthroat. It didn't matter if we were playing Candyland
or Monopoly or Risk. If you cheated, you were banished to
your bedroom. I only cheated twice. Once, when I was six
years old and too little to understand my dad knew exactly
what I was doing. Then once again when I was sixteen and
I thought I was smart enough to pull one over on my dad.
Didn't happen—and yeah, I was banished to my room, just
like when I was six. Only this time, I snuck out my bedroom
window and walked over to a friend's house. When I came
back three hours later, Dad was waiting in my bedroom. My
return didn't go well. And that's all I'm going to say about
that. I found out years later that my friend's mom called my
mom to tell her where I was. My dad wasn't all-knowing,
like I thought.

Now you know one of the dark secrets from my past.
Here's a question for you: Where did the Jolly Rancher Candy
Company originate? Joe

P.S. I admit defeat on the snowflake question. I googled it
and found out the world's largest snowflake, according to the

Guinness World Records, was 15 inches in diameter and 8 inches thick.

Joe spent the rest of the afternoon in front of his laptop, with random trips back to the kitchen for a Pepsi or a bottle of water. The sandwich sat in his stomach like a huge wad of chewing gum. Between kitchen runs, he alternated reading chapters of his manuscript, googling book trends and book sales, and skimming recent reviews for his work.

Two hours later, the space behind his eyes ached. The only thing he'd written was a comment on iread4thrillz85's two-star review of his last book, a reader who thought the plot was predictable and that he—or she—could write a better ending than Tate Merrick.

Joe would like to see iread4thrillz85 try.

He deleted the comment and closed the tab. He knew better than to get stuck in the mental maze of reading reviews. It was one thing to read funny one-star reviews for someone else's book. He had no emotional connection to any of those. But when he read reviews for any of his books? Too personal, both the positive and the negative.

When his friend Tucker texted him half an hour later with a brief, **Mallory says we have way too much food. Want to come for dinner?** he replied, **I'll be right over,** shut down his laptop, grabbed his keys, and turned his back on all things related to books.

Tucker and Mallory's apartment was also in Highlands Ranch and was almost like a second home. Tucker and Joe had met in college and Joe had been Tucker's best man when he married Mallory. The trio shared a love of CrossFit and Mallory treated him like a brother—just the right mix of love and sass.

When Joe arrived, Tucker slapped him on the back as he toed off his shoes. "Dinner's ready."

Joe followed him to the combo living room and dining room, inhaling the aroma of tomato sauce and Italian seasonings. "It's good to be here."

"I hope you like chicken parmigiana." Mallory appeared wearing a bright pink apron and set a platter of chicken breasts coated with breadcrumbs, tomato sauce, and melted cheese at one edge of the small square table.

"Are you kidding? I started drooling the minute Tucker opened the door." He dropped into a chair where a Pepsi was already waiting for him. "If I was home, I'd be throwing a bagged salad onto a plate and slicing up some store-bought chicken on top of it."

Tucker carried in a basket of rolls and a salad. "No bagged salad here. And the parmigiana? It's Mallory's grandmother's recipe. It's one of the reasons I married her."

"It's true." Mallory motioned for Joe to hand her his plate. "Tucker, bless the food, please, and then I'll serve."

Tucker removed his Rockies baseball cap, hanging it on the back of his chair, and did as Mallory requested, then passed Joe the salad.

Tucker palmed a roll, and then spoke around a bite. "How's the writing going?"

His friend didn't know he was done discussing writing—or anything related to books. "Had an interesting phone conversation with my agent earlier today."

"Interesting … how?"

"She called to talk about the manuscript I turned in a few weeks back. My editor wants me to add more romance to the story."

Tucker raised an eyebrow beneath his shaggy blond hair. "You don't write romance."

Joe leaned back in his chair and raised his hands in the air. "Thank you very much!"

Mallory added salad to her plate. "But they said, 'add romance.' That's not the same as writing a full romance novel. It could be fun, Joe."

"Fun would be hearing they love the manuscript and want normal edits." Joe sliced into the steaming chicken parmigiana.

He refused to let this conversation ruin his appetite. Romance just wasn't his thing, in fiction or in real life. He had Cassidy to thank for that. Time to focus on this delicious dinner and his good friends. Joe took a bite of Mallory's dish, savoring the chicken coated in Mozzarella cheese. Raised his glass. "Here's to your grandmother."

Mallory sipped her iced coffee, then said, "Joe, I was thinking—"

Tucker cut her off. "Honey, we weren't going to talk about this tonight."

"I never agreed not to talk about it."

"Mallory." Tucker raised his hand like a traffic cop.

"Tucker."

Joe chuckled. "Hey. Still here. Can I get in on this conversation?"

"No." Tucker shook his head.

"Absolutely." Mallory offered him a Cheshire cat smile.

Mallory's and Tucker's responses collided. "Tucker, it's okay. Let Mallory have her say."

"You're gonna regret this, man."

"Hush! He said he wants to hear what I have to say." Mallory focused on Joe. "How long have you been emailing Kylie?"

"Emailing Kylie?" Joe pressed his lips together at the unexpected question. "Five months."

"It's way past time for you to meet her."

Tucker crossed his arms over his chest. "I tried to warn you."

"Meet?"

"I was reading a magazine article that said when you connect with someone through a dating app, the first meeting should happen in three to five days. You guys are way past that."

"Kylie and I didn't meet on a dating app." Joe took a drink of his soda. "We're not dating."

There. He'd shut down that idea. He wasn't dating Kylie—or anyone else. If he could, he'd emphasize that point by standing and digging his heels into the ground, um, carpet.

Joe shoved a forkful of salad into his mouth. Chewed. Swallowed, or rather tried to swallow. He'd forgotten to put any dressing on the mix of lettuce, tomatoes, cucumbers, and red onions. He poured a generous amount of the homemade vinaigrette over the remaining salad on his plate.

Mallory had her say. No harm done.

"I didn't suggest you date her." Mallory tucked a lock of her dark hair with purple highlights behind one ear. "I suggested you meet her."

Uh-oh. Mallory wasn't done with the topic.

"Based on an article you read about couples who met on dating apps."

"Ye-es." Mallory shrugged. "It's the same thing."

"The goal for those people is dating, so it's implied they'd meet at some point."

"Come on, Joe." Mallory leaned forward. "You're being difficult."

"Calm down, Mallory." Tucker spoke up at last.

"I am calm."

Joe had to laugh. "You almost threw your roll at me."

"I didn't—" Mallory let out a huff. "You're so infuriating."

"You started this conversation."

"Joe, be honest. You're just going to email this woman forever?"

"Sure."

"I refuse to believe you've never thought of meeting her."

Now Mallory had backed him into a corner. He could keep protesting. Say she was wrong. But that would be a lie. And Joe didn't lie. It was the latent Boy Scout in him.

Mallory continued to stare at him across the table, waiting for his response. But Joe refused to answer. Shoved the idea aside like an annoying twinge of a toothache he didn't want to deal with because ... well really? Who wants to go to the dentist? Great. He just compared meeting Kylie to going to the dentist.

"You've got an odd look on your face. What are you thinking?" Mallory's question intruded on his thoughts.

"Nothing." Joe cleared his throat. "Fine. I have thought about meeting Kylie—but just as friends."

"Aha!" Mallory clapped her hands. "I knew it!"

"Stop gloating." Tucker pointed a finger at her.

"Sorry." Mallory didn't look the least bit repentant. "When are you going to meet? Because I know the perfect time."

Tucker leaned back in his chair. "You never should have admitted you've thought of meeting Kylie."

"I don't lie, Tucker. You know that. And I'm not planning on dating Kylie. We're just friends."

"Fine." Mallory smiled her wide grin again. "This is a perfect 'just friends' way to meet."

Joe had to laugh. "Go ahead and tell me what you were thinking."

"Invite her to the Memorial Day cookout, of course. It's casual. Low-key—"

Joe gave a sharp laugh. "There is nothing low-key about that cookout. My parents just invited themselves out from Arizona for the weekend. Abbie and her boyfriend will be there. You and Tucker... Oh, I see your evil plot."

"No evil plot." Mallory's voice was pitched just a bit too high. "It's a small group of family and friends. Casual. And with us there, you don't have to keep the conversation going all by yourself. We'll be there to help you."

"You'll be there to check Kylie out."

"I promise no flashing of scorecards. And besides, you wouldn't tell me any important details if you met her for coffee."

"Ha! You admit you want to meet Kylie too."

"Of course I do. I don't lie either, Joe Edwards."

Their laughter blended at Mallory's declaration. They were like the Three Musketeers, without the swords. They were loyal, with a heavy dose of humor.

Mallory had never cared for Cassidy. Joe had ignored her comments early on in his relationship with the country singer, but she'd been right. Cassidy was a lot of flash and bling, but no depth. Maybe it would be wise to have her meet Kylie—*if* he was going to meet her.

"Just as friends?"

Mallory stopped laughing. "Are you seriously considering inviting her to the cookout?"

"As a friend ... maybe."

Mallory raised her hand. "I vote yes."

Tucker served himself more chicken parmigiana. "We know you do. You suggested the whole thing."

"Joe will never know if he wants to date Kylie unless he meets her."

"Do not consider this an audition, Mallory." Joe resisted the urge to shake his finger at his friend.

"You already know she does, Joe. And don't try and talk her out of it. I've been listening to her mind run wild about this for a week."

"Guilty as charged." Mallory didn't try to hide her smile. "I promise to behave at the cookout. Really."

"I can just uninvite you."

"What a mean thing to do to me and Tucker."

"I didn't say I would uninvite Tucker."

Tucker threw his head back and roared as Mallory gasped. "My husband wouldn't go without me."

"Oh, I wouldn't?"

"Enough." Joe waved his napkin like a white flag. "I'll do it. I'll invite Kylie to the cookout."

"Yes!"

"If she's smart—and I know she is because we play Words with Friends together and she's wicked good—she'll decline nicely. Who wants to do a first meet in a crowd?"

"And then?"

"And then I'll do the normal thing and invite her out for coffee." He motioned to the chicken parmigiana. "May I have more, please?"

Mallory was as persistent as his mom when he was twelve years old and she'd decided he'd "cleaned" his room long enough—and it was time for her to do it right. She ignored his protests that his room was fine. That it was clean. Kicked him out of his bedroom, turned a deaf ear to his demands for privacy, and promised he would thank her later.

He was an adult now, not a middle schooler. He could hold his own against Mallory. Besides, he doubted Kylie would say yes.

. . .

Good morning, Kylie. I know you haven't answered my question about Jolly Ranchers yet, but I have another question for you. It's an easy yes or no. Would you like to come to a casual Memorial Day weekend cookout at my house on Monday the 29th? It'll be a small group of family and friends. Let me know. Email. Or text. I'll include my phone number at the end of this email. Joe

. . .

Kylie had been sitting at her desk reading *Worth the Risk* when her computer pinged, indicating a new email. She'd just finished one chapter and was debating getting a fresh cup of tea versus pressing on to the next. She should have ignored the email, but instead she skimmed her inbox and found Joe's message. *Odd.* She hadn't responded to the email he'd sent last night. Shannon would have been so proud of her. Now she sat here, reading his second email for the third time.

Joe had invited her to a cookout in ten days.

An easy yes or no question, according to him.

Why hadn't he just tossed another fun trivia question to her? Something like "How many staircases are located in Hogwarts?"

Easy answer—142.

Kylie reached for her phone and video-called Dylan. If she could, she'd dial in Zoe and Leah, too, but for now, she'd talk with Dylan, starting to talk the minute her friend's face appeared on the screen. "Joe wants to meet me."

"That's fantastic!"

"No, it's not!"

"You're not excited?"

"I called you because I need you to help me figure out how to say no."

"You're not saying no."

"He invited me to a cookout, Dylan." Kylie spoke low and slow. "Memorial Day weekend. Family. Friends. I'm not doing that."

"Don't you want to meet Joe?"

Dylan's straight-to-the-point question made Kylie pause.

"Aha! You do want to meet him. You like him, don't you?"

"I wouldn't be emailing with the guy if I didn't like him—as a friend. And yes, I've imagined meeting him."

"You said yes to both questions, which means you'll say yes to Joe's invitation."

"But a cookout? I'll be the only person who doesn't know everyone else."

"You'll be the special guest."

"I don't want to be the special guest." Kylie pressed her fingertips to her temples. "Would you want to be the unknown in a bunch of knowns?"

There was the real problem—the introvert in her was stomping her feet and screaming, *"Don't go."* She didn't want to walk into a group of new people by herself. *Sheesh.* She didn't even know what Joe looked like.

Kylie groaned. "I can't do this."

"Yes, you can. Be brave."

"I haven't told Joe that I'm widowed."

"In five months, you haven't mentioned that?"

"I assume he knows I'm single. Like I assume he's single—"

"As if he'd invite you to a cookout and then introduce you to his wife. Or his girlfriend."

"Don't make this more complicated than it already is." Kylie choked on a half laugh. "I just didn't explain single meant widowed."

Dylan gasped. "Wait ... "

"What?"

"There is one thing that definitely makes you saying yes more complicated."

"What?"

"What if someone recognizes you? I mean, Joe probably doesn't browse the romance section of the bookstore, but someone else at the cookout might read your books."

Kylie dropped the phone on the table and buried her face in her hands. "I can't go."

Joe's simple yes or no question was becoming so tangled, like when Kylie decided to try knitting—a very short-lived aspiration. Remington decided her brand-new bag of yarn was for his amusement. He'd had more fun with all that softness than she did.

"Kylie! I can't see you or hear you. Kylie!"

She should just end this call with Dylan. Never reply to Joe—act like she hadn't received his email.

"Pick up the phone."

She dropped her hands from her face. "I'm here."

"You can say yes to the cookout. Take this relationship to the next level."

"Are you kidding me?"

"I don't mean romantically. I know you're not ready for that. I mean honestly."

"Oh."

"Either before Memorial Day weekend or once you're at Joe's—your choice—you tell Joe that *single* also means *widowed*." Dylan paused. "Or you save that conversation for the next time you get together with Joe. One thing at a time."

"You're assuming I'm going to the cookout."

"It's not that complicated."

"But like you said, what if someone recognizes me? Joe only knows me as Kylie Franklin."

"That's a distinct possibility because your books are crazy popular. Odds are, there will be other women there and someone recognizes you as *the* Veronica Hollins."

"What do I do?"

"Wait and see."

"That's your answer?"

"Yes. Wait and see. Meeting Joe for the first time is enough to deal with—and the possibility of explaining that you're widowed. If your writing identity is revealed, then you say, 'Surprise!'"

Dylan made it sound like she was jumping out of a huge party cake.

Surprise!

But if she said no now, she would probably never say yes to meeting Joe. They would remain in relationship limbo forever. Not that she was looking for more than friendship with him. But she knew the burden of regret. Had carried it for three years since Andrew's death.

Kylie ran her fingers through her hair. Her mouth was so dry she could barely swallow, and her teacup was empty. "I just realized something."

"What?"

"If I say no, then it's no forever."

"Meaning?"

"If I don't go to the cookout, then I won't ever meet Joe."

"You don't think he'll invite you to meet him another time?"

"He might. But I'd say no again because I would always see all the reasons not to meet."

"So then ... "

Kylie gripped the edge of her desk as she closed her eyes. Exhaled. "I'm saying yes."

"And the difficulties we just talked about?"

"They're still there, obviously."

"Will you tell Joe?"

"That single means widowed? Yes. That I'm also Veronica Hollins? If I need to jump out of that cake, I will."

Why did she feel like some superhero or secret agent being forced to reveal her identity? *Identities.*

"When are you going to give him an answer to his invitation?"

"Right now, while you're on the phone so I don't back out."

"Good idea."

"It's called accountability. Hold on." Kylie settled the phone against her laptop and hit Reply to Joe's email.

Hi, Joe, Thanks for the invitation to the cookout. I'd love to come. Please send the details and let me know if I can bring anything. Looking forward to meeting you and everyone else. Kylie

P.S. I loved Jolly Ranchers when I was a kid. They were originally made in Golden, CO.

Within seconds, the email was on its way to Joe. Things were in motion now. No stopping them.

"My yes is sent."

"Just a yes—nothing else?"

"One thing at a time, Dylan. I even told him I was looking forward to meeting him and everyone else. A blatant lie if I ever wrote one."

"You write fiction—all lies."

"Very funny." Kylie refused to smile. "I realize that's how some people view what I do for a living, but I think that's crass. There are fundamental truths in all fiction."

"I'm not one of those crass people. I'm your number one fan—well, I share that position with Leah and Zoe."

"Thank you. Now pray me through this decision, will you?"

"Absolutely. We also need to talk about what you're going to wear."

Kylie couldn't help but laugh. "Priorities, priorities."

CHAPTER 3

Joe: In all the time we've emailed, I don't think we've had the coffee versus tea conversation yet. I used to be quite the coffee drinker, but now I've switched caffeine camps and drink tea. I guess you could say I straddle the fence. What about you? And here's another question for you: Which two U.S. states produce coffee? (This is an easy question, but I'm going with it today.) Kylie

"I have a proposition for you." Shannon's statement came after a brief hello.

"I don't even know what to think about what you just said." Kylie finished tossing clean towels and washcloths into the laundry basket, shut the dryer door with a dull clang, dropped her phone on top of the pile, and then carried the plastic basket to her bedroom. "I'm listening."

"We both know you're dealing with writer's block—"

"I'm working on finishing the manuscript, Shannon. I'm getting back into the story, chapter by chapter ... "

"I know you are. But I've thought of another way to help you jump-start your writing."

"Fine. What's your proposition?" She dumped the laundry onto her deep purple bedspread, then reached for a still-warm washcloth to fold.

"Just this. You work with bestselling author Tate Merrick, who needs to add a romantic thread to his already completed military suspense."

"Tate Merrick?"

"Yes. Do you know him?"

"No ... I mean, not personally. But Andrew loved his books. He always preordered them. Our cat is named Remington after the hero in the series, Remington Gerard."

"That's a diehard fan."

"Well, Andrew wanted a Rottweiler, not a cat. He just refused to give up on the name after I adopted a stray kitten."

"Makes a little more sense. Where was I?"

"You want me to write with Tate Merrick?" As she continued to fold laundry, Remington curled up on one of the towels. Great.

"Yes. His agent contacted me, and his publisher and editors are on board with the idea. There's already a vague love interest in the book, but you're free to do what you want. Expand that character or start from scratch and create someone new."

"Why am I doing this again?"

"You're helping Merrick. He needs to connect with more female readers, and a stronger romantic thread will help him do that."

"And?"

"I'm negotiating what you'll get paid right now. This will help keep your readers happy too while you finish your manuscript. But I was also thinking it would be a great way to—"

"—deal with my writer's block. I remember."

"It's not the story you were writing when Andrew died, so writing it will be easier."

"I guess so."

"I know so. And a Tate Merrick and Veronica Hollins book will be an automatic bestseller."

"My name will be on the cover, then? Tate Merrick with Veronica Hollins." Her comment met with silence. "Shannon?"

"His publisher was thinking more of a ghostwriting gig."

"Then it's a no." Kylie held a folded towel against her body. "This isn't about ego, Shannon. I'm not a ghostwriter. If Merrick wants to gain readers, he needs my name on the cover to help him do it."

"I agree with you, but I'll need to take this request back to his agent."

"I'm glad you understand." Kylie paced her bedroom. "This isn't some high school group project where everyone gets the same grade, with no consideration for individual effort."

Shannon snorted. "You hated those too, huh?"

"Yes—but I like this idea. Andrew would be thrilled I was working with his favorite author. He'd ask me how soon we could meet Merrick for dinner." She had to laugh, imagining the scenario. She'd be lucky to get a word in past hello. "I know you'll negotiate a good contract monetarily. But it has to include a clause stipulating my name is on the cover. I'm not asking for top billing. 'With Veronica Hollins' is fine. His agent and editor already know this will help them sell more books. Guaranteed."

"I'll call his agent right after we're done talking."

"We're done then."

"Look at you, getting all bossy. If this goes through, I'll send you the contract to sign, and then you'll get the synopsis and manuscript."

"What's the timeline?"

"Three months, I think, but I'll double-check that with his agent too."

"Doable."

"Says the award-winning, bestselling romance author."

"You know it."

"Good to have you back."

"We'll take it one day at a time—if they agree to my request." She added the folded towel to the basket.

"You can tell me that I'm brilliant any time you want."

"You know I think you're brilliant, Shannon. I'll say it again when you send me that contract with the must-have clause."

"Deal."

She hadn't had a conversation like this with her agent in months. *Years.* One with a little bit of back talk. It could be fun to help Tate

Merrick. He didn't need to know she was doing it in memory of Andrew.

After the phone call, Kylie debated pulling one of Merrick's books off the shelves.

No. Not yet. She'd wait and see if the publisher agreed to her request. Then she'd skim some of the series and get a feel for his writing voice.

. . .

"No better way to start the week, right?" Joe shrugged into his windbreaker, his hair damp with sweat, as he exited the CrossFit gym with Tucker and Mallory.

"Especially when I beat my personal best for front squats." Mallory pumped the air with her fist.

Tucker pulled her in for a side hug. "Proud of you."

"Enjoy it today. Next time we're here, it's a new goal." Joe couldn't resist teasing Mallory.

"I intend to enjoy it all day long. It's going to be a fantastic Monday, even if my legs hurt." Mallory hugged Tucker back. "And on that note, we need to get home and get ready for work."

"Working remotely is great, but there are still virtual meetings to attend."

"Understood." Joe veered toward his car. "See you both Wednesday?"

"Planning on it." Tucker offered him a short salute.

"See you then." He escaped the chill of the early-morning May air as he slipped into his car, already anticipating a hot shower when he got home. He checked his phone before he started the car.

A voice message from Liza?

"Good morning. I know it's early there in Colorado, but I also know you're probably working out right now. Call me when you can. Sooner rather than later, okay?"

Typical Liza. Short, sweet, and to the point. He could sit in the car and call her, which would be sooner. Or he could wait until he was home and showered, which would be later—but not that much later.

His breath formed a small cloud inside the car. He turned on the car so it could start warming up. He'd be a good client and call his agent, as requested. But for all his reliability, Liza didn't answer her phone. Later it was, then.

Joe pulled out of the parking space and made the fifteen-minute drive to his home. Kicked off his cross-trainers just inside the door and headed upstairs to his bedroom. There was nothing better than a hot shower after working out.

Ten minutes later he sat on the edge of his bed in a comfortable pair of jeans and checked his phone. Liza had called again. Figured. He grabbed his earbud and hit REDIAL.

"Hey, Joe, thanks for returning my call."

"I'm glad we're not going to spend all day listening to each other's voicemails."

"I wanted to get back to your manuscript."

"I'm working on it, Liza." Joe finger-combed his damp hair. "But learning to write romance is not instantaneous—"

"I know that. Your editor knows that. And that's why you'll love Plan B."

"Tell me Plan B is that we're going back to the original manuscript, and I'll be a happy man."

"We're sticking with adding romance, Joe, but you don't have to write it."

"I don't follow."

"We're asking Veronica Hollins to write the romance for *Lethal Strike*."

Her words hit him like the unwelcome spray of a cold shower. "You're asking … Veronica Hollins to write the romance?"

"Let me rephrase that. Her agent has already talked with her, so Veronica Hollins has agreed to write the romance for your manuscript."

"Before you ran this idea past me?"

"We didn't want to talk with you about the idea until we knew Veronica Hollins was even interested."

"Why wouldn't she be interested? All she has to do is add a few kisses—"

"Aren't you the man who was just telling me writing romance is hard?"

"It's hard, but that doesn't mean I can't do it if you give me some time."

"And I'm telling you that you don't have to do it. Veronica Hollins is going to do it."

Joe forced himself to stay professional as he stood and paced the room. "What else are you telling me?"

"Originally, we thought this would be a ghostwriting project—"

"I like the sound of that."

"However, Veronica Hollins wants her name on the cover, as in 'Tate Merrick with Veronica Hollins'—"

"What?" Now Liza had turned the cold shower on full blast.

"And the publisher agreed."

"Liza, this is my book!"

"No one is forgetting that. But if you remember, the goal is to get more female readers. Having Veronica's name on the cover will absolutely do that."

"Veronica Hollins will write less than a third—"

"She's writing a very important part of this book—and the publisher is paying her. This doesn't affect your advance at all."

Small comfort, that.

"Liza . . . "

"Veronica's name will be on the cover, beneath yours." Liza's voice was firm. "Close your eyes and picture the words 'Tate Merrick with Veronica Hollins.'"

He tried to do what his agent asked, and all he could see was the cover of *Lethal Strike* morphing into a bodice ripper, with a shirtless Remington Gerard embracing some bosomy damsel in distress.

"What do you want me to say? Thank you?"

"That would be nice. I called because I didn't want you to be surprised by the new clause in the contract when I send it over."

Her words caused him to drop all the expectations he'd been juggling. He sat on the edge of the bed, the mattress giving beneath his weight. Liza had agreed to represent him when he was just Joe Edwards—standing on the outside looking in at the publishing world. She'd believed in him when publisher after publisher passed on his first manuscript.

"I'm not going to say thank you." Joe rubbed his hand along his unshaven jaw. "I'm going to say I'm sorry."

"No need to apologize—"

"Yes, there is. I was out of line." He cleared his throat. "This whole thing has knocked me back a few steps, to be honest."

"You're a good writer, Joe."

"You're just saying that because I'm your favorite client."

"I'm saying it because it's true." Liza's tone was firm. "You study the industry, the market. You know it's tough for everyone right now—even the best authors. Don't fight me on this. Accept some help."

"You're right."

"Was that so hard to say?"

"Yes."

Liza laughed, the boisterous sound pulling a chuckle from him.

He was scrambling to sweep his bad mood under his bed with the dust bunnies. Liza reminded him of all the times Mom had tried to help him work through a bad mood when Dad had overlooked him. Or worse, belittled his dreams.

He relaxed the fist clenched by his side. He'd learned years ago to stop caring what Dad thought of him—or to at least fake it. Then he went into a career field that was all about reviews and followers. And Dad never read one of his books.

Not that Joe cared.

"You'll sign the addendum to your contract?"

"You'll forgive me for being a jerk?"

"You're forgiven and it's forgotten."

"Email me the updated contract and I'll sign it."

"I'll do it as soon as we get off the phone."

"You're the best, Liza.

"You always say that."

"I always mean it too."

After he'd shaved and finished getting dressed, Joe checked his laptop. Sure enough, Liza's email was waiting with the subject line To My Favorite Client. He pulled up the PDF document, scrolled to the signature line, and auto signed it. Attached it to a quick two-word reply of "And done" and hit Send.

Now all he had to do was wait for Veronica Hollins to insert a sappy happily ever after into his story.

As Joe retrieved eggs from the fridge to make breakfast, his phone buzzed again. He wasn't going to get anything done today if people kept calling. He turned the heat on underneath the skillet. "Hey."

"You haven't called." His sister's tone was only half-kidding.

"You called first, Abbie. I didn't have a chance."

"I always call you first."

"Because you never give me a chance."

"Ugh." There was laughter in her voice—finally. "This is getting us nowhere."

He broke an egg into the skillet. "How's my favorite sister?"

"Have you been online?"

"Wait. That's when you say, 'I'm your only sister.'"

"Joe."

"No, I haven't been online yet. What's the big deal?"

"Then you haven't seen the headline."

"Something good about me?" Joe focused on making his breakfast.

"Something about your ex-girlfriend."

"Not interested."

"She's pregnant. It's all over the news."

Joe's hand slipped as he cracked the third egg. "Abbie. You made me break the yolk."

"That's all you have to say?"

"What do you want me to say?" He tossed the broken shell into the trash and rinsed his hands.

"It doesn't bother you that Cassidy is pregnant?"

"She's married to another guy. I don't care what she does—unless she's saying I'm the father of her baby."

"Joe!"

Now Abbie sounded like Mom. "Did you call to tell me anything else? Because I have some interesting news."

"What?"

"Veronica Hollins is going to write a romance angle for my upcoming release."

His sister's screech made him wish he'd pulled out his earbud. "I love her books! Why haven't you done this sooner?"

"Thanks for that." Joe reached for the insulated carafe and poured himself a mug of coffee.

"Oh, come on. I read all your books. But they're going to be even better with romance. I'll tell all my friends to buy them."

"Don't you already tell your friends to buy my books?"

"I do—and they usually buy them for their husbands. Or their brothers. But now all my girlfriends will buy them and read them."

His sister's response was the first hint this idea was going to work.

A bit of smoke filled the kitchen, along with the odor of burnt eggs. Joe turned back to the stove. He wrinkled his nose and coughed.

"What's wrong?"

"I ruined my breakfast." He pulled the pan from the burner and turned the heat off. "Not paying attention."

"You're good with this, Joe?"

"With Veronica Hollins helping me?" He faked positivity. "I've talked it over with my agent and we agree this is beneficial for both of us."

"I guess that's true."

"It gives us both the chance to expand our readership."

Not at all how Liza had presented the project, but he liked this new and much improved spin. This wasn't about Veronica overshadowing him. He could help her too.

Joe turned on the fan over his stove and then exited the kitchen. "You and Hudson still coming to the cookout?'

"Of course. You worried I'm going to leave you to deal with Dad yourself?"

He ignored her comment as he stretched out in his favorite chair and placed his feet on the ottoman. "You're not the only one with news."

"I thought you already told me your news."

"More news, then. I invited Kylie to the cookout."

"Kylie? Wait—she's the woman you've been talking to online, right? She's coming?"

"Yes, but just as a friend, Abbie. Don't overreact, okay?"

"This is so great. I can't wait to meet her. Oh my gosh, Cassidy would be so jealous—"

"And this is overreacting." Joe scrubbed his jaw. "Kylie and I are friends. And to make Cassidy jealous, I would have to invite her too, which I'm not doing. This is a low-key get-together."

"Got it. Low-key." Joe could almost see his sister crossing her heart as she said the words.

Just then an incoming call interrupted their conversation.

Liza again. Odd.

"Abbs, I gotta go. Liza is calling me. Wait—what I told you about Veronica Hollins?"

"I won't tell anyone. See you soon."

He disconnected and switched over to Liza's call. "Hello, again."

"I needed to touch base about one more thing."

"I'm listening."

"We were thinking it'd be nice if you'd write a personal note to Veronica Hollins that we can attach to the synopsis and manuscript of *Lethal Strike*."

He closed his eyes, swallowing the immediate *no* that sprang to his lips. "Why don't you just say I'm looking forward to working with her?"

"We'd like you to write the message, Joe. It doesn't have to be long. Just something welcoming. Write it and send it to me, please."

"Liza—"

"Just do it. I'll expect it later today."

"Fine. Anything else?"

"Can't think of anything. I'll let you get to it."

Joe tossed the phone onto the side table.

What a day.

He stared ahead for a few moments and then shook his head. Stood. Strode down the hallway to his office. Sat at his desk. Opened his laptop. Typed out four sentences. Added his name. Sent the email to Liza.

Done.

The coffee burned in his empty stomach. He abandoned his office and searched in the bathroom for the bottle of antacids, popped two tablets and washed them down with a gulp of water. The antacids left a chalky residue on his tongue no matter how much water he drank. Just like his relationship with Cassidy left a bad taste in his mouth.

Yeah. He'd keep his distance from Veronica Hollins. And it'd be wise to keep things friendly with Kylie. Casual. Just so long as everyone else remembered that too.

. . .

After returning to the front room, Kylie set the cup of fresh tea on the side table, away from the laptop she'd left on the corner of the couch. So far this morning she'd made decent progress reading *Worth the Risk*. The new writing project was already spurring her on.

Remington curled up next to her feet, barely moving as Kylie eased back onto the couch. She glanced at her inbox. Nothing from Joe, but she clicked on an email from Shannon.

Kylie, Here's the synopsis and manuscript for *Lethal Strike*. You'll notice there's also an attached message from Tate Merrick. I'm excited for you to get started. Call me if you have any questions.

A message from Tate Merrick? Kylie ignored the document and clicked on the message.

I'm looking forward to seeing what you add to *Lethal Strike*. My agent Liza speaks highly of you and of course I'm aware of your publishing success. You certainly know romance.

I agree adding this romantic thread to the overall book will attract new readers to the Remington Gerard series, and that will benefit both of us.

Tate Merrick

That was underwhelming. Reading between the lines, Merrick was less than thrilled about this project. She could give the man the benefit of the doubt and assume he saved his excitement for his books.

His words were as rough as the first draft of a novel. Needing a good rewrite. She stretched her fingers above the keyboard, and then dropped them into her lap, twisting her wedding bands. She could only hope what he'd written in the manuscript was better.

Right now? She didn't care for Tate Merrick very much. So much for taking on the project because he was Andrew's favorite author.

Could she write a romance with a man she didn't like? Technically, she wasn't writing *with* him, she was writing *for* him. They weren't working together. Of course, he'd read whatever she'd write. But they'd correspond via email. This was a professional relationship, not a personal one.

She could do this.

Kylie wanted to pick up the virtual gauntlet Tate Merrick had thrown down and toss it back his way by showing him just how well she could write a romance. He was "aware of her publishing success." *Humph!* If he was truly aware of who she was, he'd call her on the phone, invite her out to dinner—that he'd pay for—and then fall all over himself as he thanked her for helping him.

Now she sounded like some puffed-up egomaniac who was all over social media telling people to buy her books. What was wrong with her? She retrieved one of his books from the canvas bag, flipped it over, and stared at his professional photo.

Not bad looking, if you liked military types. He wore a black leather jacket over a lapis blue turtleneck that matched his eyes. Someone had planned that.

Kylie continued to stare at the photo. Wait a minute. No wonder Tate Merrick sounded so stiff. They knew each other—and not just in a "my husband loves your books" kind of way. How could she have forgotten? They'd crossed paths in the most casual of ways at a few writers' conferences. At one conference they'd ended up on the same authors' panel and Merrick had tossed a few barbs about the value of romance.

"Question for you, Mr. Merrick—what makes a book a bestseller?"

Tate Merrick waited for the microphone to be passed down to him before answering. "We've all heard the phrase 'write a page-turner'—something that keeps your reader up at night because they can't stop reading your book. The best way to do that is to make sure there's lots of suspense and tension in your book."

"And romance. Readers love romantic tension." Veronica had spoken up from her position halfway down the panel.

"A book can do well without overdosing on romance. My novels prove that." Tate Merrick maintained a firm grip on the microphone.

"And yet romance novels outsell all other genres year after year." Veronica's voice remained even, loud enough to be heard without benefit of the microphone.

"Even if readers know how the books are going to end."

"Excuse me?"

"A happily ever after every single time."

"And what's wrong with that?"

"Nothing—if you like predictable endings."

"Mr. Merrick, just because I write happily ever afters, that doesn't mean my endings are predictable."

The panel moderator stepped forward with an awkward laugh. "Alrighty then. Moving on to our next question, let's talk about book covers."

Andrew had been sitting in the audience and had laughingly chastised her for getting in a fight with his favorite author. Kylie had wanted to say, "He started it," but instead said, "I'm your favorite author, remember?"

"Can you imagine how difficult it was to watch my two favorite novelists throwing verbal punches at one another?" Of course, she'd laughed too and that was the end of it.

Here she was, years later, working with a man who had no respect for romance.

The truth is, Mr. Merrick, we need each other. We're stuck with one another, like it or not.

CHAPTER 4

Joe: It seems silly to send you an email this morning since I'll see you in a few short hours. I'm excited to meet you, as well as your family, and your friends. But first, I need to finish making my appetizer. Of course, I have a trivia question for you: What city is known as the birthplace of Memorial Day? I'll see you around one o'clock. Kylie

The drive from Monument to Denver had been an easy cruise underneath a clear blue Colorado sky. Kylie had texted Joe right before she left her house to say she was on the way, as he'd requested. He'd responded with, *Looking forward to seeing you soon.*

Kylie streamed her favorite playlist and sang along, hoping the music would distract her and calm her nerves. She'd splurged on a pedicure in a fun bright red polish, and then opted for a pair of jeans and a red boatneck top.

She didn't want to date Joe. She didn't want to date anyone. Today was about meeting him. Nothing more. *This is not a date. This is not a date.* She'd repeated the words the closer she got to Joe's. Once she turned into his neighborhood, Kylie parked on a side street and texted Dylan, Leah, and Zoe.

I'm a minute away from Joe's house.

Zoe responded first. How do you feel?

Sick to my stomach.

Dylan now. Did you make the wings?

Yeah. They smell sweet and spicy. I've been tempted to snack on them on the drive here.

Dylan again. Those are always a hit.

I'll just walk around saying, "Hi, I'm Kylie," while I hand out wings. That will make an impression.

Leah at last. I'm here! Stop texting us and go meet Joe. Tell us everything later.

I'll text when I get home.

Kylie took a moment to reapply clear lip gloss. Moments later, she eased her car into Joe's driveway and parked. An American flag hung by the front door. With Joe's military background, Memorial Day weekend was probably more than cookouts. The lawn was freshly mowed and edged, and the curtains pulled back on the wide bay window.

She rounded the car and retrieved the large ceramic bowl filled with the wings. As she bumped the front passenger door closed with her hip, the front door opened, and footsteps sounded behind her.

"You made it." The man's voice was pleasant. Welcoming.

Kylie turned. Blinked. Joe ... not Joe.

Tate Merrick?

Her grip loosened on the bowl. It slipped out of her hands and landed on the cement with a crack, chicken wings splattering everywhere.

Joe ... *Tate Merrick* rushed forward. "Are you okay?"

"Am ... am I at the right house?"

He stopped a few feet away. "I think so. You're Kylie, right?"

"But you're ... you're Tate Merrick."

He glanced away. Remade eye contact as his face flushed beneath his short brown hair. "Yeah, yeah. I am. This is awkward."

Kylie had been worried about needing to jump out of a cake and yelling "Surprise!" when Joe Edwards was hiding his own author identity from her.

His eyes narrowed as he continued to stare at her. Was he expecting a fangirl moment? Or had he recognized her?

"Do I know you?"

Kylie recognized him within seconds as Tate Merrick and in return got a hesitant, *"Do I know you?"*

"Um, yes, we've met before." She didn't say anything else, allowing him a moment to figure it out.

Nothing.

She stepped around the mess of wings, holding out her hand. "I write novels under the pen name Veronica Hollins."

His brilliant blue eyes widened.

"We met on an authors' panel at a conference a few years ago. And of course, I just agreed to write the romance for your upcoming release." She pulled her hand back since Joe ... Tate was as good as frozen in the May sunshine. "Thanks for the email saying you're looking forward to working with me."

Before Joe could respond, the front door opened again, and a young woman in a white and red gingham sundress came running toward them waving a white plastic trash bag.

"I saw what happened." She handed the bag to Joe. "Here, you can clean up the mess."

"Abbie—"

"I was watching from the front window. You knew I would." She turned to Kylie with a laugh. "And you're ... *Veronica Hollins?*"

Surprise.

Her "jump out of the cake" moment seemed a bit anticlimactic, considering Joe had jumped out of a cake first. He still seemed to be struggling with the reality she was Veronica Hollins.

The aroma of her barbecue wings lingered in the air. What a mess. There would be no walking around and saying, "Hi, I'm Kylie" to the other people at the cookout—if she even had the chance to meet them.

"Just call me Kylie. Please."

"But you are Veronica Hollins, right? I mean, your hair is shorter ... "

"Yes, I am. And yes, I decided to cut it last year." As if that was important. "And you're Abbie?"

The next moment she was engulfed in a hug as the young woman with loose brown hair pulled her close. "You're my favorite author."

Kylie met Joe's eyes over Abbie's shoulder. "Nice, Abbie. I thought I was your favorite author."

"Of course you are." Abbie released her. "But you're also my brother, so it doesn't count. Why didn't you tell me who Kylie was?"

Joe knelt and began tossing wings and pieces of the bowl into the trash bag. "Funny story. We didn't know we were both novelists."

"You're kidding me! This is hysterical."

"It's true." Kylie shrugged. "We kept things casual online. Nothing too personal. Joe told me that he had a military background."

"I do. I was in the Army. Civil affairs. And I thought Kylie taught English or literature."

Kylie focused on Abbie. "Most people don't consider 'author' as the first thing when they think of a journalism career field."

"Abbie." Joe stood, leaving the trash bag on the driveway. "Would you go get me the broom and dustpan from the kitchen so I can finish cleaning up this mess?"

"I'm talking with—"

"Please." He pulled a folded red bandana from the back pocket of his jeans and wiped his fingers.

"Fine." Abbie jogged back up the driveway.

Kylie shook her head. "That wasn't very subtle."

"I wasn't trying to be subtle." He motioned to the remaining shards of glass. "And I do need the broom. And probably the hose."

"Sorry about the mess."

"I'm sorry too. The wings smell great."

The stain on Joe's driveway was the least of their worries. Their little meet and greet had upended their five-month relationship—friendship—in less than a minute.

Abbie's face appeared in Joe's front window. His sister wasn't rushing back with the broom. Giving them a chance to recover before she and Joe had to meet everyone else?

"Reading between the lines in your email, you're not excited about adding romance to your manuscript."

"You really want to talk about this now?"

"Just answer the question."

"There wasn't a question."

Fine. He wanted a question? She'd ask him a question. "What do you have against romance?"

"I don't have anything against romance." Joe tossed the sauce-stained bandana onto the grass. "I said I was looking forward to working with you."

"I could almost hear you gritting your teeth while writing that email."

"If you're expecting me to hold your hand through this project—"

"I don't need you to hold my hand, Joe. *I* know what I've been hired to do."

"But do you know military suspense, which is what I write."

Kylie twisted her fingers. "Hostility—be it covert or overt—doesn't promote teamwork."

"We're not a team. I've written the book. All you're being paid to do is add a little romance—"

"Which will become a key element to *Lethal Strike.* This is no longer your book—it's our book. Tate Merrick with Veronica Hollins. *Me.* The goal is to appeal to my kind of readers, so this isn't about 'adding a little romance.'" Kylie air-quoted the phrase as she repeated Joe's words.

"You're just proving how impossible this idea is going to be." Joe's vivid blue eyes darkened. "You can't shovel romance into a completed military suspense manuscript."

"I'm an award-winning author. I don't shovel words. I write bestsellers."

How could she have ever liked this guy?

She and Joe had met on Words with Friends. Now they were battling with words, as if they were mortal enemies. She should get back in her car, drive home, call Shannon, and tell her to cancel the contract.

No.

She would write the romance and prove Tate Merrick wrong.

The front door opened once again and Abbie appeared, brandishing the broom over her head. Two other women followed her.

"We're coming!"

"Wha—?" Joe glanced over his shoulder and his body stiffened. "Perfect."

The trio advanced on them, Abbie grinning broadly while the other women lagged. "Here you go."

"What are you doing, Abbie?" Joe spoke in a low voice.

"I told Mom and Mallory"—her eyebrows rose—"you know. And I said of course they could come and meet her."

Kylie stepped around Joe. "Hi, I'm Kylie. Kylie Franklin." She went to shake hands with Joe's mom and was pulled into a hug. "O-okay."

"We're so excited you're here." Kylie could see both Joe and Abbie in the woman's smile and the shape of her face. "Of course, I've read all your books, but it's so nice to meet you, *Kylie*."

The other woman, who looked to be about Kylie's age, offered a small wave. "I'm Mallory. My husband Tucker went to college with Joe. He's manning the grill right now."

"Hi."

Abbie linked arms with Kylie. "Why don't we take Kylie to the backyard while you finish cleaning up this little spill?"

Kylie hesitated. "I should help—"

Joe took the broom and waved at the group of women. "Go ahead. I won't be far behind."

"I'm sorry about this."

"It's not a big deal."

A whirlwind of women had come and doused the fire flaring between her and Joe. When she'd said, *"I'm sorry about this,"* Kylie didn't know if she was talking about the mess he was cleaning up in his driveway or how they'd both hidden their professional identities or the tension simmering between them because of the writing project.

Abbie laughed as she gave her brother a quick hug. At least the other women didn't seem to notice any strain between her and Joe. But right now, Abbie was more excited about Kylie being here than Joe was.

She wouldn't be staying long.

...

Joe stood by the now cool grill in his backyard. Tucker watched Dad and Hudson playing cornhole, while Kylie sat with Mallory, Abbie, and Mom. They'd been talking for the last hour.

Joe pressed the metal tool into the grill and worked at removing the grease and grime. He looked up when Tucker tapped him on his shoulder, offering him a cold Pepsi.

"Scraping down the grill?"

"Needs to be done." He popped open the can.

"Why aren't you talking to Kylie?"

"Not going to fight my way through the crowd."

"She gets along with everyone, no denying that."

"That's true."

"Kind of funny how you're both novelists and you didn't know it."

"Ha ha."

Tucker raised an eyebrow. "Is it a problem?"

"You have no idea."

"Explain it to me."

Joe checked to make sure Hudson and Dad were still caught up in their cornhole competition. "Remember when I mentioned my publisher wanted romance added to my latest manuscript?"

"Yeah."

"They hired Veronica Hollins—Kylie—to do it."

"Wait … you didn't know this?"

"When it all went down, I didn't know Kylie was Veronica Hollins and she didn't know I was Tate Merrick. We realized all of it when we met in my driveway."

Tucker fought against a laugh. "That's crazy."

"Tell me about it."

Talking with Tucker was like watching a football instant replay of what happened earlier, but the call wouldn't be overturned. Meeting Kylie was a major false start.

Kylie's musical laugh pulled his attention to her. She'd smiled and laughed often while she'd talked with Abbie and Mom and Mallory.

Was she avoiding talking with him? Did she realize he'd been avoiding her?

"You're going to break your grill if you keep scraping that hard." Tucker removed the tool from his hand. "You're telling me this is going to be a problem?"

"I'm not happy about Veronica Hollins adding romance to my book. Today I find out Veronica Hollins and Kylie Franklin are the same person." Joe closed the grill with a metallic clang. "Yeah, it's a problem."

"No coffee date?"

"What's the point?"

"You could talk about the book."

Joe growled. "Not funny."

"Where's your sense of humor?"

"This is my career—"

"I know that, but you've got to breathe. Your publisher knows what they're doing. They don't want you to fail." Tucker paused, as if waiting for some sign of agreement from Joe. "And you've been talking to Kylie for months before this, which means you connected enough you wanted to invite her today. It wasn't just because Mallory suggested it. You enjoyed having conversations with her."

"I didn't know who she really was."

"And she didn't know who you really were." Tucker motioned toward Kylie. "She stayed, didn't she?"

"Abbie wouldn't let her leave."

"Your sister's not holding her hostage, Joe." Tucker pointed the scraper at him. "If you're not going to talk to her, someone has to."

With those words, Tucker left.

Tucker was right. Joe was letting his sister—and Mom and Mallory—take his place. Letting them get to know Kylie, which was what he'd been looking forward to ever since he'd invited her to the cookout. But now when he looked at Kylie, all he saw was bestselling author Veronica Hollins, who his publisher had hired to rescue his book.

Everything about the day should have been perfect. But he hadn't expected meeting Kylie to be so wrong.

Joe picked up a platter of leftover brats and carried it into the kitchen to find a storage container and put them in the fridge. A few moments later, Kylie joined him, carrying ketchup and mustard.

"Hey, I saw you cleaning up ... "

He motioned toward the condiments. "You didn't need to do that."

"I'm happy to help." She set the plastic bottles on the island. "Besides, I wanted to say goodbye before I left."

"You're leaving? You haven't played cornhole yet. It's ... tradition."

"I've got to get back to Remington."

Joe stopped adding brats to the plastic container. "Remington?"

"My cat. He gets antsy when I'm gone—not that he runs my life or anything—but he's been known to take his frustration out on the toilet paper roll in my bathroom."

"Remington. That's an interesting name for a cat."

"My husband, Andrew, was a huge fan of yours. He preordered all your books. In hardback."

Husband?

She paused. Cleared her throat. "He wanted a Rottweiler. Planned on naming it Remington. When I ended up adopting a stray kitten—long story—he insisted we name it Remington."

"Oh."

Joe fumbled for something else to say, but so many thoughts collided in his head. Kylie's husband was a fan. But the news of how Kylie's husband ... *Veronica's* husband had died in an accident just a few days before her last book released had made the headlines three years ago.

Another unexpected, awkward moment with Kylie Franklin. It was like she kept pulling off masks and revealing hidden parts of her life.

She'd mentioned to Abbie she'd cut her hair. It skimmed her shoulders in loose, black waves that contrasted with her honey-brown eyes. How long was it before? They'd met at writers' conferences, probably more than once. But back then, he discounted romance writers, even the bestselling ones. Now he had to work with her for three months.

They both looked away as his parents walked into the kitchen.

Dad spoke first. "Your sister said Kylie was leaving. Your mom wanted to make sure I had the chance to say goodbye."

Kylie stepped forward. "You didn't need to—"

"We haven't talked much today. My wife says you write. What kind of books—"

"Kylie has a journalism degree." Joe knew his words were too loud by the way Mom's eyes widened. He refused to look at Kylie.

"Just like you."

"Yes. Just like me."

"That's so interesting. No wonder you two hit it off."

"Yes. We both like trivia too. Kylie asked me earlier what city is known as the birthplace of Memorial Day."

Kylie nodded. "That's right. Do you know?"

"Waterloo, New York, based on a 1966 presidential proclamation—although there are some people who disagree with that."

Before he and Kylie could debate dates, his dad said, "We should get together for a family game night the next time your mother and I are in town."

"We'll have to see if that works out."

"Watch this guy, Kylie." Dad hitched a thumb in his direction. "He cheats."

"Dad, I don't cheat."

"Not anymore." His dad laughed. "It's a joke, son."

"Right."

Hysterical.

It seemed Abbie and Mom understood his request to keep Kylie's author identity on the lowdown. All this day needed was for Dad to find out Kylie wrote romance—worse, that she was adding romance to his latest book. What respect he'd worked so hard to earn would be lost. He needed to end the conversation. Now.

"I should walk Kylie to her car." He kept his tone casual. Relaxed. No hint of the headache building in his temples.

All Kylie said was yes, and then accepted Mom's hug before following him out of the house. Now they stood beside her car, the site of the earlier barbecue wing disaster.

"Thanks for inviting me today."

"Thanks for driving up."

"I enjoyed meeting everyone."

"I'm surprised Abbie didn't ask for your phone number."

"She did."

Of course she did.

"Would you rather I hadn't given it to her?"

"You're two consenting adults—" Joe groaned. "That came out totally wrong."

"Yes." Kylie's lips twisted. "A lot of things went wrong today."

"Agreed."

Kylie clicked her automatic key fob. "Thanks again, Joe." She opened the door. Slipped into the driver's seat.

Joe caught the top of the door with his hand. "Wait."

She gripped the steering wheel. "What?"

He took a step closer. "Would you ... would you like to meet for coffee sometime soon?"

"Coffee?"

"Or tea. Just you and me. We can find someplace between here and Monument."

She rubbed her bottom lip with her thumb and then, "Sure."

She sounded more hesitant than certain.

"Great. I'll ... I'll email you."

"Okay. Goodbye, Joe."

"Bye, Kylie. Drive safely." He stepped back. Moved to the top of the driveway as she started the car and backed away.

The plan had been to say a simple goodbye. He wasn't sure he could balance the reality Kylie was also Veronica Hollins. Then he'd called an audible and asked her to coffee.

Joe unwound the hose from the side of the house and rinsed the greasy stain from the driveway. Meeting for coffee was a one-time thing. A way to smooth over today. Nothing more.

CHAPTER 5

Kylie placed the bowl of fruit salad in the center of the dingy glass-top table. She pulled out one of the black wrought iron chairs set around the table at one corner of the deck on the side of her house. Her trio of friends, Dylan, Leah, and Zoe, each pulled out their own chairs, the metal legs scraping against the faded wood.

"Early June, and this is the first time I've sat outside." She dusted off the old gray cushion before she sat, then handed the cloth off to Dylan. "Here, use this and then pass it on. The cushions aren't the best, but at least we've got shade, thanks to the trees."

"I'm good. Just glad to get off my feet." Dylan arranged the bowls, napkins, and spoons. "That was a good barre class."

"Agreed."

"Aren't you glad we joined?" Zoe stretched her legs so her bare feet rested in the opposite chair.

"You mean, aren't you all glad I suggested the idea?" Dylan passed the towel to Leah.

"Once we got past the first month of not being able to move." Leah dusted off her chair and sat.

Kylie tossed the grimy towel on the ground in the corner of the deck. "There was that—and the learning curve for the moves."

Dylan sipped from her water bottle. "So ... have you heard from Joe lately?"

"I'm impressed. You waited until after class—and until we all got back here—to ask me about Joe."

"Answer the question already. I wanted to ask you all morning."

Kylie shook her head, releasing her hair from the rubber band that had held it in a ponytail. "Our emails have dropped off since the cookout disaster."

"It wasn't a complete disaster." Zoe was ever the optimist. Her bright pink glasses fit her personality.

"No, his sister Abbie is texting me now. We're trying to figure out when we can meet up."

"You gained a new friend." Leah spooned fruit salad into her bowl. "That's fun."

"And Joe and I are having coffee this week."

Zoe's smile widened. "There's still hope, right?"

"Hope for what?"

"That you and Joe have a future..."

"We do have a future—a literary one, remember? And that's the problem. We're writing a book together, and that fact has seriously tested our friendship, which is too bad."

Dylan leaned forward, her spoon poised above her bowl. "Why do you say that?"

"I like Joe."

"I knew it!" Leah rapped the table with her knuckles.

"Let me finish." Kylie sighed. "I like Joe. As a friend. Why else would I have emailed him for five months? We have similar interests. He's smart. Funny. Am I looking for romance? No."

"Kylie, do you want to be alone for the rest of your life?"

Dylan's direct question brought her up short—and the answer that spilled out surprised her.

"I haven't been alone these past three years since Andrew died." She pressed her hand to her heart. "Grief is crowded. Crowded with the memories of what Andrew and I had. Crowded with the dreams of the future we'd planned together."

"Oh Kylie..."

She sat in the shade of the trees arching over the deck and fought a sudden sting of tears. She hadn't cried in months. She didn't want to cry today, even if she was with her closest friends, the ones who had stuck with her during the toughest years of her life. Prayed her through.

She gripped the worn edges of the cushion beneath her legs. She'd ignored so many things since Andrew died. Big things, like her book. Small things, like dealing with the shabby patio furniture.

A broken heart made it easy to ignore things.

"What are you thinking, Kylie?" Zoe's words were a gentle intrusion on her jumbled thoughts.

"I'm just realizing how...*congested* life has felt since Andrew died. There's been so much to do—and so much I've avoided doing. I lost Andrew. I lost friends. Not the three of you, of course, but some of *our friends*. And to answer Dylan's question, no, I don't want to be alone like this for the rest of my life."

"Which means—" Dylan's words were a gentle prompt.

"I know what it means, but I don't think Joe is that guy."

"Why not?"

"Because he's not just Joe Edwards. He's also Tate Merrick, writer of military suspense novels. And while Joe likes me—well, he liked me—Tate Merrick doesn't."

"The story's not over—no pun intended." Again, Zoe's positivity showed up.

"This is a plot twist neither of us saw coming—*pun intended*—and I don't know if the story is salvageable." Kylie stirred the mixture of strawberries, peaches, and melon in her bowl. "I will say one thing."

"What's that?"

"I understand why Andrew liked Tate Merrick's novels so much."

Leah shifted in her seat, her feathered red hair framing a face dotted with a smattering of freckles. "Why do you say that?"

"Besides reading his manuscript, I started reading his debut novel."

"And?"

"He's a good writer. His sense of humor shows up in his novel, and I can see why he writes military suspense. He keeps you on the edge of your seat. Sorry for the cliché."

"You going to leave the guy a review?"

"No!"

"Why not?" Dylan used her napkin and brushed some dried leaves off the tabletop. "If you like the book so much, leave a review."

"I'm sure Andrew already did."

"So? You can still post one."

"Dylan, stop." Kylie swallowed a bite of fresh fruit. "It's not like Joe would notice if I left a review or not."

Kylie stared at the peeling paint on the deck railing. She hadn't even finished the book yet—but if she didn't exert some self-control, she'd stay up too late tonight and read all the way to the end.

"Y'all remember we have our monthly massages this weekend, right?" Dylan pulled out her phone and checked her calendar.

"Thanks for the reminder." Leah smiled. "Don't want to miss that."

"Want me to add on pedicures?"

Kylie groaned. "You do remember I am working under not one, but two deadlines?"

"I remember."

Kylie scanned the sun-faded wood of the deck. "I don't suppose you three would like to help me paint this deck, would you?"

"And this fits into your schedule how?" Zoe scrunched her nose beneath her glasses. "I'll be happy to research some people who could paint your deck for you."

"That would be great."

Dylan set her phone aside. "This is why you should be considering selling this house."

"Again, Dylan?"

"Yes, again." Dylan rose and walked from one end of the deck to the other, her sandals slapping against the wood. "Do you love this house—or do you love that it was the house you and Andrew bought together?"

Kylie stood and shoved her chair back in place.

Dylan tilted her head. "You're not answering."

"Neither."

"What do you mean?"

"I didn't love this house when we bought it ... and I don't love it now."

"I wasn't expecting you to say that." Dylan leaned against the railing, stepping away quickly. "Splinters. Why did you buy it then?"

"We didn't want to live in Denver, even though Andrew's job was there. And then one of his colleagues was moving and selling this house and offered him a deal, so ... "

"You took the deal," Leah summarized.

"Andrew thought it was a decent commute, straight up I-25." Kylie sighed. "But you know when it snows on the Front Range, it always snows up here in Monument. And I hate having to worry about Monument Hill."

"That's why Miles and I live in the Springs." Dylan nodded.

"No need to brag, Dylan." Kylie softened her comment with a laugh. "This is also a family neighborhood and well, I'm single. Obviously, Andrew and I had talked about kids ... "

There were so many unfinished conversations with Andrew.

"I'm sorry, Kylie." Zoe's words were gentle.

"It's reality, Zoe."

This house was caught in a time warp between her life with Andrew and her life after Andrew.

Laughter filtered over from the neighbor's yard. Their family had expanded from two children to three. She was happy for them. Truly happy for them, but she wanted to move on. Maybe Dylan was right and the best thing for her to do was to sell this house and find a place just for her.

"So can any of you suggest a Realtor?"

"Seriously?" Dylan's eyes widened.

"I'd just like to talk to someone." Kylie tried to keep her tone casual. "That's all."

"I know a Realtor who'd be happy to talk to you."

"Fine."

"You're sure? I've suggested this for more than a year now."

"I said yes. You can give her my number."

"This is so fantastic!" Dylan smothered Kylie in a hug.

"Calm down. It's a phone call."

"I'll contact her as soon as I get home."

"And on that note, I should probably head out." Leah gathered up their bowls and spoons. "Chaz probably thinks I've forgotten I'm married."

"Come on, I'll walk you all out." Remington met them at the sliding glass door. "What's that look for? You hate it out here."

Zoe stepped over him. "Only an inside cat, right?"

"Yep. Outside cats become take-out food for the wildlife. I'm thankful we saved him before he was injured—or worse."

"Got it."

Once her friends left, Kylie showered, dressed in a casual sleeveless top and shorts, and settled behind her desk. The question was which manuscript did she open? Hers or Joe's? Speaking of Joe...

She checked her inbox. Nope. No email with a funny trivia question or a one-star book review. Nothing since they'd confirmed their coffee-not-a-date five days ago.

Hmm. There was no reason she couldn't email him just to say she'd see him on Wednesday. She'd keep it brief.

Hi, Joe: I'll see you Wednesday at Top of the Day Coffee Shop in Castle Rock at 10 o'clock. I'll toss a trivia question at you: What's the record for solving a Rubik's Cube? You can tell me the answer when we see each other. Kylie

There. Nothing pushy about that, right?

She had other things to do besides worry about Joe. Or Tate Merrick. She had imaginary characters demanding her attention too. And right now, they were easier to deal with than he was.

. . .

Top of the Day Coffee Shop had an industrial steel vibe, with a high ceiling and exposed ductwork, windows allowing lots of light, scattered wood tables matched with black metallic chairs, and some padded booths along the back wall. The pungent aroma of coffee hung in the air, and the hiss of the espresso machine competed with the jazzy background music.

Coffee with Kylie would be casual, and take, what? Two hours max. They'd each enjoy their favorite caffeinated beverage, gloss over the cookout fiasco with some casual conversation, and go their separate ways—while completing their contractual obligations, of course.

Joe carried his straight black coffee to the table where Kylie waited, a denim bucket hat covering her black hair. "Nice coffee shop."

"It's nice that coffee shops also offer tea." Kylie held up her ceramic mug with a string dangling over the side with a teabag tag attached at the end.

"True." Joe tossed a tiny Rubik's Cube on the table. "The world's record for a single cube is 3.47 seconds for a 3x3x3 cube."

A quick chime of Kylie's laughter escaped. "I thought I'd stump you with that question for sure." She picked up the cube and started twisting the colored tiles. "I never liked these puzzles."

"Abbie and I used to try and beat each other at solving them."

"Who won most often?"

Joe slid into the chair across from Kylie, opting to keep his baseball cap on. No need to attract unwanted attention. "I am embarrassed to say Abbie did."

"Did your sister mention we're getting together?"

"No. I haven't talked to her recently. I'm sure when you see her that she'll tell you how she calls me all the time because I never call her."

"It's the way of brothers and sisters, I guess."

"Do you have siblings?"

"Only child. My mom was a single mom ... and you know that story. She worked hard and I was expected to work hard too. We were two independent women at a young age."

Joe raised his cup to her with a nod. "Abbie was always the tag-along little sister. I gave her such a hard time when we were younger. I still do."

"Hudson seems like a nice guy."

"We'll see. They haven't been dating that long." He waved away his words. "And now I sound like the protective older brother, which I assure you, I am not. Abbie's smart. She won't date the wrong kind of guy again."

"So she has in the past?"

"Doesn't every girl?"

"Doesn't everyone date someone wrong for them sometime in their life? It's kind of a requirement for growing up."

"Spoken like a romance writer."

"We're both writers, Joe. We both weave real life into our books." Kylie fiddled with the tea tag. "I'm sure you pull from your military experience when you're plotting Remington Gerard's exploits."

"Maybe."

"No maybe. Or you read newspapers and magazine articles ... "

"What do you do? Take notes while family members and friends talk to you? Eavesdrop at parties?"

Kylie tilted her head. And then she laughed and winked. "I take mental notes. Less obvious than pulling out a notebook. And I change names to protect the guilty."

She could have allowed his comment to get their conversation off-track, but her wink and her laugh, with its bright note, kept things positive. Several other customers in the coffee shop glanced their way. Smiled. They'd already had a more pleasant conversation than they'd had the Monday of the cookout.

"Speaking of writing..." Kylie tapped the table with her fingernails.

"Something on your mind?

"*Lethal Strike.*"

"Oh?"

"I'm thinking of naming the heroine Evangeline Day."

"Evangeline."

"Yes. It's a good name for a strong female lead. And it's nice when the hero gives her a nickname—"

"A nickname?"

"Haven't you ever given a girlfriend a nickname—something other than *honey* or *sweetheart*?

"My last girlfriend's name was Cassidy, and I called her Cassidy."

Kylie shook her head. "I was thinking Remington could call Evangeline *Eva.*"

"Eva."

"Right. Anyway, she could be an undercover agent working on a separate mission and they cross paths and Remington rescues her—"

"Of course."

"But here's the twist—at the end of the book, Eva saves his life, besides opening his heart to love."

"Wait a minute." Joe pressed his palms against the tabletop. "You want this Evangeline character to rescue Remington Gerard, the hero of *Lethal Strike*? How?"

"I thought we could brainstorm that part. And I need your help fleshing out what Evangeline's mission might be."

Kylie Franklin was trespassing.

She cupped her chin in her hand. Joe pushed his chair back—right into the person sitting behind him.

"Sorry about that." He tossed the words over his shoulder and adjusted his chair. "Kylie, you seem to be forgetting you were asked to write the romance for this book—and nothing else."

The light in her eyes dimmed. "Wait a minute ... you don't like my idea?"

"I would like your idea if it was just about romance. The name Evangeline might grow on me."

"I can't believe this!" Kylie's light brown eyes narrowed.

"Do I have to remind you there's one hero in a Tate Merrick novel—Remington Gerard?"

"I know what his name is. My cat's named after him."

Joe stood. "I'm getting a refill on my coffee before any more people get in line."

"Sit down."

"What did you say?"

"I said *sit down*." Kylie pointed to his chair. "I don't know how you handle business discussions, Mr. Merrick, but I don't walk away when I'm in the middle of a conversation."

"This isn't a business meeting—this is coffee between friends."

"Fine. I don't know how you handle any sort of conversation, but as your 'friend,' I don't like it when someone walks away when I'm talking to them."

Joe sat. Pulled off his hat. Scraped his fingers through his hair. Put his hat back on. Backward. "I apologize."

"Apology accepted."

Now she should apologize. That's how it worked. But apparently Kylie didn't understand the basic rule of apologies.

The line was getting even longer at the counter. He'd never get a refill now. Apology or not, he would leave this coffee shop with *Lethal Strike* intact.

"Kylie, you've already got your name on the cover of my book—"

"Our book, Joe."

Joe pressed his lips together.

Kylie tilted her head. "Are you ... are you counting to ten?"

"In French. It's the only thing I remember from high school French class."

Kylie grinned. "I took Spanish."

"Of course you did."

"I didn't take Spanish to annoy you—I didn't even know you back then."

Joe gripped his white coffee mug with the Top of the Day Coffee Shop logo, convinced Kylie Franklin would have gone out of her way to annoy him if they'd known each other in high school. "Let me explain how my books work. There is one hero in a Tate Merrick novel—"

"You've already said that, Joe." Kylie rested her hand on top of his for just a moment. "My question is why can't there be two?"

"Because there is one."

"Evangeline isn't the mega hero. She's more like a secondary hero. Remington retains his superhero status."

"He's not a superhero."

"I don't mean the guy wears a cape."

"Are you trying to frustrate me?"

"If it somehow gets you to be more openminded about this book, then yes."

Talking to Kylie right now was like trying to talk to his sweet Aunt Janice. She knew what she knew, and nothing you said was going to change her mind. And all the while you tried to change her mind, she smiled at you oh so lovingly, just like Kylie was doing right now. Not that Kylie loved him. Secretly, Joe was beginning to wonder if this woman wanted to destroy his career.

"You seem to forget the plot for *Lethal Strike* has been approved by my editors. I'm not rewriting it for you and some heroine you've created."

"Not really."

"What do you mean 'not really'?"

"If the plot had been approved, why was I asked to write romance for the book?"

"To reach more readers!" Joe slammed his other hand on the table. "You know this!"

"Which means we have to expand the plot." Again with the Aunt Janice smile. "And you know as well as I do that when you knock over one domino in a story, you knock over other dominoes."

"Dominoes?"

"D-o-m-i-n-o-e-s. Story elements. You change one part, you affect other parts of the plot. You bring in a new character and that affects the whole book."

"You're enjoying this, aren't you?"

"This?" She motioned between them. "Discovering that, besides being intelligent and funny, you're stubborn and opinionated? Nope. Not really enjoying it. Brainstorming a new story idea with you? I thought that could be fun."

"I'm stubborn and opinionated? What about you?"

"What about me, Joe?"

"You're just as stubborn and opinionated as I am. And you're ... you're ... "

"I'm what?"

"Nothing."

"I'm nothing." What little light there was inw Kylie's eyes dimmed even more. "Thanks for that."

This whole conversation had spun out of control like some crazy jam session where the musicians follow the music wherever it leads. It started off balanced with Kylie's laughter, and then she'd said he was intelligent and funny before tossing in the more discordant notes of opinionated and stubborn.

So was she.

Her brown eyes had lit up when she'd started discussing the book, her wavy hair brushing against her bare shoulders as she'd smiled at him. What he'd wanted to say was " ... and you're prettier than I'd imagined."

But he'd stick with stubborn and opinionated.

CHAPTER 6

The smooth surface of Palmer Lake reflected the columbine blue sky overhead, dotted with a few puffy white clouds. A breeze stirred the air, while the voices of several people who'd come early to paddleboard broke the stillness of the Sunday morning.

"You're quiet." Dylan nudged Kylie with her elbow as they walked the path around the lake.

"I'm thinking."

"I figured that. Want to think out loud, maybe?"

"I submitted a synopsis and a chapter to Joe's editor and agent before I went to church last night."

"That's great."

"And to Joe."

"That makes sense—I guess. You weren't required to do that, were you?"

"No. I could have waited until the entire manuscript was finished to show them anything, but I wanted them to see where I'm headed with the story." Kylie shrugged. "He's going to hate it."

"He, who? Joe's editor?"

"No. Joe's going to hate it."

"You don't know that."

"Yes, I do. The guy hates the whole idea of adding romance to his precious book. I also ran my idea past him when we met earlier this week."

"He hated it—isn't that a bit strong?"

"He told me, and I quote, 'Do I have to remind you that there's one hero in a Tate Merrick novel and that his name is Remington Gerard?'"

Dylan slid her sunglasses to the top of her short black hair. "He's right about that."

"Not you too!" Kylie stopped on the path that wound around the lake. "I know how Joe writes his novels. I've read one, remember?"

"You finished it?"

"Yes—and please stay on the subject. I want to make the heroine courageous too. Why can't Evangeline—that's her name—be more than just a love match for Remington Gerard?"

"Oooh, I love her name."

"I'll tell Joe that."

"He hated her name too?"

"If I suggest it, you can be certain Joe Edwards is going to hate it." Kylie clenched her fists. "It's like we're in a writing tug of war about *Lethal Strike*."

Wait. Was Dylan hiding a smile?

"What's so funny?"

"You and Joe—the way you spark off each other."

"It's more like a brush fire than a spark. I haven't second-guessed my writing like this in years. Do you know I read that chapter twice before I sent it off last night—and that was after I read it and the synopsis twice the day before." She stopped as Dylan laughed. "I'm glad you think this is funny."

"Don't you?"

"No."

"You've certainly taken your relationship to a whole new level."

"I don't think our email friendship will survive this."

"You never know. His editor will probably love your ideas."

"Doesn't matter if Joe doesn't."

"He has veto power then?"

"Probably not..."

"Then Joe just needs to get over himself."

Kylie moved down the path. "It's a difficult enough day without having to worry about Joe Edwards liking what I wrote."

"You mean because the Realtor's coming later?"

"Linda? No ... because today's Andrew's birthday."

Dylan stopped. Faced her. "Kylie! I knew that. I did. I mark it on my calendar every year so I remember. We just got talking about other things ... "

Kylie rested her hand on Dylan's arm. "I appreciate walking with you this morning. I didn't want to sit at home." She faced the lake. "We used to love to come here."

Dylan embraced her with a side hug. "You two did so much outdoors. Hiking. Camping. Skiing."

"We did. Colorado has so many opportunities to get outdoors. And Andrew was all about the next adventure. Sometimes it felt like I was trying to keep up." She took off her sunglasses and rubbed her eyes. "I didn't mean that."

"It's okay if you did."

"I was the introvert. The reader. The writer. Andrew was the techy guy, but he was a people person too. And a bit of an adrenaline junkie." She shrugged. "I-I'm not complaining."

One did not complain about her dead husband on his birthday.

"I didn't say you were."

"After reading one of Joe's books, I understand why Andrew liked Remington Gerard. Andrew would have loved to be that guy. Instead, he got a cat named after him."

"Andrew loved his life with you."

"And I loved him."

She could love Andrew and realize their relationship wasn't perfect, right? That didn't mean she loved him less. The year before he'd died had been difficult for them both. Their usual closeness marred with distance. Kylie twisted her wedding rings around her finger. One day she'd take the rings off. But not today. She couldn't celebrate her husband by removing such a tangible sign of their marriage.

A few hours later, Kylie opened her front door and greeted Linda, who swept into the house with all the poise and authority of a top-selling Realtor. Dressed in a form-fitting fuchsia dress with black heels, her honey-colored hair styled in short braids, makeup highlighting her deep brown eyes, Linda greeted her even as she scanned the open layout of the living room and dining room.

"I'm excited to meet you, Kylie. You have a great house here. I think it would sell quickly."

"If I decide to sell."

"Right—if you decide to sell. Why don't we do a casual walk-through so I can get an idea of the overall layout? Then we can sit and talk."

"As I mentioned on the phone when we spoke a few weeks ago, I'm not sure if I want to—" Kylie knew she was repeating herself, but Linda's take-charge attitude was a bit overwhelming.

"Of course. No pressure. But I'd like to see your house—just in case."

"Sure." Kylie motioned to the main living area. "Living room and the dining room. I like how open it is. Leads right into the kitchen with a small breakfast nook. Everything, including the carpet, sad to say, is original with the house."

Linda pulled out an iPad, powering it up. "I created a file on your house. It was built in 2000. Thirty-five hundred square feet. Three bedrooms. Two and a half baths. Finished walkout basement, which means someone could always add at least another bedroom. Always a huge selling point—if you decide to sell."

"Yes, the owners before us did that. And I use one of the main floor bedrooms as my office."

"Versatility. Another selling point."

Linda's "casual" walk-through lasted a good half hour as she opened closets, asked questions, and tapped notes into her iPad.

When they returned to the living room, she declined Kylie's offer of water, but requested a chance to look at the side deck.

"That's definitely something you'd need to deal with."

"Even if I don't put the house on the market, I already have someone giving me an estimate to repaint the deck."

"Smart."

Linda was pressuring her—in the most professional way possible. Yes, there were things Kylie needed to deal with, but it was like Linda had pulled out a flashlight, white gloves, and a magnifying glass.

"Of course, I can also show you homes you might be interested in buying ... " Linda paused, waiting for Kylie to supply details on where she was thinking of purchasing a new home. But she wasn't ready to provide the Realtor with that information. Not yet. Maybe never.

"Why don't I go back to my office and draw up a preliminary list of things I'd recommend you do to sell this house at an optimal price? I'll do some market research and see what other houses in this area are selling for too."

"Fine."

"In the meantime, here's my card." Linda produced a large magnetic photo card out of her bag. "You can just put that on your fridge for now. No worries about misplacing that."

"None at all."

Linda tapped the corner of the card. "It also has a QR code you can scan to download all my information right into your phone."

"I see that."

"I'm off." Linda slipped her iPad into her leather briefcase. "You have a lovely home. I'm certain it would sell quickly."

"Thanks for coming."

Kylie shut the door on the bright-colored whirlwind that was Linda. From the side window, Kylie could see the woman stop halfway down the sidewalk. Turn. Remove her iPad and take photos of her house.

Her home.

Linda saw a potential sale. She was probably already calculating her possible commission.

Kylie leaned against the closed door. What did she expect? She'd invited Linda to discuss putting her house on the market. The Realtor had done just that. After all, selling homes was her job. Her livelihood. If Kylie sold this house, she'd need to buy another house. Win-win.

What would Andrew say?

Wait. Andrew didn't have a say anymore.

. . .

Joe's routine was off—and it wasn't because it was a Monday. He didn't want to admit it but could no longer dodge the truth. After five months, he and Kylie had established a fun email relationship—something he'd anticipated each day. Then he'd succumbed to peer pressure—*thank you, Mallory!*—and ruined it when he'd discovered Kylie was Veronica Hollins, romance writer extraordinaire, the woman he was in an unwelcome business relationship with.

Since the cookout fiasco, not to mention the failed attempt to smooth things over with Kylie at coffee five days ago, every morning started with a *do I or don't I* debate about sending Kylie an email, which ended in the decision not to send an email.

Even CrossFit was not as much fun because Mallory always apologized for suggesting Joe meet Kylie. Every time, he reminded Mallory it wasn't her fault. She hadn't forced him to invite Kylie to the cookout. But Tucker would laugh and say Mallory was at least partially to blame, and then Mallory would look like she wanted to cry.

This issue was upsetting the three Musketeers to the point that Joe considered avoiding the gym to stop the ripple effect. Kylie Franklin could unsettle him personally and professionally, but the woman had no right messing with the Musketeers. Not even Cassidy had done that.

Joe sat on the edge of his bed and scratched his scruffy jaw. He needed a shave, but he wasn't motivated to do much of anything today.

He retrieved his phone from the bedside table. He'd missed a text from Liza ten minutes ago.

You available to talk?

He typed back a quick yes. His phone rang a few seconds later.

"Hi—sorry, I just saw your text."

"Having a good Monday?"

"I could complain—"

"But I won't let you." Liza laughed. "Checked your email lately?"

"Haven't been on my computer yet today."

"Veronica sent a synopsis and the first chapter for us to read."

"Great." Joe knew that one word contained no enthusiasm whatsoever.

"Joe, what is your problem?"

"Nothing."

"Exactly. You can't have a problem with what Veronica sent because you haven't read anything yet. Do that now and then call me back." A sharp *tsk* came across the phone. "Wait. I have a meeting in an hour, so leave a message if you need to."

"Got it."

Liza had given him assigned reading for the day. He was looking forward to this project as much as he used to look forward to a middle school science fair project. Mom always declared them "Dad projects." Meaning Dad chose what Joe would do, and his standards were more exacting than the teacher's.

Joe stood. He'd go for a run and then get to it. He already knew Kylie's basic idea. Now he'd have specifics to share with Liza about why what she wrote wouldn't work.

Maybe they'd fire Kylie from the project.

Liza called Joe three hours later as Joe sat in front of his laptop, rereading the chapter. "You haven't called me. Have you read what Veronica sent?"

"Just finished the chapter for the second time."

"Like it that much?"

"It doesn't work for me." He'd known that after the first reading, but saying he'd read the chapter twice would prove he'd given Kylie a chance.

"How can you say that? I loved Evangeline! And Veronica's managed to weave her into your writing style so well."

"I can say it doesn't work for me because I know where Veronica's going with this."

"And how can you know that after reading one chapter?"

"Because we met and discussed it—"

"You met Veronica? Wait a minute ... what am I missing?"

How had he forgotten Liza didn't know about the Veronica Hollins–Kylie Franklin connection?

"As crazy as it sounds, I've been emailing Kylie Franklin, also known as Veronica Hollins, for five, almost six, months."

"You met Kylie Franklin—Veronica Hollins—on a dating app?"

"No! We met on Words with Friends." Joe stood and walked away from his laptop. He needed something to drink. "You do remember I dated Cassidy Warrington for eighteen months, right? And that we broke up a year ago? I don't do dating apps."

"No, you just meet up-and-coming country stars at fundraisers."

"Whatever. Kylie and I met face-to-face for the first time over Memorial Day weekend and that's when we found out we're both authors."

"You didn't discuss careers before then?"

He pulled a can of soda from the fridge. "We didn't talk about personal stuff."

"And you didn't read the details of the contract addendum when I sent it over?"

Guilty.

"I usually do. Every single line. But this time I auto-signed it. I was in a rush to send it back to you."

"You mean you were in a huff about Veronica Hollins wanting her name on the cover." Liza's tone held a hint of laughter.

"Whatever. We're past that."

"Backing up—you and Kylie met and realized the Tate Merrick and Veronica Hollins connection. Then you met again . . . "

"And Kylie told me that she wanted to make the romantic interest more of a lead. I reminded her there's one hero in my novels. I don't want this Evangeline character stealing Remington Gerard's limelight."

"I don't think that will happen, Joe."

"You can't seriously want to move ahead with this storyline." Joe paced the hallway, the soda unopened.

"I do. And the editor likes it too. We're not looking for some weak heroine whose only reason to be in the story is standing around waiting to be kissed or rescued."

Was romance going to be his stumbling point again? Falling in love never worked out for him in real life or in fiction. Not that he was discussing that with his agent.

"This works, Joe. So you need to flexible." Liza's words left no room for argument. "Bringing on Veronica meant the story would change."

"Fine. I'm a reasonable kind of guy." Joe scratched his jaw. He still hadn't shaved. This day was getting away from him—just like this manuscript.

Forty minutes later and Joe had taken time to shave. Basic hygiene was accomplished, but he still hadn't contacted Kylie, which was Liza's last request before she'd hung up.

"Talk this over with Veronica. Kylie. Pick a name. Start acting like a team player, Joe."

He stood in his office as he pulled up Kylie's number. Professional call. Professional environment. Professional demeanor.

"Hello, this is Kylie."

"Uh, hello, this is Joe. Joe Edwards."

A moment's silence and then, "Hi. This is a surprise."

"I read the chapter you sent."

"Oh? What did you think?"

"I ... we thought you did a good job matching my writing style."

"We? You've talked with your editor?"

"Liza, my agent." He turned his back on the window where the bright summer sunshine streamed in. "She called earlier to see if I'd seen the email with your chapter. She and my editor thought your writing blended well with my writing voice."

"What did you think, Joe?"

He'd been waiting for her to ask that question. Wondering what he would say. "I was thinking maybe you could make Evangeline something other than an undercover agent. Maybe a doctor?"

"Why?"

"It could work in the story. If Evangeline is a doctor or some other kind of professional, then she doesn't compete with Remington Gerard—"

"What did your agent think of that idea?"

"I haven't mentioned it to her."

"What did she say about the chapter beside the fact my writing blends well with your writing style?" Kylie kept hitting him with questions like she was an interrogator.

"I'm sure she'll email you—"

"Joe. Did she say anything else?"

Joe paced a few steps. "Liza said she and my editor like both the synopsis you submitted and the chapter."

"Then I see no reason to change what I wrote this early in the process. Let's go ahead with this, okay?"

And that was the end of the phone call. Kylie wished him a cheery goodbye. He managed a grunt as she hung up.

He was backed into a corner by a trio of strong women. Make that four women—one of them fictional. He stalked to the bathroom in search of antacids. His throat was burning, and he'd had one cup of coffee today. One.

CHAPTER 7

There'd been no more emails from Joe, not that she expected them—not after their last phone call. With the support of his editor and agent, the synopsis and first chapter were given the go-ahead. Evangeline was alive and well in *Lethal Strike*, whether Joe liked it or not.

And they all knew he didn't like it.

But the more she wrote, the more Kylie loved the feisty heroine.

This Saturday though, she was ignoring both Joe's story and hers and having brunch with Abbie in Denver.

"This is fun." Kylie motioned around the restaurant, its rustic brick wall decorated with artwork by local artists, including watercolors, pen and ink, and pastels. "I've never eaten at Colorado Breakfast Café before. Thanks for suggesting it."

"It's different, and the food is fantastic." Abbie's hair was straight today, reaching past her shoulders. She wore a bright orange top and black capris. "I'm thankful we finally managed to get time together."

Kylie stared at her plate, and the remaining biscuits and gravy. "As delicious as this is, I'm not sure I'm going to be able to finish it."

"That's what to-go boxes are for, right?"

"Absolutely." Kylie savored another bite of buttermilk biscuit soaked in sausage gravy. "How are you and Hudson doing?"

Abbie offered her a smile that warmed blue eyes that were so much like Joe's. "Hudson and I are doing great."

"How did you and he meet?"

"I took a cooking class. Something I've always wanted to do. Hudson was in the same class. One session we had to team up with another student and Hudson and I randomly ended up together."

"That's a fun meet-cute."

"Right? You're welcome to use it in a book."

"Thanks. I'll remind you that you said so."

"After the first time, whenever there was a partner assignment, we navigated toward one another." Abbie moved her plate of blueberry pancakes to the side. "The last night of class, he asked if I'd like to get dessert and I said yes. And here we are four months later."

"Have you taken another cooking class together?"

"No, but we enjoy trying out new recipes. We've gone to one of those paint-and-go places where you paint your own canvas, which was fun. We're thinking about taking scuba lessons together—"

Kylie stilled, then forced her lips to curve into a smile. "Nice."

"Oh, Kylie." Abbie's eyes widened. "I'm sorry. I wasn't thinking ... "

"It's okay, Abbie. Andrew loved scuba diving. I did, too, but wasn't as big of a fan. His death was a horrible accident."

That was what happened. She'd be having a normal day. A good day. And then she collided with the awful memory of Andrew's death.

Kylie twisted her hands together beneath the table in their high-back booth, pulling her rings on, off, on, off. Before she realized what she was doing, Kylie retrieved her wallet from her purse, opened the section where she kept her change, and tossed her rings inside. Closed it. Returned her wallet to the bottom of her purse.

Andrew could have made another choice three years ago.

She'd finally broken down and asked him not to go. Why did he need to squeeze a third dive in the last day of their Greece vacation? Her book release in three days loomed over her. Would her readers like what she'd written in the third book of the series? Why hadn't Andrew recognized how stressed she was, despite their time away?

"Do you mind if I ask how things are going with you and Joe?"

Abbie's question jerked Kylie back to the present.

"Th-there's nothing going on with your brother and me."

"Nothing at all?"

Kylie leaned back in the booth, the noise in the restaurant fading. "Did he tell you that we're working together?"

"Yes, he did. But I haven't told anyone else—not even Hudson." She lowered her voice. "Between you and me, I think it's a brilliant idea."

"Just keep this brilliant idea here."

"I will." She made an exaggerated zipping motion across her lips that caused Kylie to laugh before she sobered. "Joe warned me not to tell anyone too."

Abbie seemed trustworthy, but Kylie knew her less than she knew Joe. And this project would be wrecked if it was leaked to the public, the surprise element deflating like a balloon that had a small hole in it.

Abbie reached across the table and squeezed her hand. "I promise, Kylie. I won't tell anyone."

Fine. She'd trust Abbie. And just because Joe was fighting her on the project didn't mean he wasn't reliable. Afterall, he was being honest about how he felt ... to the point of rudeness.

Later, as they packaged up their leftovers and paid for their meals, Abbie spoke up. "I hesitate to mention this ... "

"What?"

Abbie chewed her bottom lip. "Joe has an event near here at the To Be Read bookstore."

Kylie stepped down, half in, half out of the booth. "Now?"

"It started about half an hour ago. I was hoping we could drop in."

Bad idea. Bad idea.

"I don't know, Abbie."

"We don't have to stay, Kylie. But it would be so fun to just wave at Joe."

"You go. I'll head home."

"We can stay in back. It's so close we can walk there. Please come with me."

"Fine, but I can stay in the back by myself. There's no need for you to do that." Kylie couldn't believe she was agreeing to this. "Let's stash the food in our cars before we go."

"Oh, thank you! This will be so fun."

Fun. That was so not true.

During the walk to the bookstore, past an eclectic assortment of small restaurants and shops, Kylie considered turning around and returning to her car, climbing in, and driving back to Monument.

As they crossed the street, Abbie hooked her arm through Kylie's, forcing her to slow down. "You okay?"

"Honestly? No. But we're here now."

"Oh look! There's Joe's photo in the window."

Sure enough, a large poster announced that Joe, or rather Tate Merrick, would be at the store today signing books and doing a reading from his newest release, *Freedom Force.*

Kylie held the door open for Abbie. "You go first. I'll follow."

They were greeted with the aroma of fresh coffee, thanks to the coffee and tea shop off to the right with a colorful chalkboard sign displaying a variety of beverage choices.

Within a few steps, they were inside the actual bookstore, which had a tall bank of windows in the front and then opened into a maze of wooden bookshelves that reminded her of an old-fashioned elementary school library. The maroon carpet was faded, and the light fixtures were dated, but it was a bookstore—one of Kylie's most beloved places.

For just a moment, she was tempted to stop and inhale the aroma of all the books and magazines, one of her absolute favorite "perfumes" in the world. A close second? A library.

But she couldn't do that. Someone was sure to notice a woman standing in the To Be Read bookstore breathing in and out with a stupid grin on her face.

Kylie wandered through the section containing greeting cards, journals, and calendars—past customers reading books at small tables. But why was it so dark? Wait. She was still wearing her sunglasses. *Ridiculous.* If she didn't want to be noticed, she needed to remove her sunglasses and just be a normal person in a bookstore. *Act natural.* People were here today for Tate Merrick.

Before she could take another step, a woman wearing a T-shirt that said "Sorry, I can't, I have plans with my book" came up next to her, carrying an insulated coffee cup. She glanced at Kylie. Once. Twice. Stepped closer.

"It *is* you! Veronica Hollins. I wondered if you'd be here today."

What? Why would the woman wonder if she'd be here?

"Um, yes." She kept her voice as low as possible, motioning to the front. "I'm here to see my friend Tate Merrick."

The woman clutched her arm, forcing Kylie to stand still. "I saw you come into the store, and I knew it was you, even with your hair cut."

The woman's voice was getting louder, causing people to glance their way.

Kylie pulled her into a corner behind a bookshelf. "Sorry, I just don't want to distract people from Tate's book signing."

"If I bought one of your books, would you sign it for me?"

"I'm not here to sign books ... "

"Please? I've read every single book you've ever written!"

Desperate times, desperate measures—at least that's what Hippocrates said.

"Sure. If you buy one book—just one—I'll sign it for you, but under one condition."

"What's that?"

"Please don't tell anyone else I'm here."

"I won't, but you know other people are going to notice."

She needed a hat. "I'll come back downstairs and sign the book in just a few moments, okay?"

"Thank you so much." With a wave and a smile, the woman U-turned and headed toward the romance section. She should have asked the woman to look for a hat for her to wear.

Who knew? The woman might end up finding a book or two written by not-her-competition author Madison Thomas and forget all about her. That was the big fear driving this whole plan to write with Joe, right?

A large staircase led to where Joe was speaking, the wall alongside it lined with framed caricatures of famous authors. Kylie tiptoed up the steps. A wooden table was set up in the middle of the bookshelf-lined room, with yet another tall banner of Tate Merrick positioned behind it. A short stack of his most recent release was set to one side, as well as some of his older books in another pile, a few pens scattered nearby. A crowd of men and some women—more than she'd expected—as well as several teens, sat in rows of metal chairs, listening as Joe read a scene from his book. Abbie was headed for a seat in the last row, but Kylie remained standing on the top step of the staircase.

This quick drop-in on Joe's book signing was becoming an unwanted spotlight on her. At the moment, the crowd's attention was on Joe. Ten minutes. She'd give this no more than ten minutes. Then she'd text Abbie that she was leaving, sign her determined fan's book, and head back to her car.

...

The day had gone well, in the sense that people had shown up. Even Liza was here, thanks to an overnight layover in Colorado while she visited several publishers and another client. Now his agent stood off to one side near one of two large pillars plastered with poems while he neared the end of the scene in *Freedom Force* he was reading to the crowd of about thirty people. Joe hadn't counted. He'd leave that to Liza. He'd been surprised to see ten women in the crowd—those he'd counted—which was higher than normal.

As Joe turned the page, motion in the crowd caught his eye. Someone leaving? No, Abbie arriving late. His little sister making good on her promise to stop by.

Joe forced his attention to stay on the half page left in the scene. He finished reading the paragraphs, and then closed the book. "Thanks for being here today. I have a few moments left before the staff kicks me out." Laughter rippled through the group. "I'd be happy to answer a few questions."

A twenty-something young man in the front row spoke up. "You mentioned earlier this is one of your favorite scenes in the book. Why?"

"It's a pivotal scene in the plot. It also took me several rewrites to land the scene. The first time through I was in Remington's head too much, so I had to figure out who else to bring into the scene to add more dialogue. More tension. It's satisfying when a scene finally comes together."

Joe pointed to a teen boy three rows back who'd raised his hand. "Did you have a question?"

"Are you working on your next book already?"

"Yes, you've probably seen the title is *Lethal Strike*."

"Any surprises for your readers?"

"I always work on surprising my readers in every book I write."

A woman in a frilly top sitting with another woman raised her hand, wiggling her fingers. "I'm in an Instagram celebrity book club and someone mentioned you're changing things up in this next book. They said you're writing with Veronica Hollins and adding a new romantic character. Is it true?"

Joe's mind went blank, and he shot Liza a quick look. "I'm sorry ... where did you hear this?"

"A celebrity book club. On Instagram. They were talking about it earlier this week—how romance is coming to Remington Gerard, thanks to Veronica Hollins. I'm a huge fan of hers. We're all looking forward to reading our first Tate Merrick novel."

Joe gripped his book with both hands. "There have been love interests in my other books."

"Not really." The first man who'd asked a question joined the conversation. "I mean, if you add a strong secondary character and lots of romance, my wife will read your book."

A strong secondary character. Did this guy imagine himself as some sort of wannabe writer?

What was supposed to be a casual, wrap-it-up question and answer session was unraveling like so many of his conversations with his dad.

Liza appeared at his side. "I'll take it from here. You be ready to sign a few more books when I'm done."

He could handle this situation just fine. But Liza took the microphone and shooed him to the side.

"Thank you so much for coming today." Her smile encompassed the entire room. "All we can say at this time is to check Tate's website and other social media sites for updates on *Lethal Strike's* release—and the questions you're asking today."

"So you're saying—" Wannabe writer guy was not giving up.

"I am not confirming nor denying anything at this point. Thank you."

People stood as Joe moved back toward the desk, a few reaching out to shake his hand.

"Isn't that Veronica Hollins?" A woman's voice rose above the noise in the room.

What?

It couldn't be. Veronica—*Kylie*—wouldn't be here.

"It is!"

Sure enough, Kylie stood poised on the top step of the staircase. Abbie rose and moved next to her, the two women exchanging frantic whispers.

"Veronica! I'm thrilled you were able to stop by after all." Liza took control of the situation, motioning Kylie forward. "Please, come up and say hello to everyone."

Kylie's *Are you out of your mind?* expression was unmistakable. *Work with us here, Kylie.*

"I know some of the people have read your novels, and everyone else would love to meet you. Then they can go home and tell their wives, their sisters, and their moms about you." Liza tilted the microphone toward her.

Abbie took her hand and tugged her forward. Kylie stumbled one, two short steps on her platform sandals, and then advanced without a glance at Joe, a smile frozen on her face. As she took the microphone, she held it away from them and whispered something to Liza, who merely shook her head.

"Hi, I'm Veronica Hollins." As she spoke, her smile relaxed, and she seemed to connect with the crowd. "I write contemporary romance, which I'm sure some of you have no interest in reading ... "

"I'm a fan!"

"Me too!"

"My wife reads all your books. She's going to wish she'd come with me today."

Laughter rippled through the crowd.

"Well, Tate and I are friends"—she gave him a quick glance—"and I'm so excited everyone came out for his book signing. My husband was a huge fan and always preordered his books."

"Veronica, when is your next book coming out?" This from a woman who'd remained standing in the aisle.

"I'm working on it right now." Kylie seemed relaxed, even as she stood there wearing a pair of casual jean capris and a floral top.

"I'm so sorry about your husband ... "

Kylie gripped the microphone with both hands, but her smile remained. "Thank you. It's been hard to write the past few years, as you can imagine, but I'm falling back in love with the story and hope to have it released soon."

"What about writing with Tate? Are you working on *Lethal Strike* with him?"

"As his agent said, I won't confirm or deny—"

"Veronica! Be honest with us!"

"Honestly? I think every book can benefit from a good love story." And then she gave a slow wink.

Joe stiffened as the women in the room applauded and cheered. Liza and Kylie hugged like they were old friends.

"Anyway, today isn't about me. I see some more of Tate's books on the table here waiting to be signed."

She handed the microphone back to Liza and beelined to the back of the room but was mobbed—that was the most accurate description—*mobbed* by all the women. The next thing Joe knew, Kylie was swept past him in a laughing wave of women, including Abbie and even a few of the men, and someone said, "...of course they'll have copies of your books you can sign for us."

As Liza followed, Joe stopped her. "What just happened?"

"Some great PR." Liza looked as happy as if he'd just won an award.

"Are you kidding me?"

"No! This is going to create great buzz for *Lethal Strike*. We need to build on it."

"I want to know who's talking about Kylie... *Veronica* writing with me."

"We may never know."

"Can you at least try to find out?"

"Right now, I'm going downstairs to connect with Veronica's fans. You finish up here."

Great. Just great. His agent just abandoned him for Veronica Hollins.

...

Kylie was so over this day—and she wanted out of this bookstore. She'd looked forward to a relaxed Saturday brunch with Abbie. After that, she'd planned to go home, drink copious amounts of tea, and write.

But she'd ended up at Joe's—Tate Merrick's—book signing and then been manipulated by his agent into talking to the attendees. Spending forty-five minutes doing her own impromptu book signing had been nowhere in her plans for today. She'd apologized to the store manager, who'd hugged her, brought her a bottle of water, thanked her for the business, and then reminded her for the third time to please schedule something when her new book released.

Now all Kylie needed was her purse, which she'd left upstairs on the desk when Liza had called her up front, and then forgotten it in the flurry of activity afterward. Liza had assured her that she'd tucked it away underneath the desk.

"Veronica!"

Joe.

Tate Merrick.

Whomever.

The man advanced on her the minute she reached the upstairs room. "I want to talk to you."

"And I want to go home." She waved toward the small group of people that remained. "I'm sure you'd much rather talk to them."

"What was that all about?" He rested his hands on his hips.

For a moment, Kylie was distracted by the way Joe Edwards's plain, blue silk shirt hinted at his muscular build. Wondered if he always wore shirts that coordinated with his eyes when he did book signings.

Pay attention.

"What are you talking about?"

"The whole 'I won't confirm or deny' bit and then the wink." Joe's eyes were a stormy blue. "What was that?"

"That was me keeping to the script. I echoed what your agent said."

"Liza did not wink." Joe gave a slow-motion, exaggerated wink.

"It's called working the crowd, Joe. Leave them guessing."

"What about that schlock every book needs a good love story?"

"Schlock? I said every book can benefit from a good love story. Have you ever read *Gone with the Wind*? *The Great Gatsby*? *Pride and Prejudice*?"

"Have you read *The Call of the Wild*? *The Hunt for Red October*?"

"I'm an award-winning, bestselling romance writer, Joe. I believe with all my heart romance makes a book—every book—better. And romance makes readers—every reader—happy."

"Tell that to Jack London or Tom Clancy."

"I can't. They're dead." Kylie refused to blink and break eye contact with Joe. "But I'm certain their wives would have liked their books better if they'd added romance to them."

"Do you hear yourself?" Joe held out his hands. "You're talking about classics!"

"The question is, are you listening to me? Romance enriches the reading experience."

It was like they were standing in his driveway again, where Joe didn't recognize her. Was she always going to have to convince Joe Edwards that she had value as a writer?

The few remaining people in the front of the room were watching them—and Abbie and Liza stood midway up the staircase, catching the entire interaction.

Perfect.

No was a complete sentence. She should have said no when Abbie asked her to come to Joe's book signing this morning and just gone home. Oddly enough, she had no guilt about not telling the crowd no, she wasn't writing with Joe. It was fun to leave them guessing.

"Are you the one telling people we're writing together?"

Joe's question jolted her away from the sudden realization that she'd had fun today. "What?"

"Did you plant those women at my event?" He stepped toward her. "Contact some of your fans and tell them to come—"

"I didn't even know about your book event until Abbie told me. Wait. Maybe you're the one telling people. You told your sister, right?" She advanced on him, jabbing her index finger into his chest. "And let's get this straight, Joe. We are not *writing together*. I'm writing the romance, not you."

He grabbed her hand, imprisoning it in his own. "Stop with the poking."

She leaned in closer, lowering her voice. "You stop with your arrogant attitude, or I'll tell my agent I won't do this project."

"I never wanted you on this project."

The few remaining attendees had moved forward.

"Nothing to see here, folks. Nothing to see here." Liza moved past the small crowd of half a dozen people.

Joe was nothing more than a schoolyard bully—but her own behavior was no better. And here came his agent like some recess monitor, intent on separating them. Joe needed to learn she wasn't a pushover, but arguing in public wasn't right.

One teen laughed, tucking his phone into his back pocket. "Oh, there's plenty to see here."

"Right." His buddy grinned.

Wait . . . had he taken a photo? Video?

"I hope you got my good side." Kylie smiled, trying to lighten the mood even as she eased her hand from Joe's grip.

The kid laughed again. Waved and left.

A woman about Kylie's age stepped forward. "I'd love to have a photo with you, Veronica."

Liza rushed up the remaining stairs. "If you give me your phone, I'll take a photo of you with Veronica and Tate."

"That would be wonderful."

"Tate, you stand on one side of—what's your name?"

"Nancy."

"You stand here." She guided him into position. "Veronica, you're there."

"This is so wonderful! I can't wait to tell my friends!"

"Everybody, smile!" Liza took a rapid series of photos. "If you post a photo on Instagram or Facebook, Nancy, please tag Tate Merrick—"

"And me too." Kylie offered her a hug. "There aren't any more of my books in the store, but if you contact me through my website, I'll send you an autographed copy."

"Oh, I bought one earlier."

"Thank you so much."

Kylie had forgotten how much she loved to connect with readers. The thrill of taking photos with them. Sharing the experience on social media.

Her face hurt from smiling, but in a good way. At least she'd put on the most basic of makeup this morning. She'd walk out of here with a smile on her face. An I-love-writing smile.

It'd been too long. And today, it'd been despite Tate Merrick.

CHAPTER 8

Remington acted as if she'd been gone all weekend, not just most of Saturday. He followed Kylie around the kitchen, his tail twitching, while she threw her leftover breakfast in the trash and then cooked chicken strips in the air fryer and sliced them over spring salad with wedges of tomatoes and cucumbers. Once she settled against the pillows on her bed, Remington snuggled against her side and fell asleep while Kylie sipped iced tea and nibbled on her quick dinner.

Now to conjure up the energy to open her laptop and write a brief scene. Before Kylie could select her manuscript, an incoming video call from Shannon appeared on her laptop screen and interrupted her feeble good intentions.

Her agent skipped a customary hello. "You want to explain why you're all over the internet?"

"I-I'm what?" Kylie's hand jerked, sloshing cold tea over the side of her glass.

"Google Alerts—I have them set up for mentions of Veronica Hollins. You're quite a sensation right now. You and Tate Merrick."

"Please tell me you're kidding." Kylie balanced her laptop as she set her plate and glass on her bedside table cluttered with too many books waiting to be read.

"Go to your Instagram account. You're tagged in some kid's video."

Kylie dabbed at her wet hand with a napkin. "No … no … "

She grabbed her phone from the bedside table and opened her Instagram account. Clicked the link indicating she'd been tagged, which took her to a video. A video of her arguing with Joe. The teen had even gotten the part where she'd poked Joe in the chest.

Went to @TateMerrickAuthor's book signing and saw this go down between him and @VeronicaHollinsAuthor. Rumor is they're writing a book together, but not sure how that's going to happen if they can't get along. #tatemerrickauthor #veronicahollinsauthor #rumors #isittrue #fiction #bookreaders #militarysuspense #contemporaryromance

"You still there?" Shannon's question pulled her away from watching the clip a second time.

"Yes. This video is—"

"Short, but just long enough to be incriminating?"

"I was going to say bad. 'Incriminating' makes it sound like I slapped the guy."

"You poked the man's chest with some serious intent, Kylie."

"Didn't any of my fans post photos? I signed books for at least ten women."

"That would explain some of the other photos I've seen. Why were you signing books at a Tate Merrick event?"

Kylie shifted to the edge of the bed, tossing her phone back on the table. "Long story short—" Kylie groaned. "Wait, I can't make this a short story."

"You've lost me."

"When I agreed to write romance for Tate Merrick, what I didn't realize is that I already knew him—"

"Authors know authors, Kylie. It happens."

"Let me finish, please. I know Tate Merrick personally, and by that, I mean I know Joe Edwards, the guy who writes as Tate Merrick."

"Is there a problem with the fact he writes under a pen name? You also use a pen name."

"Exactly! That's the problem!"

"And you lost me again." Shannon's dangly earrings bobbled as she shook her head.

"I met Joe Edwards online playing Words with Friends. We'd been chatting for more than five months."

"Oh ... "

"It's not like that. We were friends. Nothing more."

"If you say so."

"I do say so. Right after we signed the contracts, Joe invited me to a cookout. Our first time to meet face-to-face."

"How'd that go?"

"Realizing we were Veronica Hollins and Tate Merrick?" Kylie heard her bowl of wings hitting Joe's driveway. "Not good. At all."

"Bit of a shock?"

"You are a master of understatement, Shannon." Kylie gripped the edges of her laptop. "Joe isn't happy about adding romance to his book."

"He agreed—"

"You can agree to something and not be happy about it. Fast-forward to today. Even though things were, um, tense between Joe and me, his younger sister and I connected at the cookout, and not in just the 'I love your books' kind of way. I'm not sure how Joe feels about that either."

"The man can't stop you from being friends with his sister."

"You're right. I know you're right. It's just been a stressful day." Kylie took a moment to sip her tea, the cool liquid easing the ache in her throat. "We went to breakfast today and then she mentioned Joe had a book signing nearby. She asked if we could drop in. I agreed. I wish I hadn't, but I did."

"Kylie ... "

"Those women posting photos with me? They'd heard a rumor through a celebrity online book club about Tate Merrick and Veronica Hollins writing together—how, I don't know—and came to the event hoping I might show up."

Shannon nodded. "Now this is making more sense."

"I signed some books today. And the store manager made me promise to schedule my own event when my new book releases."

"Look at you go! So why were you and Joe arguing?"

"*He* accused me of spreading the rumor. He got angry because I told him every book needs romance."

"I bet you totally won him over."

"That man is so stubborn."

"Something tells me that he feels the same way about you."

"Joe's agent was there." Kylie set her glass of tea back on her bedside table. "Her name is Liza."

"I know her. She's great."

"She certainly knew how to take advantage of what happened today. Turned what could have been a disaster into something positive."

"It's not like you're going to be able to ignore it."

Kylie shook her head. "Not you too, Shannon."

"I'm stating the obvious, don't you think? Once something like this gets out, there's no stopping it. Why not use it to our advantage? You had women showing up at Tate Merrick's book signing hoping to see you ... because of a rumor."

"I wasn't expecting you to tell me to go with what happened—"

"I called because I needed an explanation about what happened today. Relax for the rest of the weekend and we'll talk on Monday. How's that sound?"

"That sounds perfect."

"And when I say relax ... "

"I know you mean write. I was planning on doing that."

When they ended their conversation, Kylie pulled up the Instagram feed again. The video of Joe and her arguing was racking up a crazy number of likes and comments and shares.

According to Joe's agent and Shannon, this was somehow a good thing. It was as if they were standing side by side, laughing and whispering about how to keep spreading the rumor about Veronica and

Tate writing together. But she and Joe could barely tolerate being in the same room together. How were they going to manage to rewrite *Lethal Strike* now?

...

Remington didn't wake Kylie up with his customary *pat, pat, pat* the next morning, not after a mostly sleepless night. She'd lain awake until almost one o'clock, replaying how Joe's event morphed into an impromptu book signing for her, topped off with the two of them going toe to toe. She'd tossed and turned to the sound of Joe accusing her of spreading the rumor they were writing together. Tried to pray, asking God to bring something positive out of all of the mess. Eventually, she'd fallen asleep—only to dream she was scuba diving, fighting to reach the surface as her tank emptied of oxygen. She jerked awake at five-thirty and tossed aside the light blanket, reassuring herself it was just a dream. A horrible dream.

Now it was all of eight o'clock and she was on her fourth cup of black tea. She needed a real cup of coffee before church. No froth. Time for a rare Starbucks run. Kylie yawned and rubbed her gritty eyes. Maybe she should at least wash her face and brush her teeth before she left the house. Makeup was optional and not likely. She'd make do with a hat and sunglasses.

Retreating to the bathroom, she pulled her hair into a messy bun, some of the shorter pieces falling around her jawline. She lathered her face with cream cleanser, soaked a washcloth with warm water, and buried her face in the damp cotton.

Relief.

Wait. Was her phone ringing?

Kylie dropped the washcloth into the sink with a splat, grabbed a towel, and dabbed her face dry as she retrieved her phone from her bedside table. "Hello?"

"Hello, Veronica?"

The voice sounded vaguely familiar. "Yes, this is Veronica."

"This is Chelsea."

"Chelsea?"

"Chelsea Price, from The Morning Connect with Chelsea and Carmen."

As she fell onto her bed, Kylie almost sat on Remington who was curled up in the crumpled blanket. "Oh! Chelsea. Hi."

"I'm sorry I'm calling so early on a Sunday—"

"Not a problem. I'm up."

"I saw photos online of your book signing with some of your fans."

Kylie needed to stop whatever crazy assumption Chelsea Price had based on those photos. "That wasn't a true book signing. Someone spotted me in the bookstore and before I knew it, I was in the middle of a bunch of readers who wanted books autographed."

"However that happened, I was thrilled to see you out with your fans. I was wondering if you'd come on the show tomorrow morning. Something else totally spur-of-the-moment, I know. We'd do a short three-minute virtual interview. I'd love to catch up on what's going on with you, let all your readers know when that novel they've been waiting for is going to be released. Maybe address the rumor about you writing with Tate Merrick?"

Fielding "let's do a catch-up interview" phone call was what her life was like before Andrew died—only back then Shannon usually notified her of requests. Kylie pulled her hair from the messy bun, strands feathering her face. There was no way she could say yes to Chelsea. Nothing glamorous to see here. She hadn't done anything like this in years.

"Chelsea, thanks so much for calling me, but there's nothing to say—"

"Social media indicates otherwise." Chelsea's laugh was infectious.

"You know how social media doesn't tell the whole story."

"Which is why I'm calling you." Chelsea wasn't taking no for an answer.

Fine. Kylie wouldn't say no. She'd say *not now.* "How about this? When I'm ready to talk about my book release, I'll call you first, okay?"

"And the Tate Merrick rumor?"

"If it becomes something to talk about, then I promise I'll talk with you first. Deal?"

Chelsea hesitated for a few moments. And then—"Deal."

"By the way, Chelsea, I love your book club *Find Your Next Read.*"

"I'm looking forward to announcing your book as a selection in the coming months."

"Thanks for saying that."

"I mean it."

They said goodbye a moment later. The conversation was relaxed, almost like she'd been talking to a friend, not someone who was after a story.

Kylie pulled Remington into her arms, ignoring how he protested her attempt to steal a cuddle. He tolerated her attention for less than ten seconds before he abandoned her. Sometimes she wished Remington were a dog, but that was so disloyal. Remington had been faithful to her for years, in his own cat way.

Kylie needed to tell Shannon. There was nothing definite, but Chelsea had requested an interview. She'd given Chelsea an open-ended promise for something in the future, and that needed to be on her agent's or her publishing house marketing manager's radar.

Shannon had told her to relax today, which meant she was supposed to write. But exhaustion didn't lend itself to creativity. Her phone rang again right after she'd sent a text to Shannon.

"Hello?"

"You didn't tell me that you were writing again."

"Mom." *So much for the hopes of a simple call.* "There's not a lot to tell. I'm a writer. I write."

"Really, Kylie? The biggest news about your writing career in recent years is how you haven't released a book since your husband died."

Thank you for that, Mom.

Not that she said those words out loud. She'd learned long ago to not step into the ring with her mom. "How are you and Peter doing?"

"We're fine. Enjoying the RV. We thought we might come through Colorado later this summer."

"Oh. Okay." She should have tried to sound more enthusiastic. "Keep me posted. I'm on a double deadline right now, so I won't be up to a lot of entertaining."

"I didn't ask you to entertain us, Kylie. I just thought we could have dinner one night."

"Dinner will probably work—"

She'd make no promises to her mother. Just like her mother made no promises to her. Ever.

Kylie ended her second unexpected conversation of the day, but the first one with Chelsea had been easier. Kylie's guard had been down with her mom—*thank you, lack of sleep*—so she hadn't let the call go to voicemail, as usual. It was always wiser to listen to the message and then bide her time and try to connect when her mother wouldn't be available. Voicemail was best with the two of them. Communication, yes, but with the right amount of distance.

Kylie turned her phone on Do Not Disturb and left it in her bedroom. No more real people today. She'd skip both Starbucks and church today—too many real people—and make herself a fresh cup of tea. After some quiet time on the deck to resettle her heart, she'd fire up her computer, and spend some time with Evangeline and Remington. Fictional characters she could handle. If they didn't do what she wanted, there was always a delete key.

CHAPTER 9

Any day that started with hiking the Incline in Manitou was a good day, but the fact that it was a Monday made today even better. Joe hadn't even asked Tucker and Mallory to join him. Today, he preferred solitude over time with his two friends. He'd left his phone at home.

The sun was just starting to make an appearance as he started the ascent. He'd acknowledged other hikers with a nod or a quick wave but focused most of his attention on reaching the top, where he skipped the usual selfie. Then he turned around and focused on the descent.

He didn't do church much anymore—had left behind the requirement when he went to college and struggled to find a trustworthy community since then. But here, in the outdoors, he sometimes wished he had more of a relationship with God. Even though he knew it wasn't fair of him, when he thought of God, the image looked and sounded like his dad. Just another opportunity to not measure up.

Better to hike by himself and admit he could enjoy what God had made. By the time he'd reached the parking lot again, the tightness in his back and shoulders had eased.

He returned home, relishing the silence in the car, ready to face the day. He hadn't anticipated the multiple texts and voicemails from Liza racked up on the phone sitting on his dresser. Breakfast and a shower would have to wait. He allowed himself time to make a pot of coffee, change into a clean T-shirt, and then grabbed his earbuds and poured himself a mug as the call connected.

"You sleep in?"

"Hardly. I just got back home after hiking the Incline."

"One of the major differences between you and me is I'm happy working out in my home gym."

"If this phone call is about Saturday's disaster, I just left all that stress at the bottom of the mountain—"

"It's not a disaster."

"How can you say that? My sister updated me all day Sunday on how many likes and comments that ridiculous video is getting."

"Haven't you heard the saying, 'Love me. Hate me. Just don't ignore me?'"

"Yes, I have. An American athlete named Daniel Cormier said it. His exact words were, 'You can love me, you can hate me, but just don't be indifferent. Care about it enough to watch.'"

"I don't know how you keep all that stuff in your head and still have room to plot new stories." Liza laughed. "My point is, you're not being ignored."

Joe carried his coffee to the living room and relaxed into his chair. "Do you want to know what the real point is, Liza?"

"Tell me."

"The real point is I can't work with Veronica Hollins."

There. He'd said it.

"You signed a contract. She signed a contract. Even more important, she wrote a great chapter. You're going to have to be reasonable and figure out some way to work with the woman."

Here he was again, back to doing science fair projects with Dad. *"Do it. Just do it."*

He needed a second cup of coffee, but his body refused to budge from the chair.

Liza wanted him to be reasonable? To figure out some way to work with an opinionated romance writer? Fine. Joe was a reasonable man. Veronica Hollins was the one being unreasonable.

That was it! He'd reason with her.

He finished the phone call with Liza. Opened the Notes app on his phone. All he needed was a nice, logical list of what Veronica should do and should not do in his book.

1. *I am the lead author.* Enough said.
2. *Remington Gerard is the hero. Keep him front and center 70 percent ... no, 60 percent of the time.* There. Evangeline would have a decent amount of time onstage.
3. *This is a military suspense. This is not a romance book.* Ha! He could almost hear the little boy at the beginning of *The Princess Bride* asking if it was a kissing book. No. *Lethal Strike* is not a kissing book.
4. *Any rescuing at the end of the book ... reread #2.*

All working relationships needed guidelines. Now there were four simple steps for Veronica to remember. Joe resisted the urge to underline the first point on the list. He'd kept the list short. Four easy-to-recall rules that would ensure their writing relationship ran smoothly.

Joe added his mug to the half-full dishwasher and pulled a cold Pepsi from the fridge. He was back in charge. Today was going to be a good day.

His watch buzzed, indicating a text from Liza about an online meeting later. Had he forgotten something? He checked his calendar on his phone. Nope. Nothing there. He scanned the rest of the text. **We scheduled a video call. It's at noon your time. Does that work?**

Yes. "We" means?

Me and Charlotte. I'll send you the link in a bit.

Fine.

An impromptu meeting with Liza and his editor. What was that about? He wasn't being called to the principal's office. What happened over the weekend wasn't his fault. Besides, he was an adult. No one could give him detention.

Joe retreated to the shower, rinsing layers of dirt and sweat off his body. He'd send the list to Veronica and then spend some time with his online author group. Connect with his readers in a positive way.

A few minutes before noon, he clicked on the meeting link, expecting to wait for Liza to let him into the virtual site. But he was on-screen almost immediately. Liza greeted him.

"Charlotte is running a few minutes late, but you'll recognize Veronica Hollins. Let me introduce you to her agent, Shannon Wells, and her editor, Fiona Morgan."

Wait. A. Minute.

Liza had set him up. For what, he didn't know. All he could do was smile at all the other people in their little screen boxes and act like he was fine with whatever was going on. If he'd known there were going to be additional people here, he would have worn something other than a plain black T-shirt. Oh well. He'd showered.

"Veronica, hello again." He forced a smile. "Shannon. Fiona. Nice to meet you."

Kylie . . . *Veronica* looked no happier than he was about the meeting. Maybe she'd been ambushed too. He'd stay quiet and let Liza handle things, which she did, getting things rolling once Charlotte arrived.

"I don't believe in wasting my time—or anyone else's time. Both publishers involved in this project want it to succeed. However, it's apparent Veronica Hollins and Tate Merrick are having serious problems writing together."

"You got that right." Joe crossed his arms.

"Your microphone is not muted, Joe." Liza's reprimand held no humor.

"I'm just agreeing with you."

"Also, we're not wasting our time trying to discover who leaked the information about the two of you writing together." Liza was all business today. "We think it may have been a harmless mistake. Nothing malicious. It could have even happened through one of our publishing houses. We're going to continue with the 'neither confirm nor deny' route for the time being and announce it formally when we're more prepared."

"Will you keep us updated on that?" Kylie's attitude was no-nonsense. She sat in front of a beautiful row of bookshelves, her hair pulled back from her face.

"Yes, of course we'll keep you and Joe in the loop." Liza hadn't smiled once during the meeting. "As I mentioned before, the biggest difficulty right now is between Veronica Hollins and Tate Merrick—and your struggle to write together."

"I think I've found a way to fix that." Joe might as well show everyone that he was a team player. "I sent Ky—Veronica an email with some basic guidelines—"

"Really? I didn't see that email—"

"Read the email after the meeting, Kylie," Shannon interrupted. "We have a suggestion for the two of you."

"More than a suggestion," Liza added.

"Yes." Shannon nodded. "We want the two of you to write together."

Joe made eye contact with Liza—as much as he could do that via a video screen. "We are writing together."

"When we say *write together*, we mean you should get together and write. In the same room. Face-to-face." Shannon motioned between Joe and Kylie.

Oh.

Kylie sat silent in her little window.

Liza took over. "Shannon and I talked for a long time yesterday. We both know how you and Kylie became friends first online. The two of you got along for five months as Kylie and Joe."

"Right." Shannon nodded. "Tate and Veronica clash. Joe and Kylie are friends. Go back to the beginning, when you were just Joe and Kylie, and then figure out how to write this book."

"That's an absurd idea." Joe shoved his chair back.

"Why?"

"Because we're not just Joe and Kylie anymore."

"You both ask your readers to suspend belief every time they pick up one of your books. To go with you on fictional journeys. We're asking you to set aside your egos—there, I said it—and remember you started out as friends. Look at each other and see Kylie, not Veronica Hollins. See Joe, not Tate Merrick."

"I'm willing to try." Kylie half raised her hand, as if they were in a classroom and not a virtual meeting.

"Seriously?" Joe raked his fingers through his hair.

"Yes. It's worth a try. I want this book to succeed." Maybe Kylie was attempting to make amends for her part in the book signing fiasco. Her expression seemed softer than it had been at the beginning of the meeting.

"Thanks for that."

He had to go along with this preposterous idea if he didn't want to look like a complete jerk. Kylie was willing, but of course she would want the book to succeed. She couldn't lose the opportunity to have her name on the cover of his book.

And he wanted this book to succeed too. He may have forgotten that.

"Great." He pumped as much enthusiasm as he could into that one word. "Sounds like a plan."

"Then we're done here," Liza spoke up and the others nodded in agreement. "We'll let you and Kylie figure out the specifics."

"Submit your chapters to both me"—the name below the box Identified the woman as Fiona Morgan, Kylie's editor—"and Shannon. I don't need to see them before the deadline, but if you're done early—"

"I know. Early is great, just don't be late." Kylie smiled.

Within minutes, they'd all signed off. Joe stared at the blank computer screen. If it wasn't such a long drive to the Incline, he'd be tempted to hike it again to work off the tightness that had returned to his shoulders and neck.

One thing was certain—he'd already sent Kylie one email with his suggestions today. She could email *him* with her suggestions of how to make this brilliant plan work.

CHAPTER 10

When Kylie had woken up and realized it was Wednesday, which meant Joe was coming over, her first thought had been *Today is going to be the longest day of my life.*

No. That day had happened three years ago. The day in Greece when Andrew had kissed her goodbye. Told her he'd be back in a few hours and left her to pack, ignoring her silence. Her hurt. And then hadn't returned from his scuba diving excursion—and so much had been left unsaid. Unfinished.

Joe Edwards coming over to talk about their writing project? No big deal. And yet, Kylie had been up since six o'clock. No, earlier than that, but she'd forced herself to stay in bed until six. She'd equally forced herself to not fret over what she wore. Cotton capris and a fitted T-shirt. No curling her hair. Just a touch of makeup.

Now it was all of eight forty-five. Kylie should have told Joe to come at nine o'clock instead of ten because waiting for him to show up was undermining her bravado. Her *false* bravado.

At least the weather was cooperating today, promising to be sunny but not too warm, so they could sit outside, if Joe was agreeable. Then again, she doubted he'd agree to anything she suggested.

Dylan, Leah, and Zoe had encouraged her to be hospitable. Fine. She'd bolstered her courage with kindness. She'd made chocolate chip cookie bars. Simple enough. Bought a single-cup Keurig because Joe drank coffee, so she could at least offer him the choice between caffeinated or decaf pods. Her coffee maker had been ignored since the day she'd returned from Greece after Andrew died. Who knew if it even worked anymore.

For what seemed the hundredth time that morning, her phone pinged with a group text from her trio of friends.

Dylan: How ya doing?

> Just as nervous as I was five minutes ago when Zoe texted me, but I'm determined to not let Joe see how anxious I am about all this.

Leah: Ha! He's probably nervous too.

> Hardly. He'll walk in here all confident and bossy—

Dylan: I was going to ask if you need a chaperone, but it sounds like you probably need a referee.

> A chaperone?

Dylan: Two unaccompanied adults ...

> Don't be ridiculous, Dylan. Nothing is going to happen between Joe and me.

Zoe: You're writing a romance ...

> It's make-believe.

Her falling in love with Joe Edwards would be like Batman falling in love with Catwoman. Wait a minute. There was some attraction between those two, wasn't there? And was Catwoman a villain or a heroine? Was she both?

Kylie twisted her hands together. Stared at her bare left hand. Where were her wedding rings? When had she taken them off?

GOT TO GO! I DON'T KNOW WHERE MY WEDDING RINGS ARE!

Kylie tossed her phone aside. Ran to her bathroom. Had she taken them off last night when she'd washed her face? Not beside her sink. A frantic scan of her dresser revealed nothing but a jumble of receipts and bracelets and earrings overflowing the small jewelry dish.

Kylie forced herself to stop. Covered her face with her hands, her fingers pressing into her eyelids.

Think. Think.

When was the last time she had them on?

Her purse, maybe?

She sprinted back down the hallway, grabbed her purse from its customary spot on the padded chair at the kitchen counter. Turned it upside down, dumping the contents onto the granite. Keys ... wallet ...

Wallet.

Kylie opened the change section and there! Among the mix of pennies and nickels and dimes and quarters were her rings. She dug them out of the coins as eagerly as any treasure hunter who'd found the one elusive object after years of searching. Clasped them in her closed fist, then pressed her hand against her heart.

Found.

But even as her heart stopped racing, she knew that she wouldn't put the diamond ring and slim gold band back on her finger. At first, she'd worn them because she couldn't imagine taking them off. Then she'd worn them out of habit.

What a horrible realization.

Outside, a car pulled up in front of her house.

Joe.

Kylie scrambled and stuffed the items back in her purse. Ran down the hall again and put the rings on the small pewter dish on her dresser. Fast-walked back to the front door. She could only hope she wouldn't be panting when she opened the door to greet Joe.

She waited ten seconds after he rapped on the door. Plastered a smile on her face. "Welcome."

"Thanks for having me over." He wore cargo shorts that revealed muscular legs and a navy T-shirt that accentuated his eyes. A laptop bag was slung over his shoulder.

"Not a problem. Come on in."

He toed off his shoes and held up a paper bag. "I, uh, brought some bagels."

"Oh? Thanks. I made chocolate chip cookies."

"My favorite."

"I wasn't going to force you to drink tea, but all I can offer is a one-cup Keurig option."

He raised a to-go cup. "I picked up something on the way here, but that will be great later."

Kylie motioned behind her. "I thought we could either work here in the living room or out on my deck. I have an umbrella over the table, so the sun won't be a problem. And there are outlets for our laptops."

"Outdoors works for me."

"Okay. Do you want to get something to eat now or just get to work?"

"I'm not hungry, so we can go ahead and get started."

"Perfect."

No need to give Joe a tour of the house. They were being friendly, but still not getting personal. She picked up her laptop and iced tea from the kitchen island. Joe followed behind her as she led the way to the deck.

"This is nice." Joe shrugged the laptop bag off his shoulder.

"The deck's a bit worn, but it's a nice morning to be outside. I've always liked writing out here."

"I can understand why."

"Before we get started, I wanted to give you something." She placed a legal-size white envelope on the table in front of him and then claimed the seat across the table.

"What's this?" He flipped over the envelope, which was labeled in plain print letters with his name. Nothing more.

"Go ahead and open it."

Joe did as she directed, his forehead furrowing. He dumped shredded pieces of paper onto the table. "Again . . . what is this?"

"That is a copy of the email you sent me with your *rules*."

His piercing blue eyes connected with hers. "You shredded it?"

"Yes. Have to say, I enjoyed watching that piece of paper run through my shredder." Kylie crossed her arms. "Did you know the idea for a paper shredder was patented in 1909, but the first one wasn't made until 1935?"

"Trivia, Kylie?"

"I thought the information was interesting."

The trivia was a cover-up for her nervousness. When in doubt, spout trivia. She didn't regret what she'd done—shredding those ridiculous guidelines—but she didn't know how Joe would react.

Joe's fingers sifted through the paper. He appeared to be at a loss for words. Served him right for being so pompous.

"Did you even read them?"

"Yes, I read them. That's why I shredded them."

"Would you mind telling me which of the rules you had a problem with?"

Kylie laughed. "Which one? I had a problem with all of them, Joe."

"They made perfect sense."

"This"—she waved between them—"is not a dictatorship. We're working *together*, so you don't get to throw rules around."

"I wrote a logical list so things would run smoothly."

"Again, you're not the boss here. Our publishers, agents, and editors want us to work together."

He tapped the pile of shredded paper. "I want to discuss the rules."

"There are no rules. I shredded them."

"You're being unreasonable."

"I'm being unreasonable?" Kylie shoved her chair back. Stood. "You know what? I think you should go ahead and leave."

Joe's eyes widened. "I just got here."

"I was expecting to talk about the story. To write. I am not discussing those ridiculous rules with you."

Joe stared at her.

Kylie turned and walked away.

"Where are you going?"

"I'm done here. You know where the front door is."

This had been a complete waste of her time. While she put on her makeup, she'd repeated, *"I'm Kylie Franklin, not Veronica Hollins. I'm Kylie Franklin, not Veronica Hollins."* She'd fooled herself into thinking they could start over, make a success of his book ... their book, for both their sakes.

As was his custom, Remington waited just inside the sliding glass door, pacing her step for step as she left Joe behind. In some ways, her cat was as reliable as the hero in Joe's books. A bit of a loner too. Joe could write a great hero, but the man didn't know how to be one.

. . .

Kylie Franklin had kicked him out of her house.

It'd taken him an hour to drive to Monument, and within thirty minutes of inviting him in, she'd tossed him out. Now he sat in his car, staring at her closed front door while he called Tucker.

"Joe?" A woman's voice answered.

"Mallory? I thought I called Tucker."

"You did. I answered his phone. He ran into the store and left his phone in the car."

"Oh ... "

"You okay?"

Joe slipped on his sunglasses. "Kylie Franklin just kicked me out of her house."

"She *what?*"

"We were supposed to get together today and write, but you know that already." Joe shifted in the seat. "I was there less than half an hour and she kicked me out."

"What did you do?"

"Why would you think I did something?"

"Let me rephrase that. Tell me what happened."

"I brought bagels—"

"That's nice."

"You told me to, Mallory. You said, 'It would be nice if you brought something, like bagels.'" He tapped the steering wheel with his keys.

"How were you supposed to know Kylie doesn't like bagels?"

Joe rested his head back against the seat. "It wasn't the bagels. She handed me an envelope. In it was a printout of an email I'd sent her. Shredded to pieces—"

"Hold on, Joe. Tucker's back. Let me put you on speaker."

Joe waited as a car door opened and closed.

Mallory said, "I'm talking to Joe."

"What's going on?"

"Joe was just saying things didn't go so well with Kylie this morning."

"She kicked me out of her house, Tucker."

Tucker chuckled. "Did you make a pass at her?"

"No, I didn't make a pass at—"

"He took her bagels."

"And that's why she kicked you out?"

"No."

Mallory sighed. "He was saying something about an envelope—"

"I sent her an email with some basic, logical rules to help us write together." Joe leaned forward, arms across the steering wheel. "After I got here, she handed me an envelope with the email shredded to pieces."

Twin bursts of laughter greeted his announcement—the unexpected sound of betrayal. Why weren't Tucker and Mallory—two-thirds of the three Musketeers—championing him? Defending him? Why wasn't Kylie's front door opening so she could run outside and apologize? Or at least return the bag of bagels?

Nope. The door remained shut.

He'd been right all along. Writing with Kylie Franklin was a bad idea. Coming here today had proven that once again.

"You guys done laughing?"

"You don't find this funny?" Tucker choked back a laugh.

"I find Kylie Franklin impossible to work with."

"You can be sure she feels the same way about you, Tate."

"Thanks. Wait. What did you say, Mallory?"

"I called you Tate."

"I heard you. Why?"

"You told us the idea was that you work together as Kylie and Joe," Tucker said. "Who wrote that email? Tate Merrick or Joe Edwards?"

"And who showed up at Kylie's today?" Now Mallory spoke up. "Tate Merrick or Joe Edwards?"

"Are you two tag-teaming me?"

"Kylie was expecting her friend Joe to show up today." There was no hint of humor in Mallory's voice. "I don't think that happened."

"I sent the email before the virtual meeting."

"Then the first thing you should have done, Joe, was apologize for that email from Tate Merrick. So you go do that." Mallory wasn't allowing Tucker to get a word in edgewise. "And then you apologize for showing up as Tate Merrick. And then you ask if you can start over."

Mallory's words hit in rapid succession. One. Two. Three.

A mom walked past the car, pushing a stroller. Waved. Smiled. Joe waved back. Mallory and his sister had the annoying tendency of thinking they were relationship experts. That they were right.

Joe was tired of being told he was wrong.

"He's not doing that, Mallory."

Thank you, Tucker. "I'm not doing that."

"Why not?"

"Because all I did was set some realistic boundaries so we could work together—"

"All you did was make Kylie angry." Mallory was not backing down.

"She's not the only one who's angry."

Mallory's laugh was brief. "You two seem to be making great progress."

"I can do without the sarcasm." Joe tugged at the front of his T-shirt, which was damp with sweat.

"I wasn't being sarcastic."

He'd been looking forward to a few good hours of writing. He'd gone from one challenge to another. Couldn't one person support him? Stand by him? Well, Tucker was. Sort of. There was that.

"I think I'm done here for the day."

"You're really not going to apologize?"

"No. I'm not. I'm going to call it a day at"—he glanced at his watch—"ten forty-five and drive another hour back home after accomplishing nothing."

"Do you want to come over?" Tucker issued the invitation.

"No. Thank you." He added the gratitude to sound a little less grumpy. "I can write without Kylie."

CHAPTER 11

Kylie stepped around Dylan and added a trio of mugs to the assortment on the kitchen island. There wasn't that much room left, especially since her friend had deposited a six-pack of ginger ale and a large bag of white cheddar popcorn on one corner.

Dylan picked up a sunshine-yellow mug decorated with an old-fashioned VW van. "You want to tell me why you're cleaning out your kitchen cabinets on a Wednesday afternoon?"

"It just seemed like a good idea."

Dylan had the nerve to laugh. "Right. You had nothing better to do and then you thought, 'Dylan called. I'll have her come over and help me get rid of all my coffee cups.' Makes perfect sense."

"Leah and Zoe were invited too. It's not my fault they were too busy to come to the great cupboard cleanout." Kylie motioned to the colorful assortment of mugs lined up on the island. "I don't need these, not when I don't drink coffee anymore. Feel free to take any you want."

"Why don't you tell me what happened with Joe." Dylan picked up Remington and held him close, scratching under his chin.

"I told you when you called. It didn't go well."

"And I told you that I was coming over, bringing popcorn and ginger ale"—she pointed to the items—"and that I expected details when I got here. Talk to me."

"I need to deal with this mess."

"We can deal with the mugs while you spill the specifics. You're not keeping any of these, right?" At Kylie's nod yes, she released

Remington and put two mugs in the box on the floor. "Look, two mugs gone."

"I didn't see which ones those were."

"It doesn't matter. Talk."

What Kylie wanted to do was take all the coffee mugs outside and throw them against the back wall of the garage.

Pressure had been building inside her all day, ever since she'd stalked away from Joe. Would talking to Dylan ease the heaviness or cause it to overflow in a rush of ugliness? Ceramic glass clinked together as her friend added two more mugs to the box.

If she was going to throw anything, she should wait until Dylan left.

"Tate Merrick ... Joe Edwards ... take your pick. The guy infuriates me! I'm ready to tell Shannon that I want out of the contract."

Dylan continued to pile mugs into the box.

"The man sent me a list of four rules he expected me to follow while we write together."

"What kind of rules?"

"Things like there's only one hero in a Tate Merrick book. And to remember he's the lead author—not me."

"Sounds like the guy has some serious control issues when it comes to his story."

"Exactly! How am I supposed to write with him when he won't relax control? Let me have some room to be creative?" Kylie unplugged the coffee maker and pulled it off the counter, setting it on the floor next to the box of mugs with a thud.

"What are you doing?"

"Getting rid of the coffee maker."

"Why?"

"I don't drink coffee, remember? That reminds me ... " She opened another cabinet. Pulled out the coffee bean grinder. "This should go too."

"You want to explain the Keurig and pods?"

"That was me trying to be hospitable today. Joe drinks coffee, so I bought this one-cup contraption so he wouldn't have to drink tea. Stupid of me."

"Being nice isn't stupid, Kylie."

She'd welcomed Joe into her home. Tried to be friendly. But the guy needed to realize he wasn't some sort of grand master who got to establish all the rules of engagement when it came to their writing project. She had some thoughts on the matter too, and that meant she could refuse to play by his rules.

The faint scent of coffee lingered in the air, teasing her with the memory of all the mornings when Andrew would wake her up with a fresh cup of brew and a kiss and a "Good morning, love."

Gone. Gone. Gone.

Oh, God, why couldn't she have one more morning with Andrew ... one more conversation?

Dylan had packed most of the mugs. Kylie hoisted the box, grunting against the unyielding weight, and carried it outside to the back of the garage.

Dylan followed her. "Kylie, what are you doing?"

Fine.

Kylie motioned her to stand behind her. "Don't get too close."

"What do you mean?"

Kylie grabbed the first mug—a Starbucks cup she and Andrew had bought while they were visiting New Orleans. She hefted it in her hand for a moment and then pitched it against the wall as hard and fast as she could, wanting to cheer when it shattered into a million pieces.

"Kylie!"

She ignored her friend. Pulled another mug from the box. A beautiful blue pottery one they'd picked up in Telluride. There was a matching one in the box. Threw it, closing her eyes so she could relish the sound of it hitting the side of the garage.

Yes!

When she opened her eyes, Dylan was next to her, holding a third mug. "I figured I could help you out and hand you the next one."

"You're a good friend."

"No talking. Just throw."

Kylie took the white mug etched with a large red heart and hurled it at the stucco wall.

Each throw caused her anger to flare like a fire being fed oxygen. Heat burned in her chest, even as her arm ached with the repeated throwing motion. Again. Again. Again.

Maybe by the time the last mug shattered, the flame would be extinguished.

Within fifteen minutes, Kylie's arm fell to her side. Multi-colored shards of glass littered the ground near the wall. Tears streamed down her face. "He shouldn't have done it."

"I don't think you're talking about Joe." Dylan's words were low.

"No ... Andrew shouldn't have done it." Kylie brushed away tears that dared to streak her face. "Our vacation wasn't what we'd hoped. The last year had been hard, and we weren't talking to each other like we always had."

"I didn't know ... "

"We were trying to figure it out. I mentioned counseling once, but he didn't think we needed that. I was anxious about my book release and the publisher was adding more publicity. And then the hotel called with this last-minute dive. I asked him not to go, but—"

"It was just a horrible accident." Dylan wrapped her arms around Kylie.

"I've told myself that over and over again for three years." She rested her head on her friend's shoulder. "How ironic is it that the book I worried about exceeded everyone's expectations? My husband dies—and it's my bestseller."

"I understand why it's been so hard for you to write again."

Kylie stepped back and rubbed her sore arm. "I never realized until today how angry I was ... how angry *I am* he went scuba diving that day. His choice made me feel unimportant. *Again.* A repeat of my childhood—all the times I was overlooked. Andrew wasn't listening to me ... "

The words caused her throat to ache, as if each one was a small shard of glass she was forced to swallow.

It would have been easier if she'd lied and said she was angry with Joe. But being upset about Joe and his rules was nothing compared to trying to deal with being angry with her dead husband.

Kylie pushed her hair back from her face. "I need to clean this mess up."

"I'll help you. But first"—Dylan pulled her into a gentle hug—"admitting you're angry with Andrew isn't a sin, Kylie."

Kylie heaved a sigh. "But it feels wrong."

"It's healing. It doesn't feel like it right now, but it is. All you did was break a few coffee mugs."

"A few?"

"I didn't keep count." Dylan offered her a smile. "I'll go get a trash bag and the broom. Wait here."

"I can do that—"

But her friend was already disappearing around the corner of the house. Kylie was left alone with the remnants of her anger. Bits and pieces of dozens of coffee cups she and Andrew had collected through the years she'd destroyed one by one.

She pressed the heel of her hand against her sternum. The burning that had surrounded her heart had lessened.

God, I need to forgive Andrew for choosing scuba diving instead of staying with me that day. He wasn't abandoning me. I'm just realizing I've been angry about that. And about how we bought the house, too, if I'm being honest. Help me untangle the last bit of this grief, please. To release all of the unfinished conversations, all the things I can't change, once and for all.

...

Kylie shut the door to her office on an inquisitive Remington. After Dylan left, she'd thought and prayed about what she needed to do last night and into today. She didn't need the distraction of her cat wandering in and out of the room. He peered at her through the lower glass panes before disappearing down the hallway toward the bedroom.

Have a nice nap, Rem.

She opened her laptop, positioning it just so on her desk. Pulled up the app, and then brushed her hair back from her face. Considered touching up her lips with gloss. No. This was a professional call. She wasn't glamming it up for Joe Edwards.

As soon as he connected, Kylie offered him a smile. "Good morning."

"Hello." His eyes held a question. "It goes without saying I wasn't expecting you to want to talk to me."

"Element of surprise, right?"

"You could say that."

She needed to just get on with it. "I want to apologize for walking away from you yesterday. I let my anger get the best of me."

Joe leaned back in the chair. "Apology accepted."

"I realized later I wasn't angry with you."

"You weren't?"

"I take that back." Kylie pressed her hands to the sides of her face. "I was angry about those rules. They're a bit over the top."

"I can see why you might think that." Joe rubbed his hand across his jaw.

"You can? Thanks. I-I wasn't expecting that."

"My friends Mallory and Tucker? You met them at the cookout over Memorial Day. Mallory's a straight talker. She keeps me in line."

"You told her about sending me the email?"

"Yeah. She wasn't impressed."

"Nice to know Mallory's on my side."

Joe shook his head. "Don't go trying to steal my friends, now."

"Not in the plan at all." Kylie took a deep breath. "My friend Dylan—she's known me for years. Knows about all of this. How we met online. How we're working on a book together."

"The, um, difficulties we're having working together?"

"Yes. That's a diplomatic way to put it." Kylie glanced away from the laptop screen for a moment. Refocused on Joe. "She came over yesterday. We talked, and I came to a realization."

"That you weren't angry with me—but then you just admitted you were."

"Yes and yes." Kylie laughed. "I was angrier with Andrew."

"Andrew ... your husband?" Joe's eyebrows knit together.

Kylie thought this conversation would be better face-to-face, but she wasn't about to drive up to Joe's unannounced, so the virtual call seemed like the best option. But now that it was happening, her honesty was making things awkward. Again.

She clenched her hands together beneath her desk, praying Joe didn't see the tension on her face. Either this succeeded, and she and Joe figured out how to work together, or she was done, done, done with this project and her next call was to Shannon.

"Yes, my husband, Andrew. It's been three years since he died, but I had some lingering anger. He died right before my last book released."

"I remember reading about that. I'm sorry." Joe's voice had gentled.

"Thank you. The year before he died had been stressful for our marriage. I-I don't know why I'm telling you this." She closed her eyes for a moment. "There are times I still struggle with how things were left unresolved between us ... "

"I see."

"He chose to go scuba diving even when I asked him not to. I know my husband loved me, but I was hurt. We argued and never talked things out ... "

"I can understand how you'd feel that way, Kylie."

She exhaled a slow breath. "Somehow, you sending those rules tapped into some of the same feelings I had toward Andrew. I'm still trying to unpack that. But I want to apologize and ask you to forgive me."

"Of course."

This part of the conversation was like picking up half a dozen orange caution cones along the highway, but she could still see more cones lining the road ahead.

Kylie forced herself to release her hands and flexed her fingers. Now to see if Joe would handle her suggestion for their writing together as well as he'd accepted her apology.

"I'm still hoping we can work together on *Lethal Strike*. I love the story and the opportunity to add romance to it."

"Thanks. I hope we can work together too."

"I had an idea of something we could use in the story. A suggestion I'd like you to consider."

"I'm curious to hear what you have to say." Joe sounded sincere.

"There's no denying there's been some tension between Veronica Hollins and Tate Merrick—"

Joe laughed. "If we tried to deny it, that kid's video tells the true story."

"Agreed. Have you checked the traction on that thing lately?" Kylie waved the suggestion away. "Why don't we play up that dynamic between Remington and Evangeline?"

"You mean, have them clash?"

"It would certainly add tension to the story."

Joe snorted. "No argument there."

"It's still a romance—it's just a why not/why romance."

"Meaning?"

"A why not/why. There are reasons against them falling in love—the *why not*—and then I build in reasons why they fall in love."

"Oh. Got it."

"You get it, but are you for it?"

"I love the idea."

"You do?"

"Yes. One hundred percent."

This phone call had gone better than she'd expected. Maybe her apology had smoothed the way for Joe to be open to her suggestion. He was relaxed. All Joe—not a hint of Tate Merrick in his demeanor. She liked Joe Edwards. She could work with him.

"I have only one request." Kylie could only hope Joe would agree to this final suggestion.

"What's that?"

"We keep the relationship tension on the page—between Remington and Evangeline."

"You want Tate and Veronica to declare a truce?"

"I want to finish this book, and I think you do too. We can't write together if we're fighting all the time. A truce is mandatory, wouldn't you agree?"

"It is."

"Truce?" Kylie offered him a smile.

"Truce."

"Whew." Kylie leaned back against her chair. "I feel better already."

With a little compromise, she and Joe would work together. Tension eased out of her, leaving her limp. She had lots to do today, not the least of which was writing, but all she wanted was to crawl into bed next to Remington and nap.

"When do we start?" Kylie forced herself to sit up straight, to ignore the desire for a nap.

"The sooner, the better, right?"

"Agreed."

"And we still need to avoid the public."

"Agreed."

"I can come to your place tomorrow—"

"You came here yesterday."

"I know I did." He offered her a grin. "But we didn't write, did we?"

"No, we didn't. But I think it's best if we give ourselves a break and let the truce get a good foothold. How about next Wednesday?"

There was a slight pause. "Sounds fair. What time works for you?"

"How about eleven o'clock? I'll provide lunch. Do you like tacos?"

"Yep."

"Then I'll make my award-winning tacos—"

"Award-winning?"

"You'll taste them next week and decide for yourself."

Things were relaxed between them, and they had seven days to put yesterday's misstep behind them. A warm glint of laughter shone in Joe's blue eyes. She hadn't realized how much she'd missed Joe.

CHAPTER 12

Hi, Kylie. I'll see you at eleven. Quick question: How many tacos do Americans eat annually? Joe

Joe anchored his feet to the welcome mat positioned on Kylie's front stoop. Today would go better than when he was here a week ago. He rapped on the wooden door, curving his mouth into a smile when Kylie greeted him.

"I come in peace." Joe held out a bouquet of daisies. "I have it on good authority that daisies are friendly flowers."

His pronouncement earned him a laugh as Kylie took the flowers and pressed the white blooms to her nose. "Who told you that?"

"My sister Abbie."

"She must be a fan of *You've Got Mail*. The heroine, Kathleen Kelly, believes daisies are the friendliest flowers."

"If that's a rom-com, then you're probably right about Abbie being a fan." Joe tucked his hands in his jean pockets. "I'm more of an action movie fan."

"And why am I not surprised?" She stepped back. "Thank you for these. Why don't you come in."

He paused. "For the record, I want to say that the person standing before you is Joe Edwards, not Tate Merrick. I'd be happy to show you identification to prove it."

Kylie's musical laugh was worth the joke. "The daisies prove your intentions are honorable. Come on in, Joe."

A cat lounging on the couch gave him a lazy stare. "Is this Remington, the cat I've heard so much about? We weren't properly introduced last time I was here—my fault, entirely."

Joe would be on his best behavior today.

"Yes, the cat named after your hero. He's not much of a risk-taker, preferring to take naps to tackling villains."

"Cats aren't known for being heroic."

"He's very loyal—for a cat. He pretends he's not."

Joe sniffed the air. "Something smells delicious. Your award-winning tacos, I assume?"

"Correct. Along with refried beans and guacamole. Are you hungry or do you want to work?"

"Tacos, please." Joe rubbed his hands together. "We can eat, work, and then have seconds, right?"

His comment earned him another laugh from Kylie. A nice beginning to the day. He needed to thank Abbie for suggesting the flowers. He would have just shown up with a can of Pepsi. He needed to listen to his sister more often.

Kylie sniffed the bouquet again as he followed her to the pale-yellow kitchen. Joe's main goal was to remember they'd declared a truce. Any tension stayed on the page, between their fictional characters.

Once she'd arranged the daisies in a vase and centered them on the kitchen island, Kylie served up lunch, ushering him to the table on her back deck. It didn't take long for Joe to finish off his third taco and push away. "And with that, I'll stop."

"You're full?"

"I'm not a glutton, but I put a good dent into the four and a half billion tacos Americans eat annually."

"Joe! You didn't let me answer the question." Kylie pretended to pout.

"Sorry. That just slipped out. I'll be more careful in the future. And for the record, your tacos are some of the best I've had."

Kylie's face tinged with pink. "I'm glad you like them."

"That's an understatement. The guacamole is just as good. I'll be glad to hit the gym tomorrow."

"You go to a gym?"

"Mallory, Tucker, and I like to do Cross Fit. And I love to hike." Joe wiped his hands with a napkin. "What about you?"

"My friend Dylan is always pushing our group of friends—there are four of us—to try something new. Right now, we're trying barre classes. I also like to paddleboard, although it's been a while since I've done that."

"Was that something you and your husband used to do?"

"Yes. That and kayaking. Andrew loved being outdoors. I tried to keep up, but he did a lot with his buddies, which was great, especially when I was on deadline."

"You're not outdoorsy?"

"I am, but not as much as Andrew was. A hike? Yes. Camping in the winter? Never did that. He went BASE jumping. I did not. I like snorkeling, he liked..."

"Scuba diving."

Kylie stood and gathered their dishes, averting her gaze. "I took the classes. Did a few dives. It just wasn't my thing."

"The best couples learn to adjust to one another, don't you think?"

"I do."

"What do I know? I've never been married." He gathered up their glasses and followed Kylie to the kitchen. "It's not like I have any real expertise."

Did declaring a truce demand they talk about personal topics like what made a good marriage?

Kylie opened a cabinet, oddly empty except for three porcelain teacups. It wasn't his business if Kylie only had three teacups. They'd declared a truce, not promised to share all their idiosyncrasies with one another.

"You want coffee?" Kylie paused, her hand on one of the cups.

"No. I'm good. I'll just get some more water."

"Water sounds good." She closed the cupboard and retrieved two water bottles from the fridge. "Ready to go discuss our book?"

He tamped down his instant resistance to the word *our*. They'd declared a truce. He needed to think of *Lethal Strike* as their book, not as his book. He could do this.

Joe followed Kylie to the deck again. "Tell me what you're thinking."

"Let me get set up here." Kylie slipped into the seat across from him, opening her laptop.

Joe half rose. "Wait. Should I go get my laptop?"

"I'm a fanatic about note-taking. Right now, we're just brainstorming. When it gets down to writing, then you'll need your laptop."

"Okay. What were you thinking?"

"You said you'd never been married."

It was as if his single status was pulled under a microscope and magnified. Did he want to continue this conversation?

"Right." He nodded. "I was almost engaged."

"Almost?"

"I had the ring. According to Abbie it was a stunner." Joe cleared his throat. "I, um, never got to propose to Cassidy because she eloped with some other guy. You may have read about that on social media."

"I saw the headlines, yes. That must have been hard."

"Public humiliation. Yeah. Not a fan." He tried to laugh but couldn't.

"I'm sorry, Joe. You were in love with her, so I won't try to make things better with some platitude. Believe me, I heard them all after Andrew died."

"I appreciate that." Joe gulped some water, easing the dryness in his throat. "Abbie just told me Cassidy's pregnant, but I won't be sending a baby gift."

Kylie nodded her understanding.

"So, almost engaged, never married. How does this relate to ... our book?" There. He said it.

"I've been reading your novels. Because my husband was such a huge fan, I have access to all of them. Obviously, Remington Gerard has never been married. Or engaged."

"Right."

"We can either play with that and Evangeline is the woman who opens his heart to love, as I've mentioned before. Or—"

"Or?"

"We can weave into this story that they've met before and clashed—and then have their relationship become romantic. What do you think?"

Kylie was offering him a choice about how the romance might work, rather than playing the Queen of Romance role and insisting it go a certain way. She sat across from him, her posture relaxed.

This was his chance to exert control. She'd opened the door and asked him what he thought. He had the freedom to say without looking like a jerk.

Thank God Kylie couldn't read his mind and see he'd mentally violated their truce already.

"You're the romance expert. Do you think one way would work better than the other?"

"Doing it the second way—where they've met before—will take extra writing. We need to consider that."

"We've already lost some time." Joe steepled his fingers.

"True. Why don't we keep it simple and write it straightforward, where their personalities clash because they do things differently. Despite that, they fall in love."

"That's smart."

"We agree then?" Kylie tilted her head.

"Yes." That hadn't been too hard. "How do you see us working together?"

"Our publishers, editors, and agents want us writing together, but I don't think that means we have to get together every day. It's not like they've put up video monitors to watch us."

"Sounds like you've been reading too much military suspense."

"More than usual." Kylie winked. "I don't know about you, but I'm also working on finishing the last book in my series—the one I never released after Andrew died."

"And I need to come up with something else to show my editors."

Kylie took a few moments to type something into her computer. "What if I send you my chapters on Monday and then we meet together on Wednesday?"

"That sounds like a reasonable schedule." Joe leaned back in his chair. "If you have any questions about Remington Gerard, just text or call me."

"I'll do that—and I do have one question."

"Fire away."

"How would you like him to be injured?" Her hands were poised above her keyboard.

"Injured?"

"He's been injured before. I don't want to repeat something you've already written. If there's a scene in *Lethal Strike* where he's injured that you think I can add Evangeline into, let me know."

"I don't get it."

"If he gets injured and Evangeline is there, it allows them to emotionally bond."

"Can I just say that when I sprained my ankle playing basketball, I didn't feel like bonding with anyone."

"It's a romance trope, Joe." Kylie shoved her chair back and motioned for him to follow her back inside. "Come here."

Her office bore no resemblance to his, with its overly organized bookshelves. "Color-coordinated books?"

"Isn't it fantastic? Don't ask how long that took me to accomplish." She went to a row of shelves on the right side of the room. Pulled one, two, three books from the top shelf. "Here."

He held the books away from his body. "What are these?"

"My first three books. Like every writer, I got better the more books I wrote, but these will make my point."

"Am I supposed to read these?" He shuffled through the trio of books.

"Of course. I don't want you to use them as doorstops. I've read your books to understand Remington Gerard and how a military suspense works." She patted his shoulder. "You now have a reading assignment."

Kylie hadn't mentioned their truce included reading romances. She might as well have asked him to watch a Hallmark movie marathon. The woman was trying to hide a smirk—and failing.

"There's only one way I'm agreeing to this."

"And that is?"

"You send me home with some of your tacos too."

CHAPTER 13

There's something about Saturday morning breakfast with your best friends. Something comforting about having a favorite breakfast restaurant in Colorado Springs, where the hostess recognizes you, greets everyone in your group by name. Where your favorite waitress knows who in your group wanted coffee and how, and that Kylie was the lone holdout for hot tea.

Kylie sat in the corner booth and waited to speak, letting her teabag steep in the little silver pot, while their waitress served everyone their different breakfast entrees and refilled their waters. Between the location at the back of the restaurant and one of her favorite summer hats, she was almost guaranteed anonymity.

"Today is about more than just breakfast with friends."

"What do you mean?" Dylan cut her waffle into small bites and doused them with syrup. Her friend would have a definite sugar rush by the time she was done eating. "Are we celebrating the start of July?"

"Why not? And don't get me wrong. I love having breakfast with you all." Kylie poured tea into her red mug. "You've been the best of friends to me the past three years."

"Friends stick together—no matter what." Zoe, who was sitting across from her, raised her Café Mocha in the air in a small salute.

"That's right." Dylan nodded.

"Besides, you usually pick up the tab, so why wouldn't we come to breakfast?" Leah arched her eyebrow and laughed.

"Leah, that's a terrible thing to say." Zoe frowned so that her eyebrows came together over her pink glasses.

"Kylie knows I'm joking."

She did. Kylie knew each of these women so well, and they knew her. These three women had rallied around her after Andrew died. Dylan had been waiting for her the day she returned from Greece and stayed with her the first two months, insisting she didn't want Kylie to be alone until she was ready, even if it meant leaving her husband, Miles, alone at night for eight weeks. Zoe still sent hand-written notes of encouragement with scripture verses that had started after Andrew's memorial service. And Leah's ability to make her tears turn to laughter had pulled Kylie away from the edge of despair so many times.

"Are we going to plan something for your birthday in a few days?" Dylan would be the one to mention that.

"No—"

"That's a great idea!" Zoe was always ready for a party.

"I vote yes!" Leah raised her hand.

"That's not what I wanted to talk about."

Dylan motioned to the other women at the table. "We want to talk about it."

"My birthday is not a big deal."

"You're a Fourth of July baby! Growing up with fireworks on your birthday didn't automatically make it a big deal?"

"Single mom. Worked a lot. As a kid, my birthdays were low-key." Kylie used her fork to pull away pieces of her hash browns. "I'm juggling two deadlines. I'll probably watch fireworks on TV."

Mentioning her birthday always made her uncomfortable. When she'd married Andrew, she'd finally had someone who wanted to celebrate her on her birthday. Since his death, she'd retreated to the norm of ignoring her birthday again.

Kylie moved more bits of her hash browns around her plate. Staying quiet, going unnoticed during all the fireworks was just fine with her.

"Back to what I was saying." Kylie wiped her hands on the cloth napkin. "The three of you aren't just my closest friends, you've also been the best advance readers for my books."

Her friends froze. Stared at her, waiting for her to say more. It was almost comical how their actions mirrored each other's. "I need your help again."

Leah spoke first, never blinking. "If you mean you have something for us to read—at last!—I am so in!"

"That's exactly what I mean."

"Yes! Absolutely yes." Zoe clapped her hands.

Dylan, who was sitting to her right, half turned to face her. "You finished your book?"

"I didn't say that." Kylie cradled the mug of tea in her hands. "But it's coming along."

"And?"

"And I like it. A lot."

"This is so wonderful!" The smile on Zoe's face probably matched Kylie's.

"That's not all—and this part I need you to keep between the four of us, okay?"

"It's true, isn't it?" Leah's words were a low whisper as she leaned in from the left.

"What's true?"

"You're writing with"—Leah glanced around the restaurant—"*Tate Merrick*."

Kylie almost expected a background *duh-duh-duh* and couldn't hold back a laugh, smothering it with her hand. "Yes. Yes, I am."

Zoe's eyes widened behind her glasses. "Do we get to read that manuscript too?"

"Are you up for not one but two manuscripts, both with a quick turnaround?"

"Are you kidding?" Zoe's question ended on a high note. "Send us what you've got whenever you're ready. Am I right?"

The other two women cheered, attracting the attention of people sitting nearby.

Kylie shushed them, even as she savored being with friends who supported and believed in her. "I know your feedback will make my writing better. I can finish this manuscript with your help—and make sure I get Evangeline right too."

"Evangeline?"

"That's the name I chose for the love interest for Remington Gerard, the hero in Tate Merrick's novel."

"It's perfect! So romantic."

The other diners who'd glanced their way probably thought they were just a group of women out for a fun breakfast. But this was so much more. Dylan, Leah, and Zoe had stayed with her when the ground beneath her feet fell away. They'd grabbed her hands, stopping her from plunging into the black abyss of grief.

Leah relaxed against the booth. "You want to tell us anything more about Joe, also known as Tate Merrick?"

"No. Not really."

"Oh come on, Kylie! We all saw the video of you two arguing."

"I figured as much." She took a sip of her tea. "Isn't there something else on the internet to capture everyone's attention?"

"His ex-girlfriend is pregnant."

"So I've heard."

Zoe rested her chin on one of her upturned hands. "Are his eyes really that blue?"

Huh.

"Uh-oh. She paused." Leah was watching her much too closely. "Kylie, do you like this guy?"

"No, I don't *like* him." She added extra emphasis to the word *like.* "A few days ago, we could barely tolerate each other. But now we've declared a truce and I think we'll meet our August deadline just fine."

"That's it?"

There was nothing to say. "We've decided to be friends. Focus on the story."

"Well, I'm disappointed." Zoe slumped back against the booth.

"Sorry. Any romance will be in the manuscripts. That's good, right?"

"Yay!" Leah's and Zoe's cheers were muted, causing Kylie to laugh.

"I still think we need to celebrate your birthday, Kylie." Dylan set her plate aside, having demolished her waffle.

"I'll take a rain check." She kept her tone firm. "Any celebrating needs to be postponed until after I've turned in both these books."

"Writers. It's all about your deadlines."

"You're just realizing that?" Her phone buzzed. Mom? At least this time she checked and could let it go to voicemail.

Dylan's eyes narrowed. "Everything okay?"

Kylie turned her phone over. "My mom. I'll check the voicemail later."

"Ah."

"She called a while back to say she and her husband were traveling in their RV and would be coming through Colorado later this summer. She's probably updating me."

"Oh."

"No big deal."

"Right." Dylan nodded.

"With my deadlines, I won't have time to see them."

"And they'll take no for an answer?"

"They'll have to."

She and her mom did life better long distance. They both knew that.

And if that statement didn't scream dysfunctional mother-daughter relationship, Kylie didn't know what did. She took a casual bite of her eggs Benedict. *Mistake.* Forced herself to swallow the cold, congealed egg covered in sauce instead of spitting it into her napkin.

"What's the plan for us reading the manuscripts?" Dylan took the hint and changed the topic.

"I'm glad you asked ... " Kylie paused as their waitress returned to their table and everyone who needed to-go boxes requested one. Leah snagged the bill, causing Kylie to laugh. "I thought I was paying."

"Even if I have to be satisfied with fictional romances, you made me so happy today, this is my treat! Keep talking."

"Once we're done here, if you'll follow me to my car, I have your binders—"

"Our advance reader binders?"

"Of course! With your personalized covers. You didn't think I'd forget those, even if it has been three years." Kylie was thankful she'd remembered that fun part of the process for her friends. "I printed up *Worth the Risk*, which you haven't read yet because there wasn't any ending. I read through it again, made some changes, and added two new chapters for you to read."

"Veronica Hollins is back! I can't wait!" Leah bounced in her seat as if she'd just been told they were all going on a shopping spree—and Kylie was paying for it.

"Shhh, Leah!" Kylie shook her head. "You're also getting a second binder with the first chapter I wrote of Joe's upcoming book, *Lethal Strike*."

"Joe of the blue eyes." Zoe almost singsonged the words.

"Stop." Kylie shook her head. "Joe and I have a professional relationship that has nothing to do with his blue eyes. And if that's not one of the more ridiculous things I've ever said ... anyway, I'll send other chapters along as I'm finished. Does that work?"

"Yes." Zoe's face was as serious as if she was taking a sacred pledge. "I'll stop watching all my favorite TV series for this. What's the timeline?"

"It's quick—for both books. We have to turn Joe's manuscript in the end of August. I'd love to turn my book in by the end of September."

"Good to know." Leah scribbled her name on the restaurant receipt. "And we'll all be praying for you too."

"Thanks. I'll need it. I'm balancing this crazy mixture of nervousness and excitement."

Kylie could do this. She and Joe were in sync—finally. She had her trusted team of readers working with her again. She knew what she needed to do. She'd stay focused. No distractions.

When her phone buzzed again, she dropped it into her purse. She was doing one thing at a time and right now she was finishing up with Dylan, Zoe, and Leah. Getting them their manuscripts. She'd check her phone once she got home.

. . .

Joe was accustomed to having the house to himself. To quiet, unless the TV was on when he was watching a sports program. And he was good with that. When he'd dated Cassidy, she had music on all the time. Or she was playing her guitar, trying out a new song. She'd even brought over a portable keyboard, alternating between writing notes and lyrics, and then asking him to come listen and tell her what he thought. Not that he was a musician. Maybe that, and not her claim that he refused to commit, was the real issue in their relationship.

Last night he'd accepted Tucker and Mallory's casual invite to a Saturday evening church service. He woke up this morning still trying to figure out why he'd said yes, after years of not attending church, except for the traditional Christmas and Easter occasions.

He also found himself mulling over how the pastor's message seemed more like a conversation and less like a finger-pointing listen-to-me half hour intent on making him squirm. He just might go back—and that realization unsettled him.

Today the house was filled with friends, following a morning outing to The Incline at Castle Rock. Abbie and Mallory had called first and second chances on the shower, and then he'd insisted Tucker and Hudson take their turns. Everyone snacked on the precut veggies and fruit platters he put out on the kitchen table while they prepped lunch.

"It was fun to do The Incline today, instead of driving all the way to Manitou." Mallory tossed the beefsteak tomato slices into the large plastic bowl filled with mixed salad greens.

"I agree, but some people had to run up and down Challenge Hill a crazy number of times." Abbie nodded toward Joe, who put bottles of ranch and Thousand Island dressings on the counter.

"I can hear you, Abbie."

"I'm not just talking about you, big brother. You were trying to keep up with Mallory."

"Trying to?"

"You heard me. When you said hike Challenge Hill, the words *multiple times* were not conveyed."

"It was optional."

Mallory offered Abbie a smile, her highlighted hair still damp from the shower. "And thank you for cheering for us whenever we came back down."

Joe hooked an arm around Abbie's neck. "We could have done without you booing when we decided to go back up."

Laughter filled the kitchen.

"We get it, Abbie." Mallory set the salad aside and cleaned up her workspace. "But we're all home now. We're all cleaned up. Getting ready to eat some good food."

"Just need to throw those burgers on the grill." Joe motioned to the platter piled high with thick beef patties. "It should be heated by now."

Hudson picked up the platter. "I can do it."

"I'll help." Abbie held the back door and then followed him outside.

"Why don't we take out the fixings and the chips?" Mallory gathered up the ketchup, mustard, relish, along with the plate of sliced onions and tomatoes. "Tucker, will you get plates, cups, and plasticware?"

"Sure thing, sweetheart."

Joe didn't realize how much he'd needed a relaxed day, complete with a few runs up and down the closest incline. By the last time he'd reached the bottom, all the caffeine-fueled stress was out of his system. He finished off another liter of water. Refilled his water bottle. No Pepsi for him today. No coffee. Just water. Today was a reset.

Reality was, he'd probably down a cup of coffee—or two—while he read the pages Kylie sent him tomorrow. But even one day off caffeine was good, right?

Joe joined the group outside.

"This reminds me of Memorial Day weekend. Remember? When you met Kylie the first time?" Abbie poked her elbow into his ribs.

"Yes, I remember. Not a highlight of my life, but things have improved since then."

"Care to share with the crowd?"

"Um, the crowd wasn't listening until you raised your voice."

"I'm sure there are other people here who would be interested to know if you and Kylie are no longer fighting."

"Kylie and I don't fight."

Abbie pulled her phone from her back pocket. "Would you like me to pull up the video from your book signing?"

"Stop already." Joe reached for her phone, but Abbie stepped back with a laugh.

"Stop? This is one of my favorite things to watch. Kylie Franklin giving my big brother what for."

"Kylie and I are friends—" Joe paused. He'd almost said *now*, but he and Kylie had always been friends. Tate Merrick and Veronica Hollins were the ones who had to learn to get along.

"We're all listening, Joe." Abbie motioned to the assembled group.

"Kylie and I are working on the rewrite of *Lethal Strike*. As a matter of fact, she'll be sending me chapters tomorrow and we'll be meeting together Wednesday."

"Wait, Tuesday's July Fourth. What about our plans to watch the fireworks together?"

"What about them?"

"We'll be out late—you don't think that would interfere with your plans with Kylie on Wednesday?"

"Not that late, Abbs ... wait a minute." His sister had an odd smile on her face. "What are you plotting?"

"I know you're smarter than this." Abbie grinned. "You could adjust things this week and meet tomorrow and then invite Kylie to go with us!"

His sister's suggestion surprised him, but in a good way. He liked the idea of sitting next to Kylie while fireworks filled the night sky. When he'd left her house four days ago, she'd given him a brief hug—a half hug really, but it was the closest connection they'd had to date. Definitely the friendliest. Being poked in the chest was not friendly.

"Nice idea, Abbie, but at this late date, she probably already has plans with friends."

"You're right, but it wouldn't hurt to ask her."

"Burgers are ready." Hudson waved the spatula over his head. "Anyone hungry?"

Mallory headed toward the house. "Let me go get some napkins."

"I can do it."

"No problem, Joe."

"Just grab some from the pantry."

A few moments later, Mallory returned with a stack of napkins and a book tucked under her arm.

"You didn't find that in the pantry."

"I saw this beside your favorite chair, and I recognized the cover."

Caught. He was most definitely caught.

Mallory deposited the napkins on the table and then held the book up. "What are you doing reading Veronica Hollins's debut novel, *Love Like No Other?*"

"What?" Abbie handed her plate to Hudson and ran over to Mallory. "My brother is reading a Veronica Hollins romance?"

"If this utility bill envelope is being used as a bookmark, he's almost halfway through the book."

"Don't lose my place, please."

"You admit it!" Abbie stared at him with wide eyes and laughed.

"Have you no pride at all, dude?" Tucker slung his arm around his shoulders.

"What?" Joe shrugged away. "It's research. Kylie's read some of my novels, so she requested I read some of hers."

"And you agreed?"

"We're a team. Because of that, we're taking the time to learn about each other's genre."

It made sense. Tucker didn't need to look at him like he'd betrayed every man who ever walked into a bookstore and turned a cold shoulder on the romance section.

Mallory was flipping through the pages of Kylie's book while Abbie leaned over her shoulder, holding the envelope that had marked his place.

He'd meant to hide the book before everyone came over. But then he got caught up trying to write a synopsis for his new book idea—certainly not reading a love story—and forgot all about it. If Tucker said something about turning in his man card, he'd abandon everyone in the backyard and retreat to his office.

"If everybody's had their fun, can we eat?" Joe plucked the book out of Mallory's hands. "And this is borrowed. No burger drippings on the pages."

"You're no fun."

"Oh, you're both having too much fun—at my expense."

Abbie took Kylie's novel from Joe. "Let's be glad Dad didn't find this."

Joe's laugh locked in his throat. "I would have just said it was yours." He retrieved it and ignored Abbie's shocked expression. "Kidding. You think Dad would believe I was reading this?"

"There was a small bit on the news about you—you, being Tate Merrick—and Veronica Hollins."

"That explains why Dad called me last week and asked me about my writing."

"He did?"

"Yeah. It was odd. He never mentions my writing—unless he wants to remind me how I walked away from a perfectly good career in the military."

"He's proud of you, Joe."

Abbie saying that didn't make it true.

"It doesn't matter. I love what I'm doing."

"You say it doesn't matter, but I think it does."

"Don't worry about me. I'm a big boy."

Joe knew who he was. He didn't need to rethink his career choice every time Dad was mentioned. He just needed to get through this unpredictable joint writing project with Kylie, garner some new readers, and move on.

He eased past Mallory, who handed him the envelope with a grin. "Sorry we lost your place."

"Sure you are."

He was confident enough to handle some good-natured teasing from his close friends and his sister. He no longer doubted his career choice, and he accepted the fact Dad disapproved, that he thought Joe lost his way when he traded his military uniform for the questionable life of a peddler of fiction.

He couldn't make everyone happy. And everyone included so many people. His father. Cassidy. His readers. His publisher. Editors.

He hesitated to put Liza's name up there because he hoped his efforts, when weighed against each other, kept her happy.

Enough introspection. Or maybe, just maybe, he needed to spend some time wrestling through some of this with God again—if God would listen to him after all these years.

"Hudson!"

"Yessir!"

"You made one of those burgers rare, right?"

His sister's boyfriend grinned. "Put the biggest one on the grill last, and it's got your name on it."

"I'm a happy man, thanks to you." He rubbed his hands together as Hudson slapped the burger onto the waiting bun. "After we eat, I intend to beat all comers at cornhole."

Everyone cheered.

Abbie came up beside him. "What about inviting Kylie to the Fourth of July?"

"After we eat, I'll send her a text and see what she thinks about meeting on Tuesday and watching the fireworks with us."

"You're the best." Abbie gave him a side hug, causing him to fight to juggle his plate of food.

"You always say that when I do what you want."

"Exactly."

CHAPTER 14

Kylie: Happy Fourth of July to you! Thanks for being flexible and adjusting our meeting to today. I hope you're still considering the invite to go watch the fireworks later with me and the rest of the group. I'm looking forward to talking story with you today. Until then: What is the oldest book club in America? Your writing partner, Joe

"I'm happy to come to your house too. You know that, right? I could have done that today and saved you the trip for once." Kylie stepped back from the doorway decorated with a rustic wooden wreath of red, white, and blue stars as she invited Joe in.

"We've established a routine." He slipped off his brown flip-flops and moved past her into the living room. "Hey, Remington. Save any lives today?"

The cat didn't move from where it lay on the cream-colored couch but did give Joe a quick once-over and a yawn without raising its head from the muted blue pillow.

"He's too busy protecting his nine lives to exert himself and be heroic." Kylie leaned in for a quick hug, her hair scented with something that hinted of eucalyptus. "Want a Pepsi?"

"You have Pepsi?"

"I remembered that was your beverage of choice when I came up for Memorial Day. There's a six-pack in the fridge. As I recall, you like it straight from the can."

"Yes, ma'am, I do. Thanks." He picked up one of the deck samples from her kitchen counter. "Redoing your deck?"

"You probably noticed it's not in great shape. I hoped it just needed some basic repairs, as well as a new coat of paint. But someone gave me an estimate, and he said the supports were worn, as well as a number of the planks. He suggested replacing the entire deck. Dropped off these samples yesterday."

"That could be pricey."

"Tell me about it, especially if I'm going to sell the house. I can't put it on the market with an unsafe deck." Kylie handed him a Pepsi, retrieving a ginger ale for herself.

"You're moving?"

"Yes. Maybe." Kylie shrugged. "I've talked to a real estate agent. Once. Whether I move or not, there are things that need to be fixed around here. Andrew was not a handyman. On the weekends, he was all about the next adventure."

"The house isn't that old. What kind of projects are you talking about?"

"The Realtor sent me a list. I need to deal with curb appeal. I know, you always hear that. Repaint rooms. Parts of the fence have fallen down a few times during high winds, so I'm getting an estimate to replace it." Kylie stopped. "You didn't come here today to talk about my house."

"If you love the house, then it will be worth investing in."

"I don't." It was easier to admit this now. "I don't love this house."

"Why not?"

"The front part is open concept, but the bedrooms and my office feel closed off. Not enough light. I ... we didn't look around enough. But Andrew liked the location and he wanted to get settled before his new job started, so we bought it." She shook her head. "Enough talk about the house. I hope you're hungry. I made salad."

At the way his brows furrowed, Kylie laughed.

"Just salad?"

"You'll love this salad. It's a layered taco salad—and yes it stays with the Mexican theme. It's got all the goods. Lots and lots of taco meat, just as much cheese, kidney beans, shredded lettuce, tomatoes, red onions ... "

"I *am* going to like this salad." Joe grinned. "Did my trivia question stump you?"

"I hate to admit it, but it did. Go ahead and gloat, and then tell me the answer."

"It's the Chatauqua Institution."

"That doesn't sound like the name for a book club."

"Let me finish. The Chautauqua Institution was founded in 1874 as an educational experiment in out-of-school learning in southwestern New York State."

"Very interesting."

"I'll try to find something a bit more fun for next time."

"Please do."

Their relaxed conversation proved things had gotten back to normal between them. They needed to tell Shannon and Liza their idea was working. Kylie Franklin and Joe Edwards could get along and work together.

Joe was relaxed, dressed in jeans and a heathered navy T-shirt that highlighted his blue eyes.

"Joe of the blue eyes."

Zoe's comment from their breakfast last weekend caused Kylie's skin to heat. *We're friends. Just friends.* And for this project to be successful, they needed to remain just friends. Uncomplicated friends.

"Okay." She clapped her hands. "Let's get to work. It's still cool enough to work outside today, don't you think?"

If Joe noticed anything abrupt about her behavior, he was polite enough not to say anything as they settled in their seats at the table and set up their laptops.

"So where are we?" Joe waited for Kylie to take the lead.

"Any feedback on what's been rewritten so far?"

"I'm going out on a limb here to say I like Evangeline more than I thought I would. She's not abrasive, which is what I was expecting."

"Abrasive?" Kylie forced herself to just listen to Joe's words without getting defensive.

"Yeah. You know, brassy. She's intelligent. Strong. But she's not afraid to accept help when she needs it."

"Everybody should be able to admit when they need help, don't you think?"

"I guess. That wasn't a value taught in my family. It was all about being independent and never letting anyone consider you the weak link."

"But I thought the military was all about being a team player."

"Yes ... and no." Joe turned his soda can in his hands. "You need to be a resilient individual, strong enough to benefit the team. It's a tricky balance."

"Sounds like it." Kylie pulled a blue folder from her messenger bag, handed it to him, and then opened a similar folder.

Joe held it up. "What's this?"

"It's your copy of the outline."

"The outline?"

"I'm a plotter, remember? If you're a pantser, it's gonna make you crazy, but I like to know where we are in the story. We've established who our main characters are. Had Inciting Incidents for both. Yours for Remington? Genius."

Joe set the folder aside without opening it. "I don't remember writing an Inciting Incident ... "

"It was there—you and all your 'I don't want to take time to plot' hadn't labeled it. We've got a lot of obstacles. I can't decide if we have too many."

"Can you ever have too many obstacles?"

"We're adding romance to this story. I need to make sure we mix things up, balance out the romantic tension, with the military suspense tension."

"I'm not taking anything out of the story."

Kylie shoved her chair back. "Did you eat before you came down here?"

"What?"

"Do you get hangry?"

Joe chuckled. "That's a female thing."

"And that's sexist." Kylie stood. Pointed at him. "Sit. I promise this is not a repeat of the time I walked away from you. I'm just going to get chips and salsa."

Her initial action was reminiscent of when she'd poked him in the chest—but pointing at him and then promising to return with chips and salsa was much friendlier. Kylie could only hope he didn't hear her laugh as she disappeared into the house. Did Joe even realize he wrote a hero who was so much like him?

An hour later, they'd almost finished the chips and salsa, and Joe was on his second Pepsi. Kylie asked if he'd read any of her novels and couldn't hold back a grin when he said he enjoyed the ending of her debut novel.

"You did?"

"It was … sweet."

"Sweet?"

"Yeah. I smiled when I read the reunion between the hero and heroine." He dragged a chip through the bowl of salsa and managed to get it to his mouth without dropping any on the table or his shirt.

"Thanks, Joe. Coming from a military suspense guy like you, that's a win."

"I've already started the second book."

"Whoa. I was not expecting that."

"Hey, you've read how many of my books?"

"I had to stop at three. Meeting my daily word count for both of these projects is more important right now."

"I will match your three."

She held out her hand. "Deal, my friend."

"Deal."

As he clasped her hand, her fingers slid against his palm, causing her arm to tingle. Kylie was having a moment straight out of one of her books.

And enough of that. She was an author, the one who wrote about these kinds of reactions for her fictional characters. She did not have this kind of response to Joe Edwards.

What had Joe just said? She needed to pay attention to his words, not some random tingles.

" ... so about tonight ... "

"Yes?"

It almost sounded like Joe was trying to ask her out on a date. But that couldn't be right.

Joe was *not* asking her out.

Just put him in the friend zone, girl, and leave him there.

"The gang ... "—since when did Joe call his friends a gang?— "is going to watch the fireworks in Glendale. Did you decide if you wanted to go with us?"

Oh. The fireworks. How had she forgotten about that?

Because she never did anything on the Fourth of July. Ever. "I was planning on watching the fireworks on TV."

"That's kind of underwhelming."

"True, but with the deadlines and everything, it makes sense. Thanks for the invitation, but—"

"Kylie?" The muffled sound of a woman's voice came from inside the house. "Are you home?"

Kylie bolted from her chair. "No ... no ... "

As she moved toward the sliding glass door leading into the house, it opened, and her mother, dressed in black slacks and a red top with hair dyed some crazy new combination of colors, stepped out. "You *are* home."

"Mom. What are you doing here?"

"Did you even listen to my voicemail? I told you we'd be in the Springs in time for your birthday." She opened her arms for a hug, but Kylie didn't move in for an embrace. "Happy birthday!"

"I-I didn't ... I'm on deadline."

As her mother finished off the hug, she must have caught sight of Joe over Kylie's shoulder. "And who is this?"

Kylie stepped back. Turned. Joe had risen and was offering a particularly charming smile.

"This is Joe Edwards, a-a good friend."

Oh, God, please don't let Mom recognize Joe as Tate Merrick. Her mother wasn't much of a book reader, so there was hope.

"Nice to meet you, Mrs. Franklin."

"It's Mrs. Hunter now." Her mother tucked a lock of her permed hair, which was an odd mix of red and fuchsia, behind one ear. "And it's nice to meet you, Joe."

"I'm sorry you didn't listen to my message, Kylie, but Peter and I were hoping we could take you out for your birthday ... "

"Mom, you know I don't make a big deal about my birthday." Kylie almost choked on the words. "Besides, I'm ... I'm going to watch the fireworks with Joe and a group of friends tonight."

"Right." Joe didn't miss a beat. "You're welcome to join us, of course."

Kylie stiffened. *Please say no. Please say no.*

"I'll have to check with Peter. He's in the RV with Rocko."

"Rocko?"

"Our dog."

"You have a dog?"

"Yes. Rocko is a six-month-old mini pin. Come on out and say hello to Peter and you can meet him."

"S-sure. Let's do that."

For the first time in her life, Kylie regretted not listening to one of her mother's voicemails. If she had, this fiasco could have been avoided. She'd need to be more careful in the future and apologize to Joe for using him as an out once Mom left. Kylie could only hope Mom and Peter wouldn't take him up on the invitation to go to the fireworks.

. . .

"You're sure you're okay with this?" Kylie pulled the layered taco salad from the fridge.

"You want to tell me why you didn't mention today is your birthday?" Joe ignored her question.

"I don't make a big deal about my birthday."

"That's obvious."

"It's no big deal."

It's never been a big deal.

"You've said that already. And yes, I'm fine with eating taco salad in the RV with your mom and her husband." Joe grinned. "We have to think of little Rocko. He's no match for Remington."

Kylie muffled a laugh.

"You know I'm right."

"Joe. Stop."

"Remington Gerard takes down Rocko the mini pin . . ."

Kylie leaned against him, giving in to her laughter. "That name does not fit that dog."

"You are so right." His chuckle was low in her ear. "But it can't be helped. You going to be okay?"

"I can manage lunch with Mom and Peter just fine. Thanks for sticking around."

"Hey, I'm not passing up taco salad. I just hope I don't have to fight Peter for seconds."

"You're a good sport."

"The fireworks start at dark. Do you want to just follow me back to my house after lunch—"

"Joe, it's okay. I'm sorry I said that."

"You're standing me up?"

She offered him a smile. "You even invited Mom."

"Well, I understand why they're not coming. Rocko might get scared because of all the fireworks tonight. But you have no excuse not to come."

"I should stay home and write..."

"Bring your laptop. We can both get a few hours of writing in before the fireworks. I'll text Abbie and Mallory and tell them you're coming. They'll be thrilled too."

"It does sound like fun. I haven't been to fireworks in years."

"Okay then. I'm texting them." When he was finished messaging his friends, Joe put his phone into the back pocket of his shorts. Tucked a Pepsi and a ginger ale in the crook of his arm. "I've got the salad dressing and the sour cream and salsa. Anything else?"

"Mom's supplying the silverware and plates. We're all good."

She could get through lunch with Mom and Peter because she had tonight to look forward to. She'd concentrate on the good things today—and Joe Edwards was most definitely one of them.

...

Kylie had never seen Joe Edwards like this before.

Relaxed. Talkative. Laughing. The Joe she'd gotten to know, in a sense, through their emails. The Joe she'd wanted to meet face-to-face at the Memorial Day cookout weeks ago. But back then, he'd retreated behind the grill, paying more attention to the brats than to her.

Today? He'd stayed by her side—well, except when they'd had a few hours to write. He'd hunkered down in a well-worn leather chair in his living room, and she'd chosen one corner of his couch to focus on the story of Remington and Evangeline.

Earlier, he'd sat beside her during lunch in Mom and Peter's RV, talking sports with Peter, all the while tolerating Rocko, who'd decided Joe was his new favorite person, and had climbed into his lap and fallen asleep. Kylie had steered the conversation to all the different states and towns Mom and Peter had visited. Away from anything personal.

"Having a nice birthday?" Joe bumped her shoulder, pulling her attention back to the present as they walked the edges of the crowd in Infinity Stadium. He'd changed into a short-sleeve Henley and jeans and had added a Broncos ball cap and tinted sunglasses.

"The best in years." Kylie tugged the brim of her white bucket hat lower. It was an easy complement to her red, white, and blue striped tank top and lightweight cotton pants. "Thank you for this."

"This? Just a few thousand of my closest friends gathered to celebrate you."

His words brought a smile to her face. "How did you pull it off on such short notice?"

"Wait until you see what we have planned for later."

She motioned to the lineup of various food trucks. "The food options are great."

"None of them have topped your salad."

"Flatterer."

"I'm just sorry there weren't any leftovers."

"I promise to make another batch soon to make good on my promise to you."

Joe maneuvered around a family with a toddler dressed in red, white, and blue in a wagon. "I'm happy to let you do that."

"I bet you are."

"So, you mentioned earlier that your birthdays weren't a big deal growing up. Was it hard for your mom because she was single?"

"Yeah. I think being a single mom is one of the hardest challenges in the world."

"But you and your mom don't seem close."

"Close? No, we're not close. She was busy surviving. Looking for the next man who might be Mr. Right. And I figured out at a pretty young age that the best thing I could do was grow up and be as independent as possible."

"You're not in touch with your dad at all?"

Kylie stopped walking. "No. I-I don't know who my dad is."

"What?" Joe turned to face her as people moved around them.

"I asked my mom once ... well, more than once. On my eleventh birthday, I asked her again. She said, 'It doesn't matter, Kylie. Stop asking me, okay? It doesn't matter.'" Kylie ran her hand across her face. "Happy Birthday to me."

"I'm so sorry—"

"Mom was right. I didn't ... it didn't matter."

Enough of that.

Kylie turned and scanned the crowd. "Do you see our group?"

Joe stood behind her, his hands on her bare shoulders. "Right ... there." He pivoted her a bit to the left until she spotted Abbie and Hudson and Mallory and Tucker gathered by the blankets, chairs, and coolers they'd set up earlier to mark their spot in the stadium.

For a moment, all she noticed was the warmth of Joe's touch on her skin.

Stop.

It was one thing to write an awareness like this into one of her novels, but she did not need to wish Joe's hands still rested on her shoulders. Or wish his blue eyes weren't hidden by his sunglasses.

Or wish he could somehow hug away the ache that came whenever she allowed herself to think about her unknown father.

"Hey!" Abbie stood and waved. "Find anything good to eat?"

"Lots of good things to eat, but we just browsed the different options. I may go back for a shaved ice before the fireworks."

"Looking for something sweet? I may have just the thing." Abbie pulled one of the smaller coolers close. Produced a circular Tupperware container. Lifted the lid and grinned as she revealed a dozen floral cupcakes and then began to sing, "Happy Birthday to you ... "

"Stop!" Kylie waved her hands to shush her friend.

Joe, Hudson, Mallory, and Tucker joined in, singing louder and louder. Joe held her still, preventing her from covering her face with her hands. By the time the song ended, people all around them had joined the birthday serenade that ended with cheers and applause.

Kylie knelt on the blanket. "Thank you, but no encores, please."

Abbie handed her the tray of cupcakes. "Birthday girl gets first choice."

"Did you make these?"

"I would love to say yes. Joe texted me it was your birthday and asked if I could figure out how to celebrate you tonight. I know a great little cupcake bakery. Voila!"

Kylie selected a cupcake decorated like a daisy and settled on the blanket as Joe chose to sit in one of the portable camping chairs.

"The friendliest flower, right?" Joe tossed her a wink.

Mallory did an exaggerated double take. "Did you just quote *You've Got Mail?*"

"Why yes, I did." Joe's reply was casual. "I think it's your turn to choose a cupcake. Toss me a Pepsi, Tucker?"

"Only if you promise not to quote a chick flick again for the rest of the night."

"Hand me a Pepsi and we can discuss *Independence Day* all you want."

This birthday was well on the way to making up for all her forgettable, ignored birthdays of years past—and that was even considering Mom's surprise appearance earlier. She bit into the thick layer of buttercream icing and discovered the hidden lemon curd nestled inside the vanilla bean cupcake. Such a surprising day. And the fireworks hadn't even started.

The sun had eased its way down the sky, offering its own brilliant display of color. Bright yellow. Vivid orange. Navy blue. All faded into a charcoal sketch of the Denver skyline. As the air cooled around them, the crowd quieted, readying for the fireworks display. Kylie rubbed her hands up and down her bare arms.

"You okay?" Joe, who sat in the chair behind her, leaned over her shoulder, his voice low in her ear.

"Yes." She'd take his question at face value. "I can't believe I left my hoodie in the car. I'm a native Coloradan. I know better."

"I can run back to the car—"

"Don't do that." Abbie, who was sitting beside her. "I've got an extra blanket. Use this, Kylie."

"Thanks so much." Joe helped her arrange the light white-and-red-striped blanket around her shoulders.

"All good?" His hands rested on her shoulders again, providing another layer of warmth.

"Much better."

"Anybody need anything before the fireworks start?" Abbie was the acting hostess for the day. "Soda? Water? Cupcake?"

"We can get what we need, Abbie. We're all good." Joe patted his sister's leg. "Thanks for picking up the cupcakes."

"You're welcome."

"I'll pay you—"

"I know you're good for it, big brother."

Kylie exhaled and relaxed—right into Joe's legs. She looked over her shoulder. "Sorry about that."

"Not a problem, birthday girl. Get comfortable. Use me as a cushion." He grinned and then motioned to her hat. "And go ahead and take that off if you want. We don't have to be incognito anymore."

"You figured me out, huh?"

"I knew your agreeing to come today didn't mean we'd be setting up a book signing booth."

"Never even crossed my mind."

"You remember we'll be doing that once *Lethal Strike* releases, right?"

"Hadn't thought about it until you mentioned it."

"Will we fight over who signs first and signs where on page? Do you insist on a particular kind of pen?"

"I bring my own pens, but I'm willing to share. What's your favorite color?"

"My favorite ... "

Kylie burst out laughing as a low whistle filled the air and the first firework lit the sky.

It was as if the light burst inside her, all the incandescent bits tumbling inside her body, warming her through and through. Joe's jean-covered legs pressed into her back. For the first time in years, she made a birthday wish.

Please let Joe and me write a good book.

And let us stay friends, God.

Of course, by mentioning it to God, it was more of a prayer than a wish, but who better to trust with a wish?

Within forty minutes, the display was over. Kylie had almost forgotten anyone else was around as she'd marveled at the beauty of different fireworks. The bursts of colors. The booms and flares.

They exchanged hugs and "see you soons" and gathered up all the blankets and chairs and coolers, with Abbie insisting Kylie take the one remaining cupcake home. Then she and Joe walked to their cars and waited while the parking lot emptied.

Joe leaned against the side of her car. "Who else gets fireworks on their birthday?"

"Everybody with a Fourth of July birthday." Kylie set the pansy cupcake on top of the car and then stood beside Joe, close enough that their shoulders touched.

"Well played." Joe turned his head. "Do you know that 150 million hot dogs are eaten by Americans on the Fourth of July?"

"Trivia! My birthday is complete!"

"I've got more. People plan to spend 7.7 billion dollars on food—"

"Please tell me that you looked this up."

Joe chuckled. "I'll admit it. But we both know there were fifty-six original signers to the Declaration of Independence."

"And with that, I'm going to head home."

Joe stepped back and scanned the lot. "The crowd has disappeared."

"It has. And Remington is probably worried about me."

"Cats do not worry about their owners."

"Rem and I are very close. He wakes me up in the morning."

"So you can feed him, right?" He handed her the cupcake. "Don't forget this."

"Thank you, sir." Kylie touched his arm. "Thanks for such a wonderful birthday, Joe."

"I had a great time too."

"I'm glad to hear that."

"Do me a favor?"

"You want half my cupcake?"

"No. Just text me when you get home, please."

His kindness was an endearing end to the day.

"Sure." She went up on her tiptoes and pressed a brief kiss to his cheek.

Joe's arms slipped around her and pulled her close. Kylie allowed herself to remain in his embrace. To rest, just for a moment, in the comfort of his nearness.

When Joe brushed her hair from her face, Kylie tilted her head back. The air between them stilled as his fingertips grazed her jaw, his thumb caressing her lower lip. The intimate touch caused her breath to catch in her throat. His gaze never broke from hers as he leaned down to kiss her.

It was a tentative kiss. One filled with questions more than passion. Kylie rested both her hands against the fabric covering Joe's broad chest as his mouth melded to hers. The gentleness of his lips against hers caused warmth to course through her body.

Joe is kissing me.

Kylie pushed away from him, stumbling back into the solid reality of her car. "Stop."

Joe stared at her. "Kylie ... "

"That ... that shouldn't have happened."

"Can we talk, please?"

"No. No, there'll be no talking about"—she motioned between them—"whatever that was."

"We kissed."

"Right. Fine. We kissed. And we're not talking about it."

"We *are* talking about it right now."

"And we're done talking about it ... because we both know it shouldn't have happened." She opened her car door and escaped inside. "It's late. I need to get home."

Joe stood in the same spot. "We're just going to forget about what happened?"

"Yes. Yep. Uh-huh." She struggled to insert the key into the ignition. "We have a book to write. We're focused on that. Not kissing."

There was that word again.

Kylie almost cheered when her car started. Joe stepped forward and shut her door.

They'd leave that ... that *mistake* in the parking lot, along with the birthday cupcake that Kylie had dropped when Joe held her.

CHAPTER 15

Joe had never been more thankful for a Friday night and that Tucker and Mallory took him up on his offer of a movie night, complete with him buying pizzas.

He and Kylie hadn't met Wednesday, which was probably a good thing after their *"we're not talking about it"* kiss. He'd watched ESPN nonstop. Worked on his book proposal. He needed a break.

He carried the warm pizza boxes up the sidewalk to where Tucker waited in the open front doorway.

"Greetings. I can take one of those."

Joe held onto the boxes. "No problem. I've got them balanced."

"Just take them to the kitchen. Did you get the usual?"

"No. I went with Hawaiian and veggie this time."

Tucker blocked the doorway. "Then you can turn right around and leave."

"Of course I got the usual. Meat Lovers and Meat Lovers."

"That's better."

Joe moved past him. "I knew Mallory was the woman for you when she proclaimed that was her favorite pizza."

"I knew she was the woman for me when she could put up with you."

"That is also true."

After depositing the pizzas on the kitchen counter and giving Mallory a hug, Joe collapsed on the couch. "I'm ready to relax."

"Thanks for picking up the pizzas."

"No problem. What movie are we watching?"

Tucker handed him a Pepsi. "Mallory thought we could play a game to select a movie."

"Can't we just pick a movie?"

"This will be fun." Mallory stood in front of the two men. "I picked four different movies—action, classic musical, western, and a rom-com. You choose a number between one and four, and that's how we decide which movie we watch."

Joe rested his elbows on his knees. "We're adults. Not kids. Can't we just watch a movie?"

Mallory didn't budge. "Come on, Joe."

"Two out of the four categories I don't even want to watch."

"You have a fifty-fifty chance of getting something you do want to watch. Play along or I'll just pick—"

"Three."

"Great! We're watching *Spider-Man: Across the Spider-Verse.*"

"What? That's not an action movie."

"Technically it is. And the animation is spectacular." Tucker pulled the DVD from the pile on the coffee table.

"I could always go with the musical." Mallory waved a DVD of *Singin' in the Rain.*

"I'm getting pizza." Joe pushed off the couch and strode to the kitchen. All he wanted was a relaxing evening with his friends. He hadn't planned on trying his luck at picking a movie and then ending up with a cartoon.

He opened one of the delivery boxes and selected a slice. Took a bite of the gooey cheese and salty blend of sausage, pepperoni, pork, and beef without bothering to get a plate. He needed his Pepsi. And a napkin. And a plate.

And he needed to stop thinking about that kiss with Kylie.

Mallory appeared in the doorway. "Is the plan to eat while you stand in the kitchen?"

"Sorry." Joe swallowed the bite of pizza. "It smelled so good, I couldn't wait."

"The paper plates and napkins are right here." Mallory moved them closer to the two pizza boxes. "And you can get another soda from the fridge."

"Can we eat first and have dessert while we watch the movie?" Joe took another bite of pizza.

"You assume I made dessert."

"I smell the brownies, Mallory. I assume there's vanilla ice cream in the freezer."

Mallory's eyes narrowed. "You seem off. What's wrong?"

He could lie. Postpone the inevitable. But there was the whole Boy Scout thing.

"I kissed Kylie."

"Yes! I've been waiting for you to tell us this!" Mallory did a little jig around the kitchen.

"You're the only one excited about that kiss."

"What? No, come on ... "

Joe found the glass pan of brownies on the back of the stove, pulled a fork from the drawer, and dug in. "It's true."

Tucker joined them in the kitchen. "Are we eating pizza or not? Hey! The brownies are for later."

Mallory hugged her husband. "Joe kissed Kylie!"

"And he's celebrating by skipping pizza and going straight to dessert?" Tucker reached for the pan, but Joe twisted away.

Mallory pulled some sodas from the fridge. "Did you kiss her on the Fourth of July?"

"Yes."

"I knew it! There were sparks flying back and forth between you two all evening."

"You're way off here, Mallory." Joe shoveled another bite of chocolatey brownie into his mouth.

"I can't be. There were sparks that led to a kiss ... "

"And then Kylie jumped into her car and drove home. *Pffft.* End of story."

"If that's how she reacted when you kissed her, it just means you're out of practice. Kiss her again." Tucker piled three slices of pizza on his plate.

He and Tucker joked about everything. But this? Joe didn't want to laugh off what had happened between him and Kylie on the Fourth of July. The brownies sat in his stomach like a glob of cement—and Mallory made brownies just the way he liked them. Rich and gooey. Might as well be eating dry oatmeal.

Why was he talking about that kiss? Kylie refused to talk about it, and here he was, discussing it with Mallory and Tucker.

"You realized what happened, right?" Mallory took the dessert from him, handing him a plate with a trio of pizza slices.

"I just told you—I kissed Kylie and she bolted."

"I'm talking about *why* she ran." Mallory paused for a moment. "Joe, I bet you're the first man she's kissed since her husband died three years ago."

"What? No."

"Think about it. She never finished the last book in her series. There's been nothing in the headlines about her dating anyone."

"You're her first kiss." Tucker grinned.

"I'm not her first kiss."

"You know what I mean. Mallory's right."

"It wasn't that she didn't like kissing you." Mallory faced him, as serious as he'd ever seen her. "It's that she's confused."

"She's not the only one who's confused. Isn't a kiss just a kiss?"

Tucker paused with a slice of pizza halfway to his mouth. "Don't start quoting poems or song lyrics—"

"I didn't quote anything. I was just saying it was one kiss."

And yet what he'd shared with Kylie had all the unexpectedness of a first kiss, with the promise of more. Was he looking for more after what had happened with Cassidy?

"You haven't texted her?" Mallory handed him a napkin. "Haven't called her?"

"She was very clear we weren't talking about it."

"She didn't mean that."

"Pretty sure she did. She said, and I quote, 'We have a book to write. We're focused on that. Not kissing.' And then she drove off. Left behind her cupcake, just like Cinderella left behind her glass slipper."

Tucker laughed. "Do you hear yourself?"

"It's so romantic."

Tucker stared at his wife. "It was a cupcake, Mallory!"

"The first thing you have to do is text her or email her. Tell her you're sorry."

Joe set his plate on the kitchen counter. "I'm supposed to apologize for kissing her?"

"Not exactly." Mallory crossed her arms.

"You're not helping here, Mallory."

"You're still working on the book, right?"

"Yes."

"You have to communicate with her."

"Yes."

"Well then, just email her … or text … say you wanted to see how she was doing. That you had a good time the other night, but you know things ended on an awkward note—"

"That's an understatement!" He dragged his fingers through his hair.

This whole conversation made him feel like a middle schooler. He was an adult. Tucker hadn't weighed in on this whole situation that much. He kept plowing through pizza.

Did he want another opinion? "Nothing to say, Tuck?"

"I told you—kiss her again."

"That's all you got?"

"The second kiss will tell you how she really feels about you. If she runs away again, then give up, man."

"I don't even know how I feel about her."

"Then why did you kiss her?"

"Because it felt right."

"There you go."

"What does that mean?"

"You haven't wanted to kiss anyone since things ended with Cassidy. Haven't wanted to date anyone. And then Kylie comes along ... something's there."

"It's not that simple."

Mallory offered him a gentle smile. "Falling in love never is."

"I never said I was in love with her."

Tucker just grinned at him.

"I'm not in love with Kylie Franklin."

"Why did you kiss her?"

That was a good question. A very good question.

. . .

Kylie carried the stack of dirty dishes into the kitchen and set them in the sink. Leah followed behind her with a couple of glasses. "Just put those on the counter. I'll clean up later."

"The pasta carbonara was delicious, Kylie." Zoe set the cloth napkins on the kitchen island.

"Happy to feed you all. You're helping me out giving me feedback on my story."

"No pun intended, right?"

Laughter filled the kitchen and even as she joined in, Kylie allowed the sound to embrace her and fill the emptiness in her heart. She needed more times like these.

"That is so bad, Zoe. I didn't even realize what I said ... "

"Can I get the recipe for the pasta?" Dylan ladled the now-cooled mixture into a plastic container to store in the fridge. "Miles will love it."

"Sure, Dylan. It's not that difficult."

"Kylie, you could serve us peanut butter and jelly sandwiches and I would be happy." Leah refilled her glass with iced tea. "I'm so excited about your manuscript."

"Did you like it?" Kylie held up her hands. "Wait, don't say anything until we're all sitting down and can go round-robin and focus."

"Can I get coffee?" Zoe opened the cabinet. "Wait... where are all your mugs? There are only three teacups in here."

"Yes, I got rid of all the coffee mugs, and the coffeepot. I do have a one-cup Keurig. How many of you want coffee?"

"I've got tea." Leah held up her glass.

"I brought my own." Dylan retrieved her insulated tumbler from near her purse.

"Then we're good. One cup of Keurig coffee for Zoe and tea for me."

Dylan, loyal friend that she was, saved the day, not mentioning Kylie's vent-and-toss with all her coffee mugs. Kylie hadn't even thought about there being a problem on a night like tonight. One of the problems. She hadn't been sleeping. She kept thinking about Joe kissing her.

And that was not going to be discussed tonight.

Kylie took one of the remaining teacups and added boiling water to it, along with a teabag, the faint scent of Irish Breakfast tea reaching her nose. "You all brought your binders, right?"

Zoe nodded as she finished doctoring her coffee, as Leah and Dylan agreed.

"Let's go to the living room and get started."

Zoe and Dylan claimed the couch, while Leah took the over-stuffed chair and Kylie settled on the floor. It didn't take long for Remington to wander over and curl up next to her.

"For tonight, I just wanted you to reread what I'd already written. No new chapters. I've edited them a bit. Were you all able to get through the reading?"

A chorus of yeses greeted her question.

"Does the story still work for you?" Kylie pulled her copy of the manuscript up on her laptop.

"I love *Worth the Risk*. Opening with Dianna trying to forget that Jeremy had kissed her? So good." Leah spoke up first. "I was thinking about how the kiss happens before the book opens and wondering if you should put it on the page."

Kylie stared at the first page of her manuscript. "I-I hadn't thought about rewriting the opening scene."

Or the fact that she and her imaginary character were struggling with the same problem.

Dylan took a sip of her coffee and then chimed in. "How fun would it be to see their kiss? In a lot of romance novels, authors wait a few chapters for a kiss, and then it's an almost-kiss. Your readers might be expecting the ex-boyfriend to show up—but not a kiss in chapter one."

Kylie couldn't tell her friends that she hadn't been expecting this either. She touched her thumb to her bottom lip.

No.

She wouldn't be using that in the scene. She'd come up with something else that created a sense of intimacy between Dianna and Jeremy—*if* she rewrote the scene.

Two hours later, they'd talked through the manuscript, transitioning from overall ideas of the manuscript to chapter-by-chapter thoughts. As always, Kylie thanked Leah for the punctuation and grammar errors she zeroed in on, insisting she'd missed her true calling as proofreader. Zoe still excelled at catching plot inconsistencies, while Dylan had a knack for dialogue.

"And this is why you're my advance readers. I'm a better writer because of the three of you." Kylie closed her laptop. "I'll be adding four more chapters to your binders tonight before you leave."

"I'm so excited you're finishing this book." Zoe hugged her binder.

"Honestly? I am too."

"How many chapters do you have left to write?"

"I'm into the third act—I'm at eighty-five thousand words. I need another fifteen thousand before I can turn it in to my editors." Kylie stood and stretched. "I need good words. A good ending—one worth all the waiting."

Leah applauded her words. "That's great!"

"Especially since I'm also working on Joe's manuscript."

Zoe took her teacup to the kitchen. "How's that going?"

"Fine. We're good." And that's all she'd say about Joe.

"You guys ended up meeting on your birthday, didn't you?"

"I can't believe I didn't tell you!" Kylie turned to face her friends. "My mom and her husband showed up on my birthday."

"*What?*" All three women spoke at the same time.

"She'd said they were coming through Colorado later this summer. Then I missed a voicemail where she said she'd be here for my birthday. She walked in and surprised me while Joe was here."

"What did you do?" Leah pushed her curly hair away from her face.

"We had lunch with them in their RV with their miniature pinscher Rocko." Kylie laughed, trying to describe Rocko sound asleep on Joe's lap.

She'd end the story there. No need to tell them all about what happened later that night. There'd be too many questions and it was already going on ten o'clock.

Rocko and Joe. Yep. She'd think about that tonight if... when she had difficulty falling asleep.

Dylan lingered behind when Leah and Zoe left, offering to help her clean the kitchen.

"It's not a problem. I'm just going to load the dishwasher. There's not that many—"

"Coffee cups," Dylan interrupted her. "You might want to get a few more so you're ready for our next dinner. Go to a thrift store."

"Good idea."

"I'll deal with the dishes while you tell me more about Joe."

"There's nothing more to tell."

"Come on, Kylie. I've known you for years. What's going on?"

Kylie leaned her back against the counter and wrapped her arms around her waist. "Joe invited me to go see the fireworks with him and his sister, Abbie, and some friends."

"Okay. That's nice, but nothing too exciting. I thought he tried to kiss you or something."

"He did."

"*He did?*"

Kylie didn't make eye contact with Dylan. "After the fireworks, when we were by ourselves, waiting for the parking lot to empty, he kissed me."

Dylan hugged her. "This is so fantastic!"

"No ... no, it's not."

"What's wrong?"

"I told Joe the kiss was a mistake. Got in my car and left him standing in the parking lot. We haven't talked since then."

"A mistake? Why?"

"Because ... because ... I don't know." Kylie's words were a verbal shrug.

"Kylie, it's okay if you have feelings for Joe—"

"Oh, I have feelings, all right. He makes me angry ... he makes me laugh ... he makes me excited about writing again ... and he frustrates me ... "

Dylan laughed. "That's a lot of conflicted feelings. Are you falling in love with him?"

"No. Absolutely not." Kylie paced the kitchen.

"Why not?"

"It complicates things."

"Will you take a breath for a minute?" Dylan stood in front of her, forcing her to stop walking circles around the island. "Yes, love is risky. You know that better than I do. But are you telling me that you're not willing to ever fall in love again?"

"It's too soon."

"It's been three years."

"I know how long it's been." Kylie circled the kitchen island again.

"How long do you have to wait before you can have a relationship with someone again? Will five years be long enough? Ten?"

"I wasn't expecting this ... this whatever it is ... with Joe."

"Says the bestselling romance writer."

"What?"

"You write these amazing novels where imaginary characters fall in love with one another. Usually, they're not the so-called perfect match. Or it happens at the most inconvenient time. Or it's the whole opposites-attract trope."

"Are you saying Joe and I are a romantic trope?"

"I'm saying don't be afraid of what's happening between the two of you."

"I'm not afraid."

Yes. Yes, she was. She'd just told her best friend a straight-up lie.

Dylan stared right back at her and, good friend that she was, she didn't call Kylie on it.

"I'm completely, totally afraid of what's happening with Joe. The kiss was so unexpected ... and I wish he'd kiss me again."

Dylan took one of her hands and whispered, "What are you going to do?"

"I'm not going to tell him that." Kylie's laugh was weak. "I told him we weren't talking about what happened, and we haven't."

"You haven't heard from him?"

"Nothing. He's probably regretting that kiss."

"You don't know that."

"Dylan, what should I do?"

"In my what-should-I-do moments—and I have plenty of them—I've learned that's the best time to pray. Let's take a few minutes and ask God for some clear direction. Can we do that?"

Just like she had so many other times in their friendship—so many times since Andrew had died—Dylan anchored Kylie to their shared faith.

"Yes. I've been trying to pray, but maybe if the two of us pray together ... "

"God's listening. He'll help you, Kylie. And then I'll finish these dishes and we'll wrap this night up and get some sleep."

"Can we pray about that too? I haven't slept well since my birthday."

"That must have been some kiss."

CHAPTER 16

Kylie: I hope you're doing okay. I plan to be at your house on Wednesday, regular time, to discuss this week's chapters. Here's a quick trivia Q&A for you: Which author wrote his last novel in crayon? James Joyce. Sad to say this was because for years he was almost totally blind and wrote with red crayon on huge sheets of white paper. Your writing partner, Joe

Joe had taken Mallory's and Tucker's advice and emailed Kylie Saturday—well, most of their advice. He had no plans to kiss Kylie again. He'd kept the email short, friendly, with a bit of trivia thrown in. Kylie's response was even briefer—a quick "Sounds good. See you Wednesday."

He found himself muttering a short "Help me, God" prayer as he drove to Monument on Wednesday. Did God pay attention to mutters from someone who hadn't talked to him in years? He hoped so.

Kylie let him in with a smile, but she resorted to a side hug that offered him the familiar hint of eucalyptus competing with the spicy aroma coming from her kitchen.

"What smells so good?"

"Chicken fajita soup, continuing with the Mexican theme for lunch."

"Sounds fantastic." He dropped his laptop bag on the couch.

"You want to eat first?"

"That works for me. Tucker and I had a killer workout this morning." So far, so good at keeping things normal.

"Mallory wasn't there?"

"She's out of town for her job, so Tucker's solo for a few days. We're going to meet up for dinner later."

"If you like the soup, I can send leftovers home with you."

"I've liked everything you've cooked, Kylie." Joe leaned down and picked up Remington, who offered him a friendly meow. "Been on any secret missions lately?"

Just as he hoped, his question earned him one of Kylie's musical laughs. If he could keep her laughing, it would be a good day.

"I was thinking we'd stay inside today." Kylie led him into the kitchen and opened the fridge and retrieved their customary Pepsi and ginger ale.

"Fine with me. Any particular reason why?"

"It's only going to get hotter—"

"True." Joe popped open his can of soda with a soft hiss of carbonation.

"I also want to stay off the deck until it's replaced."

"It's been fine all this time."

"Yeah, but it's become this ticking time bomb in my head. I don't want to push my luck, you know?"

"Do you have a start date for the deck replacement?"

"Not until late September." Kylie leaned against the kitchen counter. "Did you happen to notice that pile of stuff at the other end of the deck? I need to clear that off before then."

Joe took a swig of his soda. "Let me look at it. Maybe Tucker and I can do that for you."

"It's okay, Joe." She waved off his answer. "That's not why I mentioned it."

Joe ignored her dismissal, set his drink on the counter, and strode toward the side of the house. He was a man on a mission. He'd gotten Kylie to laugh. Maybe he could help her out and get them back on firm ground as friends again.

Footsteps sounded behind him as Kylie tried to catch up. He'd check out this pile of stuff on Kylie's deck. Text Tucker about moving it for her this weekend. Then they'd get some writing done. Easy.

Once outside, he focused on the far corner of the deck that was filled with a hodgepodge of objects.

"It's a mess, isn't it?" Kylie stood beside him, shading her eyes with one hand. "It's been so easy to ignore for too long."

"Okay, what do we have here? An old hammock. A couple of broken chairs." Joe moved around the pile, shifting the chairs out of the way to see what was farther back in the corner.

"I think there's an old grill that stopped working—"

Joe took a few more steps. The plank beneath his right foot seemed to move just a bit. He paused. All good. As he took another step, the plank gave way. The next second, his calf disappeared below the rotted deck.

"*Joe!*" Kylie's voice pierced the warm summer air.

Joe's hands slammed against the top of the rough wooden deck, his other leg bent, his knee scraping the surface. "I'm okay ... " He huffed out a breath as a jolt of electricity seemed to course through his body. "I'm okay."

"What happened?"

"Rotted board ... my foot ... went through ... "

"How badly are you hurt?" Something scraped on the deck. Was Kylie coming closer?

"Stop!"

"What? You're hurt."

"Kylie, *stop.*" A trickle of sweat slid down the side of his face. "I can't risk you falling through too."

"Wh-what do you want me to do?"

"I'm going to get myself out of ... this mess ... And get back over there." Joe grit his teeth. "Pretty sure I cut my leg. Could you ... get a towel or something so I don't bleed on your floors?"

"I'll be right back." Kylie's voice wobbled. "Please, please, be careful, Joe."

Be careful. That was the plan. He didn't want to fall any farther through the deck. His lower leg burned and ached at the same time. He needed to extract it from the hole without injuring it more. That would be tricky, what with the jagged edges of the wood plank.

Success.

His stomach roiled, and he swallowed the bile that rose against the back of his throat. Bright red blood covered his lower right leg, pouring from a deep wound on the inside of his calf near his knee. He scooted on his backside around the chairs and hammock and then stood, balancing himself against the side of the house so he could hop toward the door.

Kylie jolted to a stop just inside the sliding glass door. The piles of towels she carried almost reached her chin.

"You think you got enough?" Joe forced a laugh.

"Hush." Her face paled when she saw his blood-covered leg. "Why didn't you wait for me?"

"I don't think about how much it hurts when I'm moving."

"Oh Joe ... wait, where's your shoe?"

"Still under your deck."

He bent forward, ignoring the queasiness building in the pit of his stomach, and wrapped his bleeding leg with one of the towels.

"Put your arm over my shoulder. Lean on me. Come on." Kylie guided him into a small bedroom a few hops down the hallway. Laid a large towel on the bed. "Just lie down there."

"Thank you, ma'am." He rested his head on a pillow. Closed his eyes. "I'll apologize now if I get any blood anywhere."

"Don't worry about it."

Joe grabbed her hand. "I should probably elevate this. And do me a favor? Keep pressure on my leg, will you?"

"S-sure."

He closed his eyes again and sucked in a breath. Kylie did as he asked. "I looked at my leg. I'm no doctor, but I've done a lot of research plotting Remington Gerard's adventures. I'm pretty sure I skewered myself with a piece of wood."

"Joe ... th-that's awful."

He scrounged up a smile. "Sorry to say, but lunch and writing is postponed while I go get this looked at. Obviously, I can't drive myself—"

"Of course I'm driving you!" Kylie looked ready to swat him with the towel.

"I just thought of something ... "

"What's that?"

He rested his hand on hers again, where she held the yellow cotton towel that was becoming tinged with pink. "This is a bonding moment, right? Like Remington and Evangeline in the book?"

Her laughter was off-key. "Joe, I can't believe you said that!"

It was a poor attempt to add humor to the moment. But Kylie's eyes were clouded, and his out-of-the-blue question had earned him the smallest of laughs. Not her normal laughter, but it was something. Now to get to the hospital.

...

Joe had survived the drive to Urgent Care. Kylie had apologized for every bump in the road. He'd then acquiesced to the doctor's recommendation he go straight to an emergency room because his injury demanded more care than they could provide. He'd appreciated how quickly the staff whisked him back to be evaluated by a physician, ahead of all the other people waiting. A towel saturated in blood must scream, "Deal with this injury *now*."

Kylie couldn't grip his hand any tighter—and it still didn't distract him from the pain in his leg. Or from the ER doctor's announcement right before she left and closed the door.

"Surgery. This means I won't be meeting Tucker for pizza tonight."

"Joe!" Kylie bit her lower lip. "Is that all you can think about? Pizza?"

"Well, I didn't get any of your soup earlier, so there's that too—"

Kylie groaned. "I'm so sorry."

"Stop. You promised no more apologies. It was an accident, Kylie."

Both of their phones pinged at the same time, causing Kylie to jump and release his hand. "That must be Abbie." She retrieved his phone from her purse, handing it to him, and then skimmed her message. "She's here. Want me to go get her?"

"She'll find her way. Once you leave, they might not let you back again, although I think it helped when the nurse recognized you and confessed she's a diehard Veronica Hollins fan."

"I think she was quite taken with you and your blue eyes, Mr. Edwards."

"My blue eyes, eh? I didn't know you even noticed my eyes, Mrs. Franklin."

"Hush." Kylie wouldn't meet his gaze. This was almost as much fun as making her laugh. Now if she'd just hold his hand again.

"Oh wait, Abbie just texted that they told her to come back."

Joe appreciated Abbie coming to the hospital, but he would miss it just being him and Kylie. There was something to this whole bonding together over a crisis theory. Any uncomfortableness between them had evaporated. And even though Kylie wasn't holding his hand, she was standing close to his gurney, just like she'd stayed close to his side all day.

They were most definitely having a Remington Gerard and Evangeline Day moment all their own.

The door opened and Abbie peeked around. "There you are! I accidently walked in on this poor guy trying to pass a kidney stone or something ... "

"Abbie, you didn't."

His sister screwed her face up in a grimace. "Didn't count the doors right. Sorry it took me so long ... and never mind all that." She hugged Kylie and then faced Joe. "How's my big brother?"

"Your big brother is being sent to surgery."

"No!"

"Yep. When I injure myself, I do it thoroughly." Joe relaxed back against the plastic-covered pillow. "The doc just left to set things up. The trauma surgeon is on the way in."

"I thought you just cut your leg ... that they'd apply a big Band-Aid ... "

"Master of understatement, your brother." Kylie stood at the foot of the bed now. "He has a six-inch piece of wood from my rotted deck in his leg. And he's lost a lot of blood. They've decided surgery is the safest way to deal with the wound."

"Is this still outpatient surgery?" Abbie gripped both her hands.

"That's the plan." Tears filled Kylie's eyes.

"It was an accident." Joe's words were firm.

Kylie sniffed. "I feel horrible ... "

"Hey, at least I'm not trying to pass a kidney stone. Have you ever had one of those?"

"Joe, will you please be serious?"

The door opened again as a medical tech appeared pushing a cart filled with tubes, needles, tubing, and IV bags.

"Hello. I need to ask both of you to go to the waiting room while I get some labs on Mr. Edwards and start an IV."

"May we come back when you're done?"

"I don't see a problem with that, unless it gets busier back here."

"Okay." Abbie pressed a kiss to Joe's forehead. "Be brave. I know how you hate needles."

"I'm fine with needles. Get out of here."

Kylie started to leave.

"Hey, come here a moment." Joe grasped her hand. "You can stay. I really do hate needles."

"I'll be right back. I'll text a few people to pray for you." She leaned forward and pressed a kiss to his forehead, just like Abbie had. "Be brave."

"Thanks. See you soon?"

"See you soon."

The warmth of Kylie's lips on his skin? Almost as good as having her here holding his hand while the tech poked him with needles. While the guy searched for veins and drew his blood, he'd think about Kylie coming back.

"So, do you like to read books?"

"Me? Yeah, I like a good mystery."

"Really? Read any Tate Merrick books?"

"Who's he?"

"Never mind."

. . .

"I'm so glad you're here, Abbie." The words rushed out of Kylie on an exhale.

"I'm sorry it took me so long. I had to get a few of my clients covered by another trainer at the gym." She pulled Kylie in for a hug. Kylie choked back a sob. "You okay?"

"Joe was just going to look at this pile of junk on my deck. I told him not to worry about it ... and then ... " She pressed her palms against her eyes as if to block out the memory of Joe's accident.

"When he texted me all he said was he'd scratched his leg on a piece of wood on your deck. I'm playing catch-up here with the whole idea of his needing surgery."

"There was blood everywhere. I didn't even have time to clean it up."

"Good thing you don't get queasy at the sight of blood, right?"

"I guess so." Kylie wrapped her arms around her waist. "Did you let Tucker know? Your parents?"

"Yes. I need to update them. I gave them the same 'scratch on his leg' story. This is going to be a bit of a shock for Mom. I'll call Hudson and ask him to come down."

"You need to step outside for phone calls." Kylie motioned to the ER rules sign. "I'll text you if we can get back in to be with Joe. I'll text Dylan so she can update Zoe and Leah. I know they're praying."

"Kylie?"

"Yeah?"

"Don't blame yourself, okay?" Abbie touched her arm. "It was an accident. That's all. And Joe's healthy. He'll bounce back and be at the gym again next week."

"You're right. I know you're right."

"How about I get us something to drink?"

"A bottle of water would be great."

"Got it."

It was comforting to have Abbie here. To have her share the emotional load Kylie had been bearing all day.

The clamor of the ER held her in place. The ebb and flow of conversations. The constant shrill of the telephones. The murmur of the TV. An unrelenting cry of a toddler hunched up in his mother's arms.

Kylie had avoided doctors ... and hospitals ... all things medical after Andrew died. She hadn't even had a routine checkup. And yet, here she was. She hadn't hesitated to walk through the automatic sliding glass doors with Joe, his arm slung over her shoulders.

Quick update on Joe: He needs surgery to remove a piece of wood from his leg. He's also lost a lot of blood. Waiting on the trauma surgeon. Thanks for praying.

Kylie sent the group text to Dylan, Leah, and Zoe. Still no sign of the tech or a nurse telling them they could come back. Did anyone else need to know about Joe?

His agent.

But she didn't know Liza's phone number.

She'd had Joe's phone in her purse. Had he given it back to her? Yes. But the screen was locked.

What now?

Kylie tapped her fingernails against the screen. It wasn't late on the East Coast. She'd have to communicate with Liza the roundabout way.

Shannon: I need you to please contact Joe Edwards's agent, Liza, for me. He had an accident earlier today at my house. Injured his leg. He's having surgery as soon as they can arrange it. We are at the hospital now, waiting for the surgeon. Have Liza call me if she has any questions. Kylie

Within minutes, Shannon texted her back.

What happened? You're supposed to be writing, not hanging out at the hospital. Did your cat attack him or something? Calling Liza now. Keep me in the loop. Love you.

Kylie couldn't hold back a smile from curving her lips. She loved her agent. Shannon was always there for her, in the craziest, most unexpected moments of her life. Did agents know this kind of stuff was part of being a literary agent when they decided they wanted to represent authors for a living?

Abbie returned as Kylie sent off a thank-you text. Waved, then pantomimed drinking water and turned toward the hallway leading to the cafeteria.

More waiting.

At last, the tech appeared, motioned her to follow him.

"How's he doing?"

"Great. The trauma doc came while I was finishing up, which is why it took a little longer."

"Will he be going to surgery soon?"

"They still need to set up the OR and get the team in, so it'll be a while longer. But now that he's signed his consent form, they gave him pain meds in his IV. Mr. Edwards is nice and relaxed now."

"I'm so happy to hear that." Kylie paused before she stepped into the room to text Abbie that she was with Joe again.

Joe's eyes were closed. The lines that had bracketed his mouth and furrowed between his eyes had relaxed and he no longer gripped the thin hospital blanket between his fingers. For the first time since she'd heard the loud thud and Joe's initial grunt of pain, the tightness in Kylie's jaw and neck eased.

She sat on the edge of the chair beside the bed. Stayed silent. If he was resting, let him rest. A few moments ticked past, the monitors at the head of his bed beeping ... Then Joe shifted, turned his head. Opened his eyes and offered her a slow smile.

"Hey. You're back." His voice was achingly subdued.

"I am. I didn't want to wake you." She feathered her fingertips over his hand with the IV. "I hope that's not too painful."

"Nah. I got the kid talking about books." Joe licked his lips. "Do you know he'd never heard of Tate Merrick?"

"You're kidding me!"

"Right? I'm sittin' here, lettin' him poke needles in my arm ... and he hasn't read any of my books."

"The audacity."

"Knew you'd understand." Joe chuckled. "Didja hear the surgeon showed?"

"I don't think he planned to skip out on you."

"Wants to get paid."

"Abbie called Tucker and your parents."

"My parents ... " Joe rubbed his free hand against his chest as his words trailed off.

"They'll want to know. And I realized even though I've had your phone all day, I can't get into it. So I texted Shannon, my agent, to contact your agent about all of this. Figured she'd want to know too."

"Thanks." He muttered a few numbers.

"What's that?"

"Passcode...so you can get into my phone." He repeated the numbers. "Part of my old lock code for my high school locker."

"You still remember that?"

"You don't remember yours?"

It was almost as prosaic as Joe Fox in *You've Got Mail* using his apartment number for his Yahoo email address.

Joe had wrapped one finger around hers, keeping the connection between them. With the IV meds on board, he probably wasn't even aware—but Kylie was.

His eyes drifted closed again. A few moments later, when Abbie stepped into the room, Kylie shook her head and nodded toward Joe. Abbie's eyebrows lifted and then she mouthed a silent *"Okay."*

Kylie slipped her hand away from Joe's, praying he'd stay asleep, and moved to the end of the bed. "He's pretty worn out."

"I can imagine." Abbie handed her a bottle of water. "I talked with Tucker, who's on his way. Asked him to pick up some food for us. I figure we're in for the long haul. Hudson will come after work."

"Thanks, Abbie."

"I also talked to our parents. They want to fly up, but I told them to hold off until we see what happens after surgery. I promised Mom that I would call her when Joe's in recovery, no matter how late it was tonight."

"I'm sure they're concerned." Kylie took a sip of water, and then gulped half the bottle. "I didn't realize how thirsty I was."

"Worry takes a toll on the body."

"Yeah. I texted my agent. Asked her to call Joe's agent and tell her what happened. I have Joe's phone—" She pulled it from her purse. "Here, you probably should take it."

"No, thank you. I do not want that responsibility. He gave it to you. Keep it."

"Fine. He just told me his passcode. If—when—Liza calls, I'll talk to her. For now, I guess we just wait."

"I've never been great at waiting."

"Me either. How are you at praying?"

"A little better." Abbie nodded toward Joe. "I know it makes a difference."

"How about we pray before he goes to surgery?"

"Good idea."

Kylie put her arm around Abbie's waist, and Joe's sister leaned in closer as Kylie rested one hand on Joe's bed. Closed her eyes and leaned into the sweet comfort of prayer, allowing it to wash away the pressure of the day better than the cold water had washed away her thirst.

Everything seemed to still around them.

She should have prayed sooner. No, this wasn't about praying sooner. Or later. This was about now. And how prayer opened a corner of hope in this ER.

CHAPTER 17

Kylie was failing.

She'd been sitting in an exam room with Joe for fifteen minutes, determined to distract him from the not-unexpected reality the doctor was running late for his follow-up appointment five days after Joe's surgery. Every time she'd tried to talk to him, their conversation trailed off into silence, just like it had on their drive from his house. He'd left the Pepsi and bagel she'd brought him in her car.

Before that, Joe had stared at the news on the TV positioned in one corner of the waiting room. She'd made certain they'd arrived early at the surgeon's office, and then they weren't shown back to the exam room until a good half hour past the scheduled time for his appointment.

Now he seemed content to gaze at the abstract painting on the opposite wall. Kylie debated if the morass of golds, blacks, and reds would be better hung upside down.

Time to try again with Joe.

"Did you know that the first pair of crutches weren't invented until—"

"Until 1917 by some woman, whose name I don't remember." Joe glanced away from the painting for a moment.

"Wow. I thought I might stump you on that one."

"I looked it up this weekend."

She hesitated to ask the next question, but it forced its way out. "You feeling okay?"

"Sorry I'm lousy company this morning. I haven't slept great the last few nights. And I hate having to use crutches." He sighed and leaned his head against the exam room wall behind his chair. "Again, I'm sorry. I'm a terrible patient."

"It's okay, Joe." Kylie rested her hand on his arm. "I understand."

"I just want to be told I can toss these crutches and get back to normal again."

"That's what we're all hoping."

He turned his head and offered her a smile that didn't reach his eyes. "Thanks for bringing me today."

"Happy to. If you're up to it, we can grab an early lunch when we're done here."

"That would be fun. How about some medical trivia while we wait? Did you know one-fourth of all your bones are in your feet?"

"More than half our bones are in our hands and feet. Cat trivia— did you know cats walk like giraffes and camels?"

"What?"

"They move both their right feet first when they walk. Then they move both their left feet."

Joe reached down and scratched around his bandage. "I'm trying to visualize this. Now I'm going to have to watch Remington walk."

"Believe me, the first time I read this, I videoed Remington walking. I'll try to find one of my old videos for you."

Talking about how cats walk was pure silliness, but if it distracted Joe, it was worth it. The poor guy's jaw was covered with a scruffy growth of whiskers, and he had dark circles under his eyes, their normal blue washed out like the color of the sky over Pikes Peak before a snowstorm.

Maybe they could eat lunch at her house. Let him see Remington. Or would that be like returning to the scene of the crime?

The physician's assistant entered a few moments later. Shook Joe's hand as she introduced herself and explained she'd do the preliminary exam before the surgeon came in.

"Joe, you can sit on the exam table." The woman's actions were concise. Professional. "Is this your wife?"

Kylie refused to look at Joe. "No, no. I'm his friend and today I'm the chauffeur."

"Ah." She extended the end of the table and then retrieved some scissors and began cutting away the bandage. "I'm going to examine the wound and then rebandage it."

"Would you like me to leave?"

"That's up to Mr. Edwards. I'm fine with you being here."

"You can stay, Kylie."

"Okay." She settled back in her chair, gripping the padded arms.

With quiet precision, the PA removed the tape and gauze covering Joe's wound. "I was in the operating room with Dr. Petroni when he removed the piece of wood from your leg."

"I'm glad I was asleep for that."

"Yes, that was an impressive injury. From a fall through a deck, right?"

"My deck." Kylie couldn't hold back the admission.

"An accident, Kylie." Joe's gaze connected with hers.

"How have you been feeling?" The PA went to the computer situated at a small desk in the corner of the room.

Joe shrugged. "I've been a little achy this morning. Had a few chills through the night. Not a big deal."

"You're running a low-grade temp, according to the vitals the medical assistant took."

"I am?"

"Let me go ask the doctor to come in and see you. I'll be right back."

This appointment was not going according to plan. At all. A deep wound ... surgery ... and now a fever, even a low fever, were lining up to send this day swirling out of control. Beneath the slight beard, Kylie could tell Joe was clenching his jaw.

Everything would be fine. But she couldn't tell him that. Only Dr. Petroni could.

Kylie stood next to Joe and slipped her hand over his, where it lay on top of the thin sheet of white paper on the exam table. "How are you?"

"I'll guess we'll find out, huh?"

"Maybe they'll need to switch your antibiotics."

"Maybe."

"The doctor's office will call in a prescription if you need one. Do you want to get something to eat while we wait? I asked that already, didn't I?"

"You've got stuff to do today, Kylie."

"I cleared my schedule for you." She tried to coax a smile out of him. "We can eat out or we can go to my house, and I'll make sandwiches. Nothing fancy, but Remington would be happy to show off his camel walk for you."

He laughed and laced their fingers together as the door opened and both the physician's assistant and the surgeon entered the exam room.

"Good morning, Mr. Edwards."

"Nice to see you again, Dr. Petroni."

Kylie squeezed Joe's hand, then retreated to her chair.

"Let's see how that leg of yours looks, shall we?"

The antiseptic odor of the room seemed to sharpen as the moments lengthened. Joe's eyes closed, and he pressed his lips together, but Kylie could tell by the way he gripped the table with both hands that the doctor's thorough exam was painful. She was close, but not close enough to offer him any comfort. The PA blocked her view of Joe's leg, which was probably for the best.

Joe had been a good patient. Tucker and Abbie had made certain of that, taking turns staying with him, ensuring he took his meds around the clock.

Dr. Petroni stepped back, stripped off the vinyl gloves and tossed them in the tall waste basket. "This wound isn't looking as good as I expected. And the fever is concerning. You shouldn't have one at this point."

Joe shrugged. "It's not much of a fever, right?"

"Any fever following surgery is worrisome. We need to get a better look at this. See if we missed a fragment. I'll set up an MRI."

"And then what?"

"If the MRI reveals we missed something, we'll have to go back in and remove it. The infection won't resolve—or it could get worse if we don't."

Kylie spoke before Joe. "You're talking a second surgery?"

"I'm not making any decisions until we see the MRI."

"How soon can we get that?"

Kylie could only imagine how much Joe would dread that, dread any additional waiting.

"I'll have my staff make some calls right now and we'll let you know in the next few minutes. My PA will go ahead and rebandage your leg while we wait. And I'll call and reserve an operating room—just in case."

Just in case.

"What kind of view will I have in that room?" As always, Joe attempted to bring some humor to the situation.

"The ceiling. But you won't care about it for long."

"*If* I have to keep that reservation."

"Exactly." And with that, Dr. Petroni exited the room.

The atmosphere around them was like it had been in the ER a few days earlier, but heavier. Joe's shoulders were slumped as the PA worked on his leg again.

How many times had Kylie wished she could push rewind, all the way back to Wednesday, before Joe volunteered to look at all the odds and ends in the corner of her deck. But she couldn't. So instead, she prayed.

The simplest of prayers. *Dear Jesus, have mercy on Joe.*

. . .

Kylie couldn't believe she was back in the hospital again. Of course, she was once again waiting. Joe hadn't been able to cancel that reservation in the OR. His humor had failed him, and he'd managed only a quiet "See you when I'm done" after she gave him an awkward hug before they'd wheeled him to the operating room.

She'd promised him that Abbie was on the way, and he'd offered a quick thumbs-up.

Dr. Petroni had said Joe's surgery would be no more than an hour, allowing him to remove the hidden piece of wood revealed on the MRI and irrigate the wound, put in some drains, and redress it. Abbie had arrived with an iced tea for Kylie and a caramel macchiato for herself. They'd waited together once again for the nurse to come back to let them know Joe was in recovery. Spent too much time scrolling through Instagram reels.

"Ms. Franklin?" A nurse in scrubs stood just inside the surgery doors.

"Yes?"

"You can come back and see Mr. Edwards now. He's been asking for you."

Kylie rose. Took two steps and stopped. "Abbie, do you want to go?"

"You go ahead. You heard the nurse, he asked for you, not me. Do me a favor and text me a photo and I'll send it to our mom, okay?"

"You're sure?"

"Go. Don't keep my poor brother waiting."

As they walked down the hallway, the nurse glanced at her again. "You're Veronica Hollins, aren't you?"

"Yes . . . "

"One of the other nurses guessed it. There's been quite a buzz on the floor about two well-known authors—one in surgery, one in the waiting room."

"I hope people keep it quiet."

"We're trained to respect our patients' privacy, and that's extended to you, too, Miss Hollins. No one will ask for autographs or post anything to social media."

"Kylie. Call me Kylie, please. Veronica is my pen name."

"I'm Sybil. I'm on all night. Let me know if you need anything."

"Thank you."

As much as she didn't want to be here, the hospital cocooned her. Joe was being well cared for. Protected. The lights in Joe's section of the recovery area were dimmed, and the lines on his face were relaxed. Anesthesia was one way to get some good sleep.

Kylie eased a chair close to the side of his bed. She'd stay quiet. Let Joe sleep for as long as he needed.

But just a few moments later, Joe shifted in the bed. Frowned. Opened his eyes and focused on her. "Hey ... you're here."

"Of course. I told you that I'd be here when surgery was over. How are you feeling?"

"A little groggy. Can't feel my leg at all."

"That's probably a good thing."

"Yeah." He moved his hands over the top of the hospital blanket and rubbed the IV site.

"Hey now. Don't mess with that." Kylie rested her hand on his.

"It hurts."

"I'm sorry. You're not a fan of needles, I know. The nurse mentioned something about IV antibiotics."

He closed his eyes for a moment and then a half smile appeared on his face. "We're holding hands again."

"Wh-what?"

He turned his hand over so that their hands met, palm to palm. "Holding hands. Again."

"We're not holding hands ... " She tried to pull her hand away.

"—like it. I like holding your hand, Kylie."

She stilled. "We don't hold hands, Joe."

" ... held my hand earlier. S'nice." His gaze was unfocused. "You like holding ... my hand?"

What was she supposed to say? "Sure. Yeah."

"I liked ... kissing you even more ... "

Joe rubbed his thumb back and forth across her skin, causing those all-too-familiar tingles to course through her arm. The nurse needed to come back and tell her it was time to leave before Joe said anything more. Before he asked her if she liked kissing him. Of course, he wouldn't remember any of this conversation in the morning.

And Abbie wanted a photo of Joe to send to their parents. How was she supposed to do that, while she was holding Joe's hand?

Sybil appeared again. If she noticed Kylie holding Joe's hand, she didn't comment. "Joe? How about we raise this bed so you can sit up?"

"Let me move out of the way." Kylie tried to ease to the end of the bed.

"You ... leaving, Kylie?" Joe refused to release her hand.

"I'm still here." She gave his hand a gentle squeeze and then stepped back. "The nurse wants you to sit up."

"I brought you some apple juice and crackers. You said that sounded good."

"No Pepsi?"

"Not yet. Let's get this apple juice down, shall we?"

"Doubt you'll be drinking any ... "

Kylie laughed. "He's going to be fine."

"Be better without this blood pressure thing."

"That's not going to happen." The nurse pulled the blanket back, revealing Joe's feet. "Can you try moving your toes for me?"

" ... feel nothing below my hip. Do I still have toes?"

"Dr. Petroni didn't touch your toes."

"Kylie, can you confirm that?"

"You can trust the nurse, but yes, I can confirm you have all ten of your toes."

"When do I get outta here?"

"We can't take you to your room until you're able to move your toes." The nurse stepped midway up the side of the bed. "Let me check your bandage and then I'll go get you some more juice. Oh, do you have someone to stay with you tonight?"

"His sister is here. She's planning on staying—"

"Abbie's here?"

"Yes, I called her. She's been keeping in touch with your parents. That reminds me." Kylie held up her phone.

"Stop." Joe turned his face away.

"Smile."

"Smile?"

"Abbie wants me to text her a photo to send your parents. I'll do that and then I'm going to let her come back."

"You're leaving?"

"Your sister should have some time with you."

"Wait. If I smile you can send a photo. Then you can hang out while I drink another juice ... maybe see me wiggle my toes ... "

"Wouldn't want to miss that."

It had been a long day. She needed to get home, but if Joe wanted her to stay, she'd stay, at least a little while longer. He'd had surgery, not her. She'd ignore the dull ache in her lower back and cheer him on while he tried to wiggle his toes.

A couple hours later, Kylie walked through her front door. Seven forty-five. Kicked off her shoes. Dropped her purse on the chair by the kitchen counter, taking her phone with her as she wandered to her bedroom. Sure enough, Remington was curled up on her pillows. She collapsed next to him to text Dylan, Leah, and Zoe, who were probably wondering what was going on since her single **Joe has to have surgery to remove another wood sliver from his leg** text earlier that day.

I'm home. Joe is in the hospital on IV antibiotics for a few days. His sister is with him. I'm exhausted. Talk to you tomorrow.

Her friends would take the hint and not text or call her.

She needed to get up. Rinse away the stress of the day with a long, hot shower. Brush her teeth. Crawl into a pair of cotton pajamas and go to sleep. Instead, she stared at the ceiling, rubbing Remington's soft fur until he purred in her ear.

"*Holding hands. Again.*" Joe's words whispered through her head. "*... held my hand earlier. S'nice.*"

Holding hands with Joe Edwards was nice. Very nice.

"*I liked ... kissing you even more ...*"

And that was a dangerous thought.

Wait a minute.

Kylie sat up. She could work with this!

She'd missed this feeling. The unexpected ping of creativity when an idea surprised her. Kylie gave her cat a quick pat. "Sorry, Rem. I have some writing to do."

She grabbed one of Joe's Pepsis from the fridge, taking a bag of popcorn with her to her desk. Opened a blank document and went to work. Faster than she expected, the scene tumbled out onto her Word document. The scene was rough, but she liked it.

Kylie scanned the first few paragraphs again.

"*Eva ... I gotta tell you something.*" *Remington's bandage-wrapped hand caught hers, forcing her to stop from walking away.*

"*What?*"

"*I liked kissing you earlier today.*"

Evangeline refused to react to his unexpected words—at least that he could see. There was no stopping the warmth that washed over her at the memory of the kiss they'd shared. The man had crashed a motorcycle and tumbled over a cliff several hundred feet. Had a head wound. He didn't know what he was saying. "*That kiss was a camouflage kiss—*"

"*That was a good kiss.*" *He gave her a lopsided smile.*

"*That kiss kept us from being spotted by the local police informant.*"

"*Doesn't mean it wasn't a good kiss.*" *Exhaustion graveled his voice.*

She couldn't reason with a man with a concussion. "*Remington, you need to get some sleep. We'll talk in the morning.*"

He gripped her hand tighter. "*Where are you going?*"

"Don't worry about me. I'm not the one who fell off a cliff."

She could only hope Joe would like the scene when he read it. Unless he remembered their conversation in the recovery room, he wouldn't know what sparked her creativity. That was fine. She'd let it sit overnight and then take her laptop with her to the hospital tomorrow and work on it again.

As she exited her office, a text came from Abbie.

All is good here. Joe wants me to tell you he can wiggle his toes and can also feel his leg again. They're staying on top of his pain meds. He insists we keep the TV on ESPN. I'm about to curl up in the recliner and try to get some sleep. You'll be back tomorrow, yes?

Yes, I'll get there by ten o'clock if that works for you.

Let me know if you want me to bring anything.

Joe says to bring any leftovers you have in your fridge.

Tell Joe I'll see what I can do about that.

CHAPTER 18

What was that noise?

Kylie rolled over, shoved the pillow off her face. Her bedroom was still dark.

Phone. Her phone was buzzing. *There.* On the bedside table. Who was calling her at five o'clock in the morning? Kylie pushed herself to a sitting position. "Hello?"

"Rise and shine." Shannon was much too happy.

"Why are you calling me?"

"You're going on The Morning Connect in an hour. You need to get ready—"

"I-I'm what?"

"Chelsea Price is doing a quick two-minute Zoom interview with you, where you will tell her yes, you and Tate Merrick are writing a book together."

Kylie stumbled out of the bed and onto her feet. "Shannon, this is either a horrible dream or some kind of terrible joke ... "

"I'd love for both of us to still be sound asleep and dreaming. But a photo of you and Joe ended up on Instagram again yesterday and created a fast burn on social media."

"What? How?" Kylie pulled a strand of hair that had stuck near her mouth away from her face.

Ugh, drool.

"Some photo of you two walking together. Joe was on crutches. We can figure out *what* and *how* later. Based on the comments, everyone's speculating you're either writing together or dating. Or both."

"We're not dating."

"I know that. You and Joe know that. But both your fan bases love speculating about what is going on. Liza and I had a late night powwow and decided it was time to come clean about you two working on *Lethal Strike*. Then I remembered your promise to Chelsea. I've been talking to The Morning Connect since oh-dark-thirty, and we're going with the story today."

This conversation was some crazy plot twist to the morning. Kylie shoved her snarled hair out of her face. How was she supposed to be ready to go on live TV in an hour? No. In less than an hour.

"You couldn't have called me last night?"

"Kylie, I need you to wake up. This all went down just a couple of hours ago." Shannon spoke in the calm tones of a mother soothing her child. "I knew you were at the hospital with Joe last night, which is why I didn't call you. But this morning—*now*—we have to deal with this."

"I'm sorry ... I'm not upset with you." Kylie leaned against the doorjamb leading into her bathroom. "I got home and then stayed up writing ... It was so late when I went to bed, I'm not even sure I brushed my teeth. This was the last thing I expected to deal with this morning."

"I need you to get ready for this interview. Remember to smile— but brush your teeth first. Keep your answers short. Talk about your book with Tate Merrick. Let viewers know you're working on your novel too."

"Thanks."

"You can do this, Kylie."

"With an adequate amount of concealer and caffeine." Kylie took a few steps toward the shower.

"Pull your hair up in a classic ponytail. No fuss. Wear purple or royal blue."

"Thanks for the tips."

"I'll be watching."

And with that, Shannon hung up.

Kylie had forty-five minutes to become award-winning, bestselling author Veronica Hollins. Someone she hadn't been in years. And she had to do it all by herself. No Andrew to cheer her on while he made her a cup of coffee. Set up her ring light while she put on her makeup. Give her a hug, while promising he wouldn't kiss her and mess up her lip gloss. Offer her a smile as he shut her office door, ensuring Remington wouldn't intrude.

The hot spray of the shower was as effective as a jolt of caffeine, but she only allowed herself three brief minutes to savor the warmth. She needed to focus. She was doing this interview for the team. For Veronica Hollins and Tate Merrick. For her and Joe. She'd survive two minutes, with the right amount of makeup, the right outfit, and a quick text to Dylan, Leah, and Zoe asking them to pray.

Two hours later, still wearing the plum-colored dress with three-quarter sleeves she'd pulled from her closet, her hair still up in a high ponytail, Kylie carried two paper bags—one containing an assortment of doughnuts, the other containing two cans of Pepsi—into the hospital. With a brief smile, she made her way past the nurses' station to Joe's room. She'd texted Abbie to let her know she was on her way but hadn't received a reply. She could only hope Joe had slept well last night.

As she knocked and pushed open the door, Kylie caught the last few words of Abbie's conversation with her brother. " ... give her a chance to explain."

"There's no good explanation for what she did, Abbie."

Huh. Joe wasn't in a good mood this morning.

"Good morning." Kylie stepped into the room and held up the two bags. "I brought doughnuts and Pepsi."

"Hey, Kylie." Abbie's smile was strained. "Doughnuts sound great, especially if you've got one with sprinkles."

Joe remained silent.

She'd try again. "How are you feeling, Joe?"

"Me? Oh, I'm fine. Of course, I'm not the one who went on TV this morning and talked about Veronica Hollins and Tate Merrick writing a book together."

Kylie paused at the foot of his bed. "You saw the interview?"

"How could I miss it? My nurse came running in and switched the TV channel, announcing you were on The Morning Connect."

"Liza didn't call and talk to you about what happened?"

"Does it sound like she did?" Joe tugged at his blankets. "The first thing I heard was your little virtual tête-à-tête with Chelsea. How long have you been planning this?"

"Planning? Joe, I found out about this interview at five o'clock this morning!"

Abbie bounced on her heels, her messy bun a testament to a restless night. "There! I told you that she had a good explanation, Joe."

"I should have been informed about it."

Kylie fisted her hands on her hips. "I was supposed to call you at five o'clock this morning while I'm trying to get ready for a short notice interview and you're recovering from surgery?"

"Yes."

"Do you hear yourself? I went on the show for us . . . "

Joe's stony gaze never wavered. "You used a lot of that interview to talk about your novel—"

"Were you using a stopwatch?" Kylie wanted to stomp her high heel against the floor. "I answered Chelsea's questions about us writing together and then yes, I told her I was working on the last book in my series. It's called publicity."

"You made sure you used that interview to your advantage and talked about romance."

Why couldn't Joe see she'd done this to help them? Why wasn't he thanking her for doing an interview after spending all day yesterday with him?

"That's because I'm a romance novelist. And because I'm adding romance to your book." She dropped the paper bags on the portable

table beside Joe's hospital bed, fighting the threat of tears. "I didn't expect you to thank me ... well, maybe I did. I thought you'd understand ... never mind. Enjoy the doughnuts and Pepsi—not that I expect you to thank me for them either."

"Kylie, don't listen to him—"

Kylie ignored Abbie, pulled open the door, and fast-walked down the hallway. This wasn't Joe's sister's fight. But Abbie caught up with her before she was halfway down the hallway.

"Kylie! Wait a minute."

Despite the urge to keep walking, Kylie stopped. Turned to face Abbie. They were friends and she wouldn't ignore her because of Joe's stupidity.

"I'm so sorry for Joe's attitude. He was upset about the interview ... well, I guess that's stating the obvious."

"I thought Liza would talk with him about what's going on."

"She just called, so they're talking now. That's why I'm here. Well, one of the reasons. You want to tell me what happened?"

Kylie produced her phone and pulled up Instagram. "This."

"That's you and Joe ... "

"Walking out of the surgeon's office yesterday on the way for Joe to get an MRI. My agent Shannon said this photo created a fast burn ... "

"I can see that from all the comments."

"Our agents decided it was time to announce Joe and I are writing together. Back when the whole book signing debacle happened, I'd promised Chelsea that I'd talk to her first if—when—there was something to talk about. Shannon woke me this morning saying I had an hour to get ready for a virtual interview on The Morning Connect."

"You're kidding me." Abbie handed her phone back.

"It's been quite the morning."

"I must say, I love the Veronica Hollins look."

Kylie shook her head. "It's amazing what panic and caffeine can produce."

"Give Joe time to cool down, okay? It's the day after surgery, and it doesn't help that our parents called last night to say they're flying up today. Mom wants to see Joe since he's had two surgeries."

"Sure. We still have a book to write together." She hugged Abbie. "Get on back there before he tries to get out of bed by himself."

A few moments later, Kylie sat in her car, staring at the front of the hospital. She had the entire day ahead of her. No sitting in Joe's room making sure he was feeling okay. Writing the ongoing adventures of Remington and Evangeline. Sharing the scene she wrote last night. Watching him sleep.

Enough.

She'd stopped treating the project like a job. Let it become personal. Gotten too close to Joe. Yes, she'd done what Liza and Shannon wanted, but she'd forgotten he was first and foremost Tate Merrick, her business partner.

There would always be a tug of war between their personal and professional lives. And for Joe, the professional would always win. All his talk about liking to hold her hand? Too much pain medication.

. . .

"Can I have a doughnut?" Joe repositioned the pillow behind his head as Abbie returned to his room.

"No."

"What do you mean no?"

"I'm not giving you a doughnut." Abbie moved one of the white paper bags away from Joe. "Not after the way you treated Kylie."

"Then let me have a Pepsi."

"Nope. Drink your water."

Joe crossed his arms over his chest. "You're being a brat, Abbie."

"Me?" She pulled a doughnut covered with a layer of white icing and neon blue sprinkles out of the bag. "Let's talk about you, big brother."

"Don't start with me—"

"Oh, I know. You just had surgery." She motioned to his leg. "Poor baby. That doesn't give you the right to beat up Kylie."

"I didn't beat up Kylie."

"You accused her of planning that interview. And she explained she found out about it at five o'clock this morning after she'd spent all of yesterday with you here, at the hospital."

"I didn't ask her—"

"Don't interrupt me." Abbie plowed right past him. "Yes, she stayed because she's your friend. She cares about you."

"She cares about her story and getting credit for my book."

"Do you hear yourself? I would like to think it's because you're less than twenty-four hours post-surgery, but I know what's wrong with you."

"You do?" Joe pulled the hospital blanket up over his chest and settled back as if waiting for a bedtime story. "Go ahead, then. Tell me what's wrong with me."

Abbie was pacing his room, as serious as some professional counselor, not the personal trainer she was. She'd eaten that doughnut and most likely hadn't tasted a bite. Abbie was his little sister, not this all-wise woman ranting at him, but he'd just invited her to continue talking.

Abbie stopped. Pointed a finger at him. "You're not mad at Kylie."

"Yes, I am—"

"I'm talking here."

"Sorry."

"The person you're really upset with?" Abbie paused and locked eyes with him. "It's Dad."

"Dad? He's not even here."

"Joe, you act like Dad is looking over your shoulder. All. The. Time."

He didn't do that. But he wasn't going to say anything because Abbie had already corrected him once for interrupting her. If he stopped arguing with her, she'd be done with her little tirade sooner. He refocused on his sister's words.

"...Dad has never approved of you leaving the military. He's never approved of you choosing to write novels, even though you're so successful." Abbie gripped the hospital bed railing. "But Joe, you're not sixteen anymore. You're not twenty-five anymore. Just live your life. Who cares what Dad thinks?"

"I do."

His admission burned his throat like he'd swallowed a boiling cup of coffee. He hadn't even known he was going to answer Abbie's rhetorical question.

His sister's eyes narrowed. "What did you say?"

She'd heard him.

"You're right, Abbie. I care about what Dad thinks."

The admission surprised him—but it also relieved him to say it. Maybe there was some truth serum in the pain medication the nurses were giving him. Or maybe they could give him something that would finally dull the ache he carried around in his heart—the persistent longing he tried to ignore.

"Why?"

"I don't know. I wish I could stop hoping he'd look at me once and be proud of me." Joe shifted in the bed, his right leg an uncomfortable weight. "This is not a conversation I want to have today."

"Joe, you're such a great guy..."

"Dad will never say that. He never has."

"I hate to admit it, but you're probably right." Abbie offered him the bag of doughnuts, waiting while he retrieved a jelly-filled one coated with a thin layer of white confectioner's sugar. "And that's Dad's problem—he won't say it. But I believe he's proud of you, even though he still wants you to live your life his way—"

"I'm not holding my breath."

"Yes, you are. And at his age, Dad's not going to change, short of a miracle."

"You're saying I give him a pass?"

"I'm saying you should let it go. Be proud of yourself and the life you've made. It's a good one. Realize there are a lot of other people who think you're amazing. Maybe think about trying to forgive him, which may take some time."

Why hadn't he noticed his little sister was so smart? So caring? Her blue eyes, the same color as his, glimmered with unshed tears. For so many years, she'd been his tagalong little sister. Today, she'd dared to confront him as an equal. To put him in his place.

"Thank you. Thank you for talking some sense into me."

"Will you apologize to Kylie?"

"If I do, will you give me another doughnut?"

"Joe!"

"Yes, I'm going to apologize to Kylie. I was way out of line today."

"You're going to ruin any chance you have to date her."

Best to ignore that comment.

"Nothing to say?" Abbie handed Joe her phone. "Let me show you this photo of you and Kylie—"

"Yeah, Liza mentioned that." Joe enlarged it. "That's us leaving the surgeon's office yesterday. Never saw anyone taking our photo."

"Some of the comments are funny. People are debating whether you two are dating."

"Why is that so funny? I could date Kylie."

"You'd be lucky if she'd even talk to you right now."

"You're right."

"Easier topic, then. What are you going to do about Dad?"

"Hope he doesn't see the TV interview?"

"*Joe!*"

"To be honest, I'm not going to think about it right now. I'm going to finish my doughnuts, drink a Pepsi, and ask you to change the channel back to ESPN."

He hadn't expected the day after surgery—his second surgery in less than a week—to be easy, but today was becoming way too complicated. He should ask Abbie to turn off the TV. Take his phone. Try and nap. The first bite of doughnut lodged in his throat. He couldn't enjoy the sweet bite of confection, not after how he'd treated Kylie.

He'd skip the Pepsi for now too. He needed to think. Maybe figure out a better prayer this time. Something more than "Help me, God." He needed help, but he also needed to change. To grow up and accept his relationship with his dad for what it was.

· · ·

Kylie: Trivia for today: Did you know that Shakespeare was the first person to use the word *apology* to mean "I'm sorry"? I didn't. But I am sorry for how I acted earlier today about your TV interview with Chelsea. I hope you can forgive me and that we can get back to Team Joe and Kylie. Rumor is, I'm getting out of the hospital tomorrow. Joe

Joe: Apology accepted. Did you know that two of Shakespeare's plays, *Hamlet* and *Much Ado About Nothing*, have been translated into Klingon? (Of course, this may only be of interest to you if you're a Star Trek fan.) Hoping you're relaxing at home now. Kylie

CHAPTER 19

Joe almost had his life back to normal now that he'd been home from the hospital for three days. Tomorrow morning Abbie would drive Mom and Dad to the Denver airport and they'd return to Arizona, which meant in less than twenty-four hours he'd have the house—and control of the remote—back to himself. Tucker would drive him to his follow-up appointment on Monday, but in a few days, he wouldn't need a chauffeur. He'd emailed Kylie and apologized, even including a bit of trivia for fun. Her response had been brief—but she had responded. There'd be time to talk more in the next few days.

For now, he needed to find Dad and tell him dinner was ready. Joe would miss Mom's cooking, but at least she'd put some meals in the freezer.

"Dad? Where are you?" He maneuvered down the hallway on his crutches. "Mom says the lemon chicken will be ready in ten minutes."

"In your office."

Joe leaned against the doorjamb, easing his weight off his right leg. "Looking for something in particular?"

"I wanted to find something to read for the flight back." Dad held up a book. "Wasn't expecting to find this."

Huh. One of Kylie's—*Veronica Hollins's*—romance novels.

"You plan on reading that?" Might as well go with humor.

"Very funny, Joe." Dad looked at the back cover, where Kylie's pro photo, one when her hair was much longer and styled in curls, took up the lower left corner. "This confirms it."

"Confirms what?"

He pushed his glasses back up his nose. "You are writing with this Veronica Hollins now."

Joe stood straighter, ignoring the ache in his knee. "She's writing with me, yes."

"She was at the cookout back in May."

"Yes. We were still working out the details of the project with our agents."

"I see." Dad flipped back to the front cover. "You write good military suspense. Why are you adding romance? Your readers don't want that."

Should Joe say thank you for the straightforward compliment or deal with the question?

"Romance is a natural part of life." Was he really defending romance novels? "Just about everyone experiences love at some point in their life. Love is important to people in the military. You ever watch any of those post-deployment videos?"

"But if you do this, you'll lose your focus on military suspense."

"My agent and editors are concerned about my overall numbers—"

"What do you mean?"

"In publishing, it's always a balance of writing what you love and writing what sells, Dad. My numbers haven't been great—"

"But you've won awards."

"Awards don't always equal sales. I've never managed to hit the bestseller list." Joe shifted his crutches. "And since when do you know about my awards?"

"You may not bother to tell me about your achievements, but your mother does."

It almost sounded as if what he did mattered to his father. But Joe knew that wasn't true. Hadn't been true for years.

Dad still held Kylie's romance novel. If Joe could have foreseen the series of events this past week, he would have hidden the book before Mom and Dad made their impromptu trip to Colorado.

"Let's be honest, Dad. You've never agreed with my decision to become a novelist. You told me it was a waste of time when I was selected to be editor of my high school paper."

Dad set the book on the desk and tucked his glasses in the pocket of his polo shirt. "Why are we talking about something that happened when you were sixteen?"

"Because it matters."

"You were a kid—"

"Who was excited about something, but his dad didn't care. And here we are—eighteen years later—and you still don't care about what's important to me."

"That's what you think?"

"It's the truth. Why do you think I don't talk to you about my writing? Do you ever wonder why I use a pen name?"

"It's your choice."

"I'm Joseph Edwards Jr. I knew you wouldn't want your name-sake to put his name out there on a novel. Nothing to be proud of, right?"

Dad shook his head. "That was your decision—"

"Just like it was my decision not to stay in the Army."

"You know I never understood why you didn't stick with the military. It's a good career field."

"I know. For you. For Grandad." Joe moved into the room, the rubber tips of the crutches making soft taps on the wood floor. He wished he could sit down, but for this conversation he needed to be eye to eye with his father. "It was irresponsible of me to not stay in until retirement, right?"

"There's a lot of stability in a military career, son."

"I wanted something different."

"To write stories. I never understood that. I followed in my father's footsteps. I just expected my son would follow in mine."

"It was no disrespect for you, Dad. I know how much you loved being in the military. And I enjoyed the eight years I was in."

"You were good at your job, and I was proud of you."

The words meant nothing. His father was proud of him only if Joe did what made sense to him. This conversation was a waste of time.

"But that doesn't mean I'm not proud of you now."

Those words kept Joe from turning and leaving the room.

"My dad wasn't a big talker and that's the kind of relationship I have with you. I grew up and did what he did, and yes, I expected you to do the same. It's a reason—not an excuse. I'm sorry, Joe." Dad's words seemed sincere. "Your mom's tried to tell me to accept we're not the same."

"Thank you. It would mean a lot if you could respect my choice even if you don't understand it."

"That's a fair request. One I can honor. Like I said, you write good books, son." His dad paused. "I'm sorry you felt you had to use a pen name."

"I should have talked to you about it, Dad."

"I can understand why you didn't. I'm glad we talked now."

"I am too." Joe tapped the floor with one of the crutches. "So . . . you're telling me that you've read my books?"

"Every single one of them. I like to tell my golf buddies about them."

"Your golf buddies?"

"I've got to have something to talk about when we're walking the course." His dad grinned. "But if you add romance, I don't know."

"Give Kylie a chance. She's writing a great character for *Lethal Strike*."

"*Lethal Strike*, huh? That's the title of the next book?"

"Yes. I don't think you'll be at a loss for things to discuss with your buddies. It's still focused on military suspense."

"I'll take your word for it."

"Thanks, Dad." Joe's attempt to shake his dad's hand was hindered by the crutches.

He was pulled off balance and into a brief hug, Dad adding a quick pat on his back. "Your mom will be glad to know about this."

Joe regained his balance, positioning the crutches on either side of his body. "You're going to tell her?"

"She's been asking me to have this conversation with you for years. You bet I am."

Joe remained behind in his office for a few moments after his dad left, sifting through their words. A single conversation had caused something to shift in their relationship. For the first time in years, he had hope for more.

Whatever just happened, God, keep it up.

...

It was good to be at Dylan's for a quiet Sunday afternoon. To get out of her house and away from the computer for a few hours. Now they sat by a card table in Dylan's family room, working on a colorful puzzle of hot air balloons. Kylie raised her glass of iced tea to her friend. "Thanks for inviting me over. Lunch was great."

"I'm glad you said yes." Dylan sorted through edge pieces. "Miles decided to go to that movie with his friends, so it's nice for us to have some time together."

"I needed a break. I've been writing every minute I can."

"Have you talked to Joe since—"

"No. I mean, he emailed me and apologized, which I appreciated. And I emailed him back."

"But you haven't talked."

Kylie added some red puzzle pieces to the pile Dylan had collected. "I heard from Abbie today."

"And?"

"He went home from the hospital last Wednesday. And his parents left for Arizona today. Joe sees the surgeon tomorrow for his follow-up appointment."

"So now the two of you get back to writing together, right?"

"I don't think so."

"I'm not following." Dylan's mouth twisted. "You said he apologized. I assume when you said you emailed back that meant you forgave him."

"I did. I do." Kylie paused. Lifted her hair off her neck. Exhaled. "I've decided to let it go."

"You've decided ... "

"Right. I've also decided I'm going to be okay."

"What does that mean?"

"I walked out of Joe's hospital room last Tuesday." She paused and counted her fingers. "That's been five days."

"Long time."

"Long enough for me to think about some things, in between writing a lot of words."

"And?" Dylan paused with a puzzle piece in her hand.

"If I'm being brutally honest, I'm also not sleeping at night, so I've had a lot of time to think ... and to pray."

"Not thinking about that kiss?" Dylan grinned.

"No. Not anymore." Kylie shrugged. "I was right when I told you that Joe wasn't going to be that guy—the one I fell in love with."

"I remember you saying that a few weeks back."

"But Joe showed me that I could love someone again. Some day. That my hope for love didn't die with Andrew."

"That was a powerful kiss."

"Dylan, I'm being serious here."

"And you think I'm not?" Her friend was no longer smiling. "When you kept thinking about Joe after he kissed you? That was a hint that you're ready to fall in love again, even if it's not with him."

"I know Joe Edwards is a handsome guy."

"You admit this now, when you tell me that you're not falling in love with him?"

Kylie shrugged. "Doesn't mean I haven't noticed his blue eyes and the muscles he's gotten from CrossFit classes."

"Kylie!" Dylan just stared at her. "You're sure you're not falling in love with him?"

"I do not want to be in a relationship with someone who doesn't trust me, even if he did apologize."

"And even if he's a good kisser?"

"Enough talking about Joe." Kylie shifted her position on the couch, abandoning any pretense she was working on the puzzle. "It was one kiss and I've forgotten about it."

"And yet, here we are, talking about it again."

"*You.* You are talking about it."

Dylan's eyes were bright with laughter. She was the only one enjoying this conversation that had gone down an unexpected rabbit trail. Kylie needed to regain control.

"Would you like to hear what else I thought about the last few days?"

"Of course."

"I'm not writing with Joe anymore."

"What? Kylie, you're quitting the project?"

"I didn't say that."

"You said you're not writing with Joe—"

"Exactly. But I didn't say I was quitting the project. I've always liked the verse that says, 'But let your statement be, 'Yes, yes, or 'No, no' ... '. I won't back out of this commitment."

"So then?"

"I can finish adding the romantic thread to *Lethal Strike* without getting together with Joe."

Dylan shook her head. "But your agents want you writing together—"

"It's not going to work. We're friends, yes, but we can't seem to work together. Any sparks we have are when our personalities clash. I'll explain to Shannon and Liza that I can't do it because of my dual deadlines with Joe's book and my book."

"That is a lot of pressure."

"Exactly. I don't have time to deal with Joe."

"I thought Joe wasn't a problem."

"He's not." Kylie closed her eyes. "Don't, Dylan. Just don't."

"You let me know when you've convinced yourself, Kylie."

There was no laughter in Dylan's eyes now. This was more like a repeat trip for Alice down the rabbit hole than a detour down a rabbit trail. Here she was again, having to convince herself... to convince Dylan that she was fine without Joe. She'd move on to the next topic of conversation.

"There's one more thing I've decided." Kylie found two puzzle pieces and fit them together.

"You have been busy the last few days."

"I'm putting my house on the market."

"What?" Dylan sputtered, choking on a sip of her drink.

"Are you okay?"

"Don't worry about me." Dylan set her glass on the side table. "Keep talking. You're selling your house?"

"It's time. Really, it's past time. I took the advice about not making any major life decisions the first year you're grieving, but I got stuck."

"You've done beautifully, Kylie. You've been so brave since Andrew died."

"Thank you. I don't know how I would have survived losing Andrew without you. And Leah. And Zoe. For a long time, it was hard to even walk into a church... not that I stopped believing in God."

"I know."

"But the three of you held onto hope for me when I couldn't."

The two of them sat in silence for a few moments.

"So." Kylie sighed. "Linda came over yesterday and I signed the contract. I'm going to have someone paint the house—interior and exterior. The deck will be replaced, and I hope I recoup the cost. Linda's recommending a good handyman to do a few repairs, including my fence. I'll have a staging company get the house ready for showings."

"I can't believe this."

"Neither can I." Kylie stretched out her legs, careful not to knock the table. "But I'm excited."

"Do you know where you want to look for your new house?"

"Down in the Springs. Linda's compiling some listings."

"You're not wasting any time."

"Not anymore. Of course, my focus is going to be writing."

Telling Dylan her decision to move made it even more real. By the time her house was on the market, it would look like she'd never lived there. But she had. With Andrew. And without him. Now it was time to move on to what God had waiting for her.

"Anything else to tell me?"

"Those three things are enough, don't you think?"

"I do. Will you still meet with me and Leah and Zoe—you know, using us as advance readers?"

"Absolutely. I need your feedback on my story."

"And Joe's novel too?"

"Yes, his too. But I need to tell you all that I'll be working fast."

"We'll keep up with you. Don't worry about that."

"I'll email the next chapters later tonight."

"That means I'll have to explain to Miles why I'm staying up late reading after you were just here."

"I need to head home." Kylie pushed herself up from the couch. "Sorry we didn't accomplish more on the puzzle."

"You want some leftovers?" Dylan motioned toward the kitchen.

"I'm fine. Besides, this way, there'll be more for Miles and you."

"Then let's get you on home."

"You kicking me out?"

"In the nicest way possible. I want those next chapters."

Kylie hugged her friend. Talking everything out with Dylan had settled things in her heart even more. These were all good decisions. Ones that embraced her future. And maybe tonight she'd sleep without dreaming Joe was kissing her.

CHAPTER 20

"Congratulations." Shannon's single word was infused with warmth. "How does it feel to turn in *Worth the Risk?*"

Kylie pushed the button on the hotel Keurig and considered her agent's question. "A bit unreal. But I'm happy with how the story ends and I think readers will like it too. My advance readers did, and I trust their insights."

"Everyone here is eager to read the book, and your fans will be thrilled."

"I'm sorry it took so long."

"We all understood, Kylie." Her agent's voice gentled.

"Thank you for sticking with me, Shannon."

"I never stopped believing in you."

"I know." Kylie sniffed. No tears today. "I have to say staying in a hotel the last ten days helped me focus."

"Nothing to do but write."

"And deal with Remington, who wasn't too happy about a change of location."

"Poor cat. How's he doing?"

"The first two days he sulked in his carrier." Kylie opened the curtains with a soft *swish*, allowing just a bit of sunshine into the room. "After that, he forgave me and claimed the exact middle of the king-size bed."

"Life with a cat."

"Exactly. When I go home the day after tomorrow, he'll be content again. I'll have a new deck and a house with new paint, inside and out, and an appointment with the home stager." She took her cup of tea from the Keurig and raised it in a toast to Remington. "I'm thankful the company had a cancellation and was able to replace my deck so much sooner."

"There's a lot going on for you right now."

"Yes, one novel is finished. One to go."

"I'm proud of you."

"We both know there'll be edits."

"There are always edits. But you can relax until you go home, right?"

"I think I've forgotten what the word 'relax' means."

"I wanted you writing again, Kylie, but I don't want you to push yourself too hard and burn out."

"I won't. The edit stage of a book is different from the writing stage. I'm almost finished with *Lethal Strike*."

"No more ghostwriting projects?"

"This wasn't ghostwriting, remember? 'Tate Merrick with Veronica Hollins' right on the cover."

"Yes. Speaking of which, I should have something to show you soon."

"No worries. It's good to be focused on my career again. Believe it or not, I've got a solid idea for a new series."

"Are you sleeping?"

Kylie sipped her tea, allowing the warmth to soothe her throat. "You're my agent, Shannon, not my mom."

That earned her a laugh. But Shannon couldn't see how Kylie hadn't unpacked her suitcases. Had never really settled into the hotel room. How she slept on the top of the bedspread, using a pillow and blanket she'd brought from home. The home she'd be putting on the market in a few short weeks.

"Are you ready to talk marketing?"

"No." Shannon's question deserved an honest answer. "Not yet. I've received some questionnaires to fill out about *Worth the Risk*. I'm expecting to see some possible cover options soon."

"You know you'll be doing interviews with Joe too."

"Of course." And didn't she sound unconcerned?

"Have you talked to him?"

"Not since the interview with Chelsea."

"I'm sorry about that."

"It's not your problem, Shannon. The important thing is we get this book done."

"You know, I always thought maybe you two would ... "

"We'd what?"

"You know ... date or something."

Kylie laughed. "You've read too many romances."

"You were friends first—"

"Yes. Online friends. But face-to-face? We don't click."

"Maybe the book project put you both under too much pressure too early in your relationship."

"Maybe the book project was a good thing because it showed us how different we are."

Why was she even having this discussion with Shannon? They were supposed to be talking about books. Not Joe Edwards.

She said goodbye and adjusted the air conditioning. After that, Kylie moved to the bed and placed the cup of tea on the table. Wrapped the blanket around her shoulders. She'd convinced herself she was fine without Joe in her life except in a professional way. Soon, there wouldn't even be that.

If only she didn't have to convince everyone else she was fine.

...

She'd done it.

It was three o'clock Wednesday morning. She had to check out in just a few hours. But she'd written "The End" for *Lethal Strike*. The chapter straddled military suspense and romance, while giving more of a nod to Joe's genre. That should make him happy.

Had she cried?

Absolutely.

The saying about tears in the writer meant tears in the reader should hold true this time.

Kylie could walk away from him ... *from this project* ... with her head high and focus on her next series. Go back to writing romantic happily ever afters.

She attached the Word document to an email for Joe. Copied both their editors, as well as Shannon and Liza.

Joe: Here it is: *Lethal Strike* by Tate Merrick with Veronica Hollins. Let me know what you think. I appreciated the opportunity to work on this project.

Kylie paused. Considered adding a trivia question. No. This was a professional email.

I hope your leg is healing well. Kylie

Pushed Send and stared at her computer screen.

This was when she celebrated finishing another writing project. Stood and did a little happy dance around the room before she collapsed and fell into a post-deadline coma. Instead, Kylie closed her laptop and pressed her hands to her face.

Why did exhaustion mirror loneliness?

Kylie swallowed back the urge to sob. She would not cry. She wouldn't. She just needed a minute to herself. But then again, she had lots of those, didn't she?

All those months she and Joe were friends—just Kylie and Joe— they'd never talked about the things that were the most important to them.

Their writing.

His breakup with Cassidy.

Her being a widow.

Faith.

And when their online anonymity was replaced by reality, their friendship couldn't bear the weight of real life and writing together.

One good kiss did not a relationship make ... except maybe in a Veronica Hollins novel.

Kylie sniffled. Blinked away the tears that filled her eyes. She didn't waste anything, so maybe she'd figure out a way to work what had happened—what had *almost* happened between her and Joe— into a Veronica Hollins novel one day, with a proper happily ever after. Maybe ten or twenty years from now.

. . .

"Did you read this?" Joe motioned to his laptop, not that Liza could see what he was doing.

"Kylie's rewrite for *Lethal Strike*? Yes, I stayed up late last night reading it. I thought it was perfect."

"You've got to be kidding me." Joe stood, walking away from the words Kylie had written.

"You don't like it?"

"No, I don't like it. What does she think she's doing?"

"She wrote an ending that blends romance and military suspense."

"Are you forgetting why she was brought on in the first place? She's supposed to add romance to the book. *Romance*."

"Yes, I remember, Joe. And I also remember how you fought us about the idea—"

"That's ancient history, Liza." Joe picked up one of Kylie's novels and stared at her photograph. Tossed it back onto the chair. "I'm talking about this complete failure of an ending. If I was a romance reader and finished this book, I would throw it against a wall."

Liza burst out laughing, making Joe want to jerk his earbud out. "Do you hear yourself? Like you're some sort of expert on romance novels."

"Liza, is this the ending you were expecting?"

"I admit, I was surprised. But that makes the ending Kylie wrote all the better. Readers will be surprised too. And it's a little open-ended, don't you think?"

"I think it's the wrong ending. Period."

"How many times have you read it?"

"Once. That's all I needed."

"I suggest you set the manuscript aside. Go work out or something. Then read it again. You might feel differently."

His goodbye was brief. Liza knew fiction, so why couldn't she see what was wrong? Joe changed into workout clothes, but instead of going to the gym, he hunkered down in front of his laptop again and opened the Word document Kylie had sent.

Evangeline pushed back from Remington's embrace. "I promised myself that I wouldn't let you kiss me."

"Why not?" Remington's arms tightened around her.

"Because it makes what I have to say so much more difficult." She forced herself to maintain eye contact. There were all types of courage, and this moment demanded she be brave.

"Eva, what's wrong?" Remington took her hand, entwining their fingers, his skin warm against hers, and then pressed a kiss against the back of her hand.

"I'm leaving in an hour for another mission."

"What ... why?"

"You know the kind of lives we have, Rem. Finish a mission. Move on to the next."

"But what about us?"

"There can't be an us. We try to stay together—try to have some semblance of normal—and we jeopardize both our lives."

"We can figure something out."

"Which one of us walks away from our job? You? I don't think so. Me? I can't."

"What do you mean you can't?"

"Some things are too complicated to explain. Love isn't enough sometimes."

Joe slammed his laptop shut. Liza was wrong. He didn't like the ending any better. "What was Kylie thinking?"

"Who are you yelling at, big brother?" Abbie appeared in the doorway of his office.

"What are you doing here?"

"Honest answer? Mom asked me to check on you. I was nearby. Decided to just drop in."

"Check on me?"

"Yeah. I told her just to call you, but I guess she thought me dropping by was more subtle than a phone call."

Joe stood and walked around his desk. "Only if you don't tell me that she asked you to do it."

"There is that." Abbie stepped aside and followed him down the hallway. "Are you going to tell me who you're yelling at?"

Joe pulled a soda from the fridge. "Want something to drink?"

"Sure, if you're offering me a Pepsi—"

Joe handed her the can and retrieved one for himself. "Kylie sent the ending for our book."

"And?"

"It's awful." He popped open the can and took a gulp of the cold soda.

"Too romantic?"

"Remington and Evangeline don't end up together."

"Joe!" Abbie almost dropped her soda. "You just told me the end of the book!"

"It's a terrible ending. Even I know the hero and heroine are supposed to end up together."

"But this book isn't a romance, right? *Lethal Strike* just has a romantic thread in it."

"Help me out here, Abbie." Joe set the can aside. "If we're trying to gain more romance readers, will it work if the hero and heroine don't end up together?"

"Maybe. Does it have the possibility of the heroine and hero getting together in the future?"

"Kylie and I aren't writing another book together. We're not even talking to each other."

"Well, then your readers can imagine a happily ever after." Abbie stopped. "Wait. Are you telling me that you haven't apologized to Kylie about how you acted when she came to the hospital after your surgery?"

"I sent an email with an apology before I got out of the hospital. She responded right away. Said she forgave me. Since then, life's been pretty hectic. We haven't gotten together to write."

"Joe, I can't believe this." Abbie stomped her foot.

"I thought we'd have a chance to talk face-to-face." Joe scrubbed his hand across his jaw. "This isn't what I wanted with Kylie."

"What do you want?"

"More than this."

"What does that mean?"

"It means this conversation is over."

"Joe, that's rude."

"I'm sorry, Abbie. I've got something to do." He hugged her, forcing Abbie to hold her soda can over her head. "Thanks for talking some sense into me. And I wouldn't mind you saying a prayer or two for me."

"A prayer?"

"Yeah. This is going to take more than me to make it happen."

"You want to tell me what 'this' is?"

He moved past his sister. "No time. You're the best, Abbs."

"You're welcome. Anytime. Nice talk."

CHAPTER 21

A bright white and red For Sale sign hung from a tall wooden post on Kylie's front lawn. The exterior of her house had a fresh coat of paint, and matching white ceramic flowerpots overflowing with vibrant summer flowers framed her front door, which had been painted periwinkle blue. The stager had stripped most of the personality from the rooms of her house, but said she loved the color-coordinated bookshelves in Kylie's office. Her desk was free of clutter once again. All signs indicating she'd faced dual deadlines? Gone. With an open house planned for the coming weekend, Kylie made certain the pristine ambiance remained when she went to bed each night.

"What a way to live, eh, Remington?" Kylie stroked his ears as she leaned back against her pillows. "Time to check email. Maybe there's a book cover to look at."

She scanned her inbox. Nothing from her publisher.

Wait.

She had an email from Joe.

Maybe he was finally letting her know he'd received the finished manuscript.

Kylie: The ending you wrote for *Lethal Strike* doesn't work. I made some changes. Let me know what you think. Thanks. Joe

What?

Kylie reread the email. She'd sent the completed manuscript with the last chapters two weeks ago. Heard nothing. And now ... *now* Joe emails her to say what she wrote didn't work? And that he made changes?

It was so typical of the man.

Kylie group-texted Dylan, Leah, and Zoe, her fingers pounding against her phone keys.

You're not going to believe this! Joe just sent me an email and said my ending for our book didn't work.

Leah responded first.

What did you say?

Nothing. He also sent a different ending.

Have you read it?

No. I don't want to read it.

Dylan: **You should read it.**

I wrote a good ending. Both the agents and editors loved it. Fine, Kylie, but you can still read Joe's ending. Did Dylan always have to be so reasonable?

Do you all think I should read it—even when I know I'm not going to like it?

LOL. Yes.

Yes.

Leah agreed.

At last, Zoe chimed in. **Yes.**

Fine.

Will you text us when you're done?

Yes, Dylan. I'll text you.

Two hours later, she still hadn't opened Joe's document. She'd cleaned out her inbox. Dusted. Eaten half a bag of white cheddar popcorn and downed two ginger ales. Showered and blow-dried her hair.

Enough stalling. She'd told her friends she'd read what Joe wrote. She was surprised no one had texted her to ask what was going on. Time to open the Word document attached to Joe's email.

"What do you mean it's best if we walk away from each other?"

"It would be safer for both of us. There's too much at risk."

So far Joe was taking the same approach she had. But he'd started with dialogue without identifying who was speaking. Hadn't set up the scene.

"Would it help if I told you I was sorry?" Joe stepped in front of the door, blocking Kylie's exit. "Because I am."

Wait a minute. What had she just read? Joe? Kylie?

"An apology won't change things."

"It might—if you give me a chance." Joe wasn't good at this, but he had to try before Kylie walked out of his life. "I admit I had a bit of an ego when we first met—"

That earned a brief sound of Kylie's musical laugh. "A bit of an ego?"

"I'll never finish what I want to say if you keep interrupting."

"Sorry."

"We're a good team. You have to see that. You challenge me like no one else ever has, and yet, I know you believe in me too."

"I do." Kylie covered her mouth with her hand. "Sorry."

"I've never met anyone like you, Kylie. I'm sorry if that sounds like a cliché. It sounded a lot better when I practiced this."

"You practiced this?"

"I wrote it down. Deleted it. Started all over again." Joe rubbed the back of his neck. "I'm sorry I acted like I didn't trust you."

"It doesn't matter."

"Yes, it does. I know you need me to trust you. And I do. Please don't walk away from what we could have together."

"There's no future for us, Joe."

"What would you say if I kissed you again?"

"You're not kissing me—"

"*I want to.*" Joe stepped closer. "*I haven't forgotten our kiss on your birthday.*"

"*I have.*"

"*Then let me remind you.*"

Kylie pushed her computer off her lap, stumbling up from her bed.

What did Joe Edwards think he was doing? Taking Remington and Evangeline's scene and turning it into something between the two of them. Saying he thought they had a future together. Apologizing. Saying . . . writing that he wanted to kiss her again?

. . .

Why was someone ringing his doorbell at ten-thirty at night?

Joe fast-stepped down the stairs from his bedroom. The bell pealed again. And now the unknown person was pounding on his door. He ran down the hallway and hauled the door open before whoever was outside could start pounding again. "*Kylie?*"

She stood in the yellow glow of the porch light and waved a fistful of papers in the air. "Explain this."

"Hello to you too."

"I said *explain this.*" There was no smile on her face, her dark hair spilling around her shoulders.

"I would if you told me what that was."

"Your so-called ending for our book."

"You read it?"

"Yes, I read it. You took out Remington. And Evangeline."

Joe stepped outside into the cool night air, causing Kylie to take a few steps back. "I wrote about us."

"This so-called chapter doesn't make any sense."

"I wrote an apology. About second chances." He took another step closer. This time Kylie didn't move, which was fine with him. "Did you get to the part about wanting to kiss you again?"

"Like I said, this doesn't make any sense ... "

"I think that part was particularly clear." He took her hand, the one that wasn't clutching the papers. "Kissing you once wasn't enough for me, Kylie."

"Joe, we are not talking about kissing ... "

"We're not?" He brushed her hair back from her face, allowing his fingertips to trail down her jawline and neck. "I'll stop talking then."

"Joe ... " Kylie's voice was husky.

He cradled her face with both his hands, watching as her eyes closed right before he kissed her—a certain sign she welcomed this. Her lips were as soft as he remembered, her mouth as sweet and enticing. He slid his arms around her, closing the last of the distance between them as he savored this long-awaited second kiss.

"What are we doing?" She whispered the words against his lips.

"If you have to ask, I must not be doing it right."

"Joe." Her gentle laugh eased the tension in his chest. "I can't believe you wrote that scene."

"Got your attention, didn't I?"

"Is that all you wanted to do?" She pressed her hand against his heart. "Get my attention?"

It seemed kissing was on hold for the moment.

"I meant everything I wrote in that scene. Now that you're here, I can tell you how sorry I am. Try to convince you to give us a chance—in between kissing you again, of course. Although I vote for more kissing and less talking."

"But did you like the ending I wrote?"

"More kissing." Joe pressed his lips to hers. "Less talking, Kylie."

With a soft whisper, the pages scattered at their feet. "I couldn't agree with you more, Joe."

"Finally."

EPILOGUE

Nine Months Later

So this was how God answered a Fourth of July birthday wish turned to prayer.

With love. Unexpected love.

"Are you ready?" Joe whispered the words, his voice low, his breath warm against her skin.

"With you here, yes." She straightened the collar of his dress shirt that complemented his eyes.

"No place else I'd rather be."

This morning? It was about being Veronica Hollins, but at least she had Tate Merrick by her side, holding her hand.

"Veronica and Tate, I'm thrilled to have you here. And you're married. How's that going?" Chelsea Price offered them her familiar friendly smile.

She was married. Again. To Joe. A year ago, she woke up each morning to Remington's *pat, pat, pat* on her face and never imagined more. Never imagined this newfound joy of life with Joe.

He'd always be "just Joe" to her.

"Want to take this one, babe?" Her husband nodded, indicating she should go ahead and answer the question.

"We're having a bit of a challenge trying to merge all the *his* and *her* stuff. Of course, it's only been two months—"

"Newlyweds with two new books that are both one and two on the bestseller list!" Chelsea motioned to the covers of *Lethal Strike* and

Worth the Risk that switched out from the original photograph from their wedding.

"The deal is, as long as mine is number one, I don't have to do the cooking." Joe's comment earned a laugh from Chelsea.

"Both of us being on the bestseller list is a crazy belated wedding present," Kylie added.

"That wasn't even on our registry." Joe pressed a kiss to her hand, which allowed the cameraman a chance to zoom in for the audience to see her ruby engagement ring and wedding band. "My wife is an amazing writer."

"We make a good team."

Chelsea motioned to the copies of the books displayed on the table in front of them. "I noticed something interesting about the dedications in both books."

"The dedication?" Joe gave a low, short laugh. "Man, I can't even remember ... I wrote that so long ago ... "

"Do authors forget their book dedications?"

Joe glanced from Chelsea to Kylie. "Yeah, we sort of do."

"What about you, Veronica?"

"Um ... now you've put me on the spot too. We've been so busy, both of us selling our houses, our books going through edits, planning our March wedding, moving into our new house, finding a church ... "

"The dedications weren't planned?" Chelsea handed Kylie a copy of *Lethal Strike* and Joe a copy of *Worth the Risk*.

"What do you mean?" Kylie shared a glance with Joe.

"On the count of three"—Chelsea held up her hand, indicating they needed to wait—"read the dedication each of you wrote."

"What?"

"Why?"

"One ... two ... three ... "

As Kylie and Joe read the words on the dedication pages, images of the pages appeared on the screen—

Dedicated to the one I love.

"Look at that." Joe spoke first.

"The two of you didn't plan this? It's just some kind of crazy coincidence?"

"This wasn't planned." Kylie's eyes filled with tears so that the words blurred. "But I ... I don't believe in coincidences. It's more of a confirmation to me."

As they switched to a commercial, Kylie stared at the words on the page.

Dedicated to the one I love.

God knew she was ready to let go of her grief a year ago. Ready to open her heart to love again. And then He'd brought Joe into her life in the most unexpected way.

Were they perfect for one another?

No. But love wasn't about perfection. It was about learning to love each other better one day at a time. It was about trusting each other. And trying again when they failed. Love was dedication.

Dedication to each other, one choice, one day at a time.

The End

ACKNOWLEDGEMENTS

Not to us, O Lord, not to us,
But to Your name give glory
Because of Your lovingkindness,
because of Your truth. Psalm 115:1 (NASB1995)

Writing *Dedicated to the One I Love* was a return to my fiction roots. I started out writing contemporary romance, took a turn to women's fiction—yes, with a romantic thread in it—and then decided it was time to revisit straight-up romance again. It's been so fun to fall in love with writing a romance again, all while my husband and I dealt with home renovations. I'm finishing this story hiding with our dog Jo in what we call "the kids' room" on the main floor of our house while our kitchen is being torn apart. Not the easiest time to be creative.

I give the biggest shout of thanks to my husband, Rob, for supporting me after I announced, "I'm writing not one, but two books for 2023!" (More on that later.) He tolerates our conversations being interrupted by discussions of imaginary characters, reads my manuscripts, makes dinners after dealing with patients in his medical practice all day, and he also stars in my Wednesday Instagram reels. (Check them out!)

Rachel Hauck walked with me from the initial "what if?" of this book all the way to helping me write the back cover copy. Our daily texts and FaceTime calls saved my sanity and grew this book into a fun, romantic romp, while her prayers anchored me to the heart of God.

Dedicated to the One I Love is my first project with my agent Cynthia Ruchti. I'm so grateful she adjusted when I shouted, "Pivot!" and changed ideas about what I wanted to write. She's a brilliant, trustworthy agent with a discerning eye when it comes to writing.

Courtney Walsh designed the oh-so-amazing cover for *Dedicated to the One I Love*. She beautifully captured the essence of Kylie and Joe's love story. Courtney is also an over-the-moon talented author.

I'm so thankful for my editors **Barbara Curtis** and **Lianne March**. It's wonderful to know I can trust my books into their capable hands.

I'm extremely grateful to **Ginny Smith**, the project manager with Books & Such Literary Management, for all her help publishing *Dedicated to the One I Love*.

I share daily prayer time via text with writer friends **Rachel Hauck, Susan May Warren, Lisa Jordan, Alena Tauriainen, Melissa Tagg, and Tari Faris**. Friendship founded in prayer is the best.

As I wrote this book, I once again found myself developing a group of friends for my heroine. I've been blessed with the best of friends. Women who've stood by me. Prayed for me. Held onto hope for me when I couldn't. I'm so thankful for Kristy, Angie, Jeanne, Dee, Jeane, Therese, Gianna, Francie, Sandy, Sara, Faith, Pamela, Susie, Sherilyn, Cara, Casey, Robin, Anne, Renee, Mary, and Libby.

Fran Shaw has always been my Safe Harbor Friend. In so many ways she's kept me going during some tough, tough months, helping me finish this novel.

For years now, **Edie Melson** starts my day by asking me, "How can I pray for you?" Her friendship is as faithful as the sunrise.

My walks and talks with my friend **Mary Agius** remind me to keep my #eyesonJesus. I'm always thankful for how often she said, "You go first" and let me talk about this book.

As always, I thank God for the many blessings He's given me—and my family is the best of those blessings. I'm thankful I wake up each morning to God's unfailing grace and lovingkindness.

Connect with
Beth K. Vogt
https://bethvogt.com/

Made in the USA
Middletown, DE
28 June 2023

33903366R00144